THE DEATH OF AN AMBITIOUS WOMAN

A CHIEF RUTH MURPHY MYSTERY

THE DEATH OF AN AMBITIOUS WOMAN

BARBARA ROSS

FIVE STAR

A part of Gale, Cengage Learning

GALE
CENGAGE Learning™

Detroit • New York • San Francisco • New Haven, Conn • Waterville, Maine • London

GALE
CENGAGE Learning™

LIBRARY OF CONGRESS CATALOGING-IN-PUBLICATION DATA

Ross, Barbara, 1953–
    The death of an ambitious woman : a Chief Ruth Murphy mystery / Barbara Ross. — 1st ed.
        p. cm.
    ISBN-13: 978-1-59414-898-9 (hardcover)
    ISBN-10: 1-59414-898-8 (hardcover)
    1. Women police chiefs—Fiction. 2. Businesswomen—Crimes against—Fiction. I. Title.
PS3618.O845245D43 2010
813'.6—dc22   2010013306

First Edition. First Printing: August 2010.
Published in 2010 in conjunction with Tekno Books and Ed Gorman.

Printed in the United States of America
1 2 3 4 5 6 7 14 13 12 11 10

This book is dedicated to my parents, Jane McKim Ross and Richard Morrow Ross, who have supported me in so many ways.

ACKNOWLEDGMENTS

I would like to thank the Newton, Massachusetts Community Police Unit for their generosity, information, and experience, and Richard Hayes and Kate MacDougall for their very different perspectives on potential conflicts between police departments and district attorneys' offices.

My stalwart writers group: Mark Ammons, Kathy Fast, Gin Mackey, Cheryl Marceau, Andrea Petersen and Leslie Wheeler supported me throughout the writing process and provided so many insights about oh, so many drafts of this story.

As always, I want to thank my family: my son Rob, daughter Kate, and especially my husband Bill. They have been with me every step of the way, and I could not have written this book without them.

CHAPTER ONE

"Sprouts." Tracey Kendall's voice crackled over her cell phone. "He likes lots of sprouts on whole wheat."

"Yeah, I know." Hannah Whiteside glanced at the granite countertop where Carson Kendall, her four-year-old charge, munched on a peanut butter and jelly sandwich. "It's your mom," she mouthed.

Carson brightened, reaching for the phone.

Hannah held up her index finger, gesturing *wait*. Returning to the phone, she said, "He's eating now."

"Good. Just checking in. I'm driving to the gym. I'm buried at the office all afternoon, but won't be late tonight. Can you start dinner?"

"Sure." Hannah's job description as the au pair included light cooking. "Here's Carson." Hannah handed Carson the phone and turned to make her own lunch, barely listening to the exchange that followed, confident the boy wouldn't tattle about the peanut butter sandwich.

"Mom!"

Hannah whirled, took one look at Carson's white face, and grabbed the phone. "Tracey?"

"SHIT!" The word exploded into the room.

Carson stared.

A split second of silence. Instinctively, Hannah pressed the receiver tightly to her ear in time to spare Carson the piercing, full-bodied scream that followed, a scream made even more

9

horrible by the reverberation of the cell phone. Hannah's mind raced, comprehending, yet rejecting what she was hearing. She stood, nailed to the spot, unable to call out. The scream melted into a cacophonous, metallic roar.

The phone went dead. Hannah felt Carson's wide eyes trained on her. Keeping her hand steady, she hung up. "Carson," she said, "why don't you go up to your room and pick a book for us to read before your nap? I need to run out to the studio and talk to your daddy."

Ruth Anderson Murphy, New Derby Acting Chief of Police, pushed her way out of the warm sunshine, through the big brass-and-glass front door into the chilly, dark hallway of police headquarters. Her step was purposeful, her mood upbeat. It was April's first warm day, a bright masterpiece in the midst of a cold, drizzly Massachusetts spring. Even better, across the street at City Hall, the rumor mill was churning out good news for a change. Word was the long-awaited consultant's report had finally landed on the mayor's desk. After a nationwide search, eighty applicants, six finalists, and months of screening and interviews, the search firm had recommended her appointment as permanent chief. The recommendation was a major hurdle, no, *the* major hurdle to be cleared in the selection process.

As Ruth passed the front desk, Lieutenant Lawry, Officer-in-Charge of the day shift, raised his eyebrows in the way that meant, "I need to talk to you." Ruth collected her mail from the vacant secretary's desk outside her office and moved back toward Lawry. Side-by-side, Ruth and Lawry were the same height, making her a tallish woman and him a shortish man. Both stood erect, Ruth's carriage reflecting her natural athleticism, Lawry's his iron self-discipline. As she sorted through the pile of envelopes, Ruth listened to Lawry's painfully patient voice as he finished taking a citizen complaint.

"So, in essence," Lawry confirmed, "as I understand it, your complaint is failure on the part of your neighbors to observe the city's pooper-scooper ordinance?"

"No, that's not what I said at all." The grand proportions of the public reception area made the tiny, gray-haired woman on the other side of the desk appear even smaller. Her wavery voice echoed around the otherwise empty room. "If you had been listening, you would have understood that the essence of my complaint is that these people deliberately cause their dog to defecate on my front lawn every day. They live four houses down from me, but the dog never goes on the intervening lawns. He always goes, he *only* goes, on my pachysandra. Same time, same lawn, every day. Don't you find that a little strange?"

Ruth knew that at almost sixty-two, Lieutenant Lawry took enormous pride in a personal regimen you could set your watch by. She suspected his sympathies were with the dog. But he said, "This happens at the same time every day?"

"Eight A.M., exactly."

"Tell you what, in the next couple of days, as soon as I have a car I can spare, I'll send someone over to observe this performance, and we'll take it from there. That okay?"

"Thank you," the little woman replied formally. "You cannot imagine how much this has been disturbing me. I look forward to chatting with your officer as soon as he has confirmed my description of events." And with that, she left, pausing only for a short wrestling match with the heavy front door.

Ruth waited while Lawry methodically finished filling out the complaint. Though she adored Lawry and he was the person she had most relied on during her six months as acting chief, she knew better than to interrupt this little ritual. After completing the required paperwork, Lawry made a note to himself about the patrol car, then picked up a personal ledger and put a mark in a column headed TMFT—Too Much Free Time. In Lawry's oft-stated opinion, many of New Derby's eighty thousand citizens had TMFT. He kept a running tally of their complaints, which he supplied to Ruth along with his other, more traditional reports.

Finally, he turned to her. "There's been a fatal car wreck on Willow Road."

"When?"

"It was reported at 12:32. One car. Late-model, luxury SUV. Hit that stone wall on the curve at the bottom of the big hill. One victim. Thirty-nine-year-old female."

"Speeding?"

"Must have been from the damage, but no skid marks."

"Witnesses?"

"No *eye*-witnesses."

"Who's out there?"

"Cable. McGrath and Moscone were in the area on their way to lunch. I just sent Kilburn and Winkle."

Ruth nodded. "Victim local?"

"Briarhill Road. Name's Kendall. She was Tracey. The husband is Stephen. There's a four-year-old son, name of Carson. Mrs. Kendall was on the cell phone with the nanny when it happened. The family reported the accident, but they didn't know where she was. Apparently she was taking a shortcut. Not much traffic on that road. A passerby called it in."

"Grisly."

"Must've been."

Ruth stared down at the day's mail still in her hands, her light mood punctured. Suburban police departments, even very large ones like New Derby's, spent about half their time dealing with automobiles—moving violations, drunk drivers, stolen cars. Fatalities, however, were rare and affected everyone. Ruth was not immune to the essential sadness of it either, the death of a relatively young woman, mother to a small boy. It was disturbing when life ended so tragically. Ruth turned the matter over in her mind. "Beautiful day, newish car, mature driver, no skid marks. A little odd," she remarked.

"Ah, but odd is our specialty." The twinkle returned to Lawry's blue eyes. For emphasis, he waved Mrs. Thurmond Bentley's dog poop complaint.

Ruth headed for her office.

"By the way, congratulations on the search firm's report," Lawry called.

Good old Lawry. He was always near the top of the grapevine.

Detective Carl Moscone turned from the salesman's car and trotted back to the spot where his partner, John McGrath, stood. The salesman hadn't been able to tell Moscone much. He'd arrived well after the accident occurred. Now, the poor guy's day was completely blown. He said it didn't matter; he just wanted to go home and hug his wife and kids. Moscone didn't have a wife or kids, but he understood.

Up on the road, Officer Cable stood ready to direct traffic around the vehicles parked along the sharp bend in the road—Cable's cruiser, the detectives' unmarked car, a fire truck and ambulance, both useless, and the salesman's mud-brown sedan just now pulling away. The accident's single victim was still in her mangled SUV.

"Must have been going at least sixty," McGrath commented.

"At least," Moscone agreed.

"That's what I said."

McGrath seemed annoyed. In fact, McGrath had seemed annoyed for the entire week they'd worked together. Moscone wondered about the three guys with seniority who'd turned down this transfer to the day shift. They were all family men, locked into schedules they'd honed over the years and dependent on the extra pay they picked up for daytime court appearances and detail work. Moscone had thought their loss his gain. Moving to day shift was a critical rung on the career ladder. And now was a good time to make a move, if the rumors were true. A new chief meant new opportunities. But after a week of sharing the cantankerous McGrath's car and caseload, Moscone was beginning to rethink things.

The two men stood in an uncomfortable silence. Moscone fished his handkerchief out of his pocket and pressed it to his nose. Despite the light spring breeze, the smell of motor oil and friction hung in the air.

"You call the medical examiner's office?" McGrath asked for the third time.

"As soon as we arrived."

McGrath glanced at his watch. "This is taking for-frigging ever." He jiggled his wrist with impatience. "We're supposed to be at lunch."

Moscone watched McGrath stomp across the grassy verge to the place where the expensive, green SUV had hit the scenic New England stone wall. The front end of the car had lifted off the ground on impact. The wheels hung in the air, splayed at odd angles. The victim was still in her seat belt, the car's air bags deployed. Neither had saved her.

McGrath reached up through the broken window and felt her neck. Then he turned and stomped back to where the freckle-faced young ambulance attendant stood by his rig. "You gonna move her?" McGrath demanded, bringing his face so close the attendant winced.

"I can't, sir, um, Detective. Regulations prohibit me from moving, um, corpses, sir."

"You a doctor?"

"No, sir, I am a trained—"

"Well, I'm not a doctor either," McGrath growled, "but I say I feel a pulse. Now get her out of here, or if this accident ever becomes a lawsuit, and it will," McGrath looked pointedly at the expensive car and its driver, "I'll testify that when I came on the scene, she was alive, and you refused to treat her."

Moscone's stomach tightened. The ambulance attendant had a panicked look in his eyes. He seemed to be weighing the threat of a mauling by McGrath now against the certainty of a mauling by his superiors later. Moscone shook his head. What was McGrath thinking, jeopardizing their reputations because he couldn't handle the wait for the M.E. and staties? It was common knowledge the acting chief hated just this kind of corner cutting.

Without waiting to see what the young attendant would decide, Moscone sprinted toward the wreck. Standing on his toes, six inches from the door, he could look straight into the driver's window. The victim's face was turned away from him, exposing a slender neck. One arm had come to rest flung over her head.

The driver's perfume, a delicate fragrance of woodland flowers, wafted through the smells of body fluids, flesh, and death. Moscone turned his face away, took a deep breath, and held it. Careful not to move closer to the car or look down into the driver's seat, he put his hand through the shattered window and felt her neck. Her flesh was cooling. The absence of movement in her carotid artery confirmed what Moscone already knew. The woman who had lived in this body wasn't there anymore.

Moscone stepped back from the car and rolled down off his toes. Taking a moment to compose himself, he inspected his pants and shoes for damage, satisfied he'd avoided the blood that dripped steadily from below the driver's door. Mission accomplished, he jogged back to the ambulance. "She's gone," he announced with finality. The young ambulance driver looked relieved.

McGrath stared at both of them. "Yeah, she's gone for sure," he said to the attendant. "Just having a little fun with you."

A patrol car pulled up behind the ambulance. "Lawry wants you two to notify the family," Sergeant Winkle called to McGrath.

"Oh, joy," McGrath responded.

Ruth sat at her desk, working through a pile of reports, budgets, plans, and projections—the detritus of the job she'd "acted in" for six months. Unlike many of her colleagues, she found paperwork enormously satisfying. When she'd been captain of New Derby's detective squad, and before that when she'd worked on the street, paperwork had offered a world of rules, order, and completion that counter-balanced the human events it sprang from, which were all too often chaotic, inexplicable, and irresolvable.

At a little after six, Ruth put the last report in her out-box, checked the item off her To Do list and packed up her briefcase. She was eager to get home.

When she pulled into the driveway, her husband Marty and the kids were already outside. Marty gestured toward their station wagon, a broad smile on his face. Ruth grinned back and called out, "Let me change!" She took the stairs to their third-floor bedroom two at a time.

Ruth and Marty had bought their first car in their third year of marriage, when they were living in Jamaica Plain and Marty was finishing up at Suffolk Law. Ruth was working a punishing beat on the Boston police force, sticking out like the token she was, frequently hazed and never accepted.

The car, a used clunker bought from Marty's Uncle Emmett, was a wonder. They were amazed they owned it, amazed the City of Boston's Credit Union looked past the student loans, the single income, and the lack of credit history. All through that first winter, Marty and Ruth shoveled the car in and out of parking spaces and cursed its intermittent heat.

Then came the first warm day. They arrived home at the same moment, a coincidence. Without saying a word, they climbed into the old car and headed west, windows open, looking for country roads. Marty and Ruth unwound with each mile, more relaxed than they'd been in months.

Since then, on the first warm spring evening every year, they took a car ride. First alone, then with James strapped in the car seat in the back, and finally with Sarah in the car seat and James riding beside her. Over time, a regular circuit evolved and they found a restaurant everybody liked that served late dinners. Certain traditions were always upheld. They never talked about it beforehand, never said, "Tonight may be the night." They just got in the car and drove away. Somehow, in nineteen years, city meetings, trials, Little League, or homework had never conflicted.

In the cluttered master bedroom at the top of the house, Ruth pulled off her uniform. It still felt strange after the ten years she'd spent as a detective in plain clothes. She kicked off the navy blue pumps and hung the suit—straight skirt and cropped jacket—in the closet. She pulled on jeans, sneakers, a cotton shirt, and grabbed a sweater.

As Marty pulled the car onto the road, they were silent. Impressed by the weight of the occasion, even James at fifteen and Sarah at twelve were not poking or squirming. Ruth let the stress seep from her shoulders.

She'd almost completely relaxed when she remembered the mayor had never called to officially inform her about the search firm's report. Odd. Mayor Rosenfeld loved to give good news. Ruth turned the tidbit over in her mind. Probably nothing to worry about. The mayor was a busy man.

She glanced at Marty as he drove. Their love, strong to begin with, had deepened and strengthened over more than twenty years, until Ruth knew she couldn't be who or what she was without her husband's quiet humor or calm intelligence. Ruth's family was her rock and it was Marty's gut-deep knowledge of what family life should be that smoothed the jagged, scary parts and made it work. Ruth exhaled happily, leaned back into the car seat, cleared her mind and closed her eyes.

By the time she opened them again, the family station wagon had come over the last rise on Willow Road, and started toward the scene of Tracey Kendall's accident. Ruth had forgotten it was on their route. Marty braked reflexively as the car gathered speed on the steep hill. As they rounded the tight curve at the bottom, Ruth turned in her seat to stare. The wreck and its driver were long gone, but she could easily make out the point of impact on the stone wall. As they moved on, the little road took them under a concrete railroad bridge and the site passed out of view.

Unease crept up on Ruth, tensing the back of her throat like an unfulfilled retch. She closed her eyes and replayed the scene—the hill, the curve, the stone wall, and the bridge abutment. If Mrs. Kendall was talking to the nanny right up until the crash, then the obvious causes—suicide, heart attack, falling asleep—were ruled out. And why on earth had the poor woman been going so fast?

CHAPTER TWO

The next morning, Ruth sat at her battered desk, her office windows open behind her. In front of her were the reports about Tracey Kendall's death and a folder containing preliminary autopsy results. The photos taken at the scene were fanned out next to the folder. Ruth studied them carefully. One kept pulling her back. It was a picture of the victim shot through the broken front windshield of the car. The M.E.'s meticulous notes indicated the photographer had taken it while crouched on the hood.

The photo was a freeze-frame portrait of Tracey Kendall's last moments on earth. In the final seconds, as her car sped toward the wall, Tracey had given up trying to brake, steer or hold on. She'd twisted to her right and begun to pull into a ball, the protective instinct of the fetal position. Her head was bowed, her dark auburn hair hung across her face. Her right arm had come to rest wrapped around her head. The preliminary autopsy said Tracey Kendall had most likely died on impact. As she read the words, Ruth felt grateful Mrs. Kendall hadn't suffered longer.

Ruth opened her briefcase and pulled out a copy of the *Metro News*, a photograph of Tracey Kendall's crumpled car splashed across the front page. The accompanying article said that Tracey Kendall, age thirty-nine, born in Southampton, Long Island, educated at the Madeira School, Princeton, and the Harvard Business School, had been a partner in a small mutual fund company by the age of thirty. Her husband, Stephen Kendall, was mentioned as "the renowned artist." Renowned, perhaps, to those who could afford art. Ruth had never heard of him.

After refolding the paper, Ruth placed the photos back in the file and tried to turn to other work, but found she couldn't. Something was off about this accident. She had heard it in Lawry's brief description, felt it even more as she rode by the scene last night.

The halls of the station house filled with the sound of voices and hard-soled feet. Roll call had ended. Ruth summoned McGrath and Moscone.

Moscone bounded into her office immediately. McGrath trailed behind.

"I'm not comfortable with the Kendall accident," Ruth announced as soon as they were seated. "I want to look into it further."

"Sure, Chief, happy to," Moscone answered eagerly.

Ruth didn't know Moscone all that well. He was tall, lean, and loose-limbed. Her impression was he had all the floppy energy of a half-grown puppy. She liked having her big desk between them, in case he jumped up and slobbered on her skirt. She found his enthusiasm both off-putting and compelling.

McGrath just seemed to find it exhausting. "What's the problem?" he grumbled.

"This death is unexplained," Ruth answered. "There's no clear cause for the accident."

"Excessive speed," Moscone offered helpfully.

"Exactly," Ruth responded. "Why was she going so fast?"

Even Moscone recognized the rhetorical nature of the question. Ruth picked up the preliminary autopsy results. "She died from the impact. There were no signs of any precipitating medical condition. I called the medical examiner's office this morning and asked them not to sign her off until we'd had a chance to look into things. They said no problem. They're waiting for the tox screens."

"That's it, then," McGrath pronounced. "She was drunk."

"So drunk she didn't hit her brakes even once? I drove by the scene last night. It's a steep hill with a sharp curve at the bottom. You'd have to be unconscious not to brake just out of instinct. The statement Moscone took from the nanny indicates Mrs. Kendall was coherent until seconds before impact."

McGrath looked wary. "Where's the car?"

"State police garage."

He rolled his eyes. "Great. They'll be done with it sometime around the Fourth of July."

"I can make some calls if I have to." Ruth wasn't going to indulge McGrath's personal black cloud. She pushed on. "Where was Mrs. Kendall going? That's a pretty deserted stretch of road."

"From her office in the Truman Executive Park to an aerobics class at Madison's Gym on the turnpike," Moscone volunteered. "It's the back way, more miles than the usual route, but no lights. Not how you'd normally go, but good for avoiding lunchtime traffic."

Ruth nodded. This made sense. "How was the family?"

Moscone shrugged. "They knew there was an accident, but they didn't know she was dead. The husband was in shock. Like he couldn't believe it. The nanny was the one who held it together, though she's barely an adult herself. She sent the kid off to a neighbor's, offered us coffee, asked all the questions about identifying the remains, and so on. The husband was totally out of it. You wouldn't believe—"

Ruth listened intently as Moscone went on to describe the Kendalls' beautiful house and grounds, the buxom nanny, the handsome, vacant husband. If Moscone wanted to talk, she would listen. She could tell he was disturbed by Tracey Kendall's death, the horror of the scene, the raw grief of the family. It was never easy, and Moscone was young.

While Moscone talked, McGrath stared at his scuffed shoes. He'd be the first officer she'd lose, Ruth supposed, ironic considering their shared history. The thought alternately angered and depressed her. She'd suggested pairing him with Moscone, hoping the young pup's enthusiasm would energize the old dog. Instead, Moscone seemed to wear McGrath out. Why was it, Ruth wondered, that Lieutenant Lawry, ten years older than McGrath, could grow, adapt, even thrive on change while McGrath spent all his energy mourning the old days? His kids were grown, his wife had finally left him, and now the old chief had retired to Florida. None of them were coming back. It was time for McGrath to move on or move out.

Moscone was still talking. Ruth knew she'd have to stop him soon or he'd describe how everyone and everything at the Kendall house had smelled. In this, Moscone's reputation preceded him. Known throughout the department as "Detective Nostrillo," he always noted the names of the perfumes and aftershaves his interviewees wore—even their brands of soap, deodorant, and shampoo. His night-shift reports were routinely passed around the day-shift squad room, fodder for department lore.

"Fine," Ruth interjected when Moscone paused for breath. "Let's talk next steps."

"Back to the family?" Moscone asked.

"Not just yet. The last people to see her were her coworkers. Go talk to them."

"Sure, Chief." Moscone rose and trotted toward the door. McGrath sighed, stood and lumbered after him.

Moscone stood alone at the offices of Fiske & Holden, listening to the pretty young receptionist juggling the phone lines. Despite what seemed to Moscone like clear instructions from the chief, McGrath had begged off the trip to Tracey Kendall's investment firm. "There's no point in both of us wasting time on this," he'd said. "You go along. I've got some pencil pushing to do."

"Hi!" The woman turned to Moscone during a quick break in the calls. The plaque on her desk said *Brenda O'Reilly, Receptionist.* She had the cadences of Boston's working-class northern suburbs in her voice. "Excuse me just a minute. It's crazy here today." She turned back to the phones. "I know," she cooed into her headset. "It is. We're all upset. I know. I don't think the family's decided anything yet. Of course, we'll let you know. I'm keeping a list of people—Can you hang on, please? I'm sure Mr. Holden will want to speak to you."

Moscone seized his chance and showed his badge.

Brenda looked it over. "We've been waiting for you guys to show up."

"What?"

"Excuse me." She turned back to her console and fielded several more calls. Moscone drummed his fingers on the eye-level countertop of her workstation. "Obsession, by Calvin Klein," he muttered to no one in particular.

Brenda returned her attention to Moscone. "Because of the accident, naturally," she continued, picking up the conversation exactly where she had left it prior to the interruptions. "He shouldn't get away with it. A few of us decided to call the police if you didn't come by today."

"Who shouldn't . . . ?" Moscone was completely confused.

"Excuse me." Brenda was drawn away by the console's incessant buzzing. "Jane!" she shouted into her headpiece. "Take the call, for God's sake. It's the third time he's phoned. Honey, please. If you're unavailable all morning, he's only going to get more nervous. I'm upset, too, but we have to do our jobs. Get a grip. That's a girl. I'm sending him through."

She turned back to Moscone. "Sorry."

"Who shouldn't get away with what?" Moscone attempted to clarify.

"The mechanic, of course. He worked on Tracey's car the morning of the crash." More buzzing and ringing. "Ooh! Sorry! Excuse me, again." This time as she turned away, she handed Moscone a business card. *Screw Loose,* it said. *Al Pace, Prop.,* with a New Derby address and telephone exchange.

"How do you know he worked on her car right before the accident?"

"I saw him. Right here in the parking lot. That's the point of his business, Screw Loose. He has a truck specially fitted out so he can do oil changes and minor repairs at your workplace." Brenda paused. "The weird part is, he wasn't even scheduled to work on Tracey's car yesterday."

"Thanks a lot." Moscone gave her his card. "I'm sorry about your boss."

"It's hard," said Brenda O'Reilly, Receptionist. "There are only seven of us in the office and we're wicked close. It's bad for business, too. The clients are nervous wrecks. Jack, that's Mr. Holden, the other partner, is trying to keep everyone calm, but as word spreads, they're calling him faster than he can call them. I'm glad I'm not him."

Ruth strode through the old headquarters building, opening doors, peering in rooms, then shutting the doors again. She'd been pleased with Moscone's call from Fiske & Holden, until she'd asked to speak to McGrath. Moscone had hemmed and hawed, but in the end had to acknowledge McGrath wasn't with him.

Now McGrath seemed to have disappeared altogether. Ruth

had paged him, beeped him, called his extension and his cell phone. No answer. Each futile attempt to reach him annoyed her more. Ruth hated shirkers and despised the little rationalizations that enabled people to avoid their duty. More than that, she suspected McGrath's failure to do what she'd asked was a direct rejection of her authority, a passive assertion of his own position that there was nothing more to Tracey Kendall's death than a tragic twist of fate.

Ruth opened the door to the detectives' squad room on the second floor. Her old desk from her years as the captain stood empty at one end of the room, awaiting the elevation of her replacement. On the other side of the room, the single desk all the detectives shared, heaped with bulging folders and office supplies, was similarly vacant. Ruth grunted in frustration and closed the door behind her.

Back downstairs, she approached Lieutenant Lawry. "Do you know where McGrath is?"

Lawry's look registered her tone. He shook his head. "Have you checked the men's room?"

Ruth glanced down the hall toward the men's locker room and the inner sanctum beyond. She was mad enough to barge right in, but she held back. There were probably younger officers in there who couldn't imagine the days before women's lockers, when men and women dressed together and shared a john. Now Ruth was the boss. Innocent lives might be scarred if she burst in there.

"Want me to check for you, Chief?" Lawry asked.

At that moment, Moscone's unmarked car pulled up in front of the big glass front door. As Ruth and Lawry watched, McGrath rocketed out of the men's locker room, down the hall, out the door, and into the passenger seat.

"No need," Ruth answered. "Problem solved."

★ ★ ★ ★ ★

McGrath braced himself against the plastic dashboard of the unmarked car as they raced down the New Derby hills toward Al Pace's address. Outside his window, the houses flying by grew progressively smaller and closer together. Al Pace lived and worked in Derby Mills, familiar territory for every cop in the city. Every third house in the Mills had a *Beware of Dog* sign posted on the chain-link fence that portioned off its tiny yard. McGrath thought at one time or another, he'd been chased by every one of those dogs.

He turned to Moscone. "Why'd you give me up?"

"She asked directly for you." Moscone was all innocence. "What was I supposed to do?"

"Say I was in the can." In fact, that's where he'd been. Just not in the one at Fiske & Holden. After he'd ditched that fool's errand this morning, he'd unplugged himself completely to get a few minutes' total isolation from his jabbering partner. Next thing he knew, a uniform burst in on his solitude to tell him Moscone had phoned the front desk four times looking for him and Murphy was on the warpath. Geez, since she'd become the acting chief, she'd completely lost her sense of humor.

As they screeched over the top of a hill and started down toward the river, McGrath swore the car actually lifted off the ground. "Slow down," he barked. "You're on the day shift now. You can't drive like a maniac. There are people around."

Moscone rounded the corner and pulled into Al Pace's driveway. Pace's business and residence stood on a narrow corner lot, a block from the river. The L-shaped house was old, built not as mill-worker housing, but as a groom's house on the prosperous farm that had preceded the mills. Along the side yard ran a building with five double doors, originally stables, now garages. A pickup truck with a custom cover was parked slightly askew at the far end of the building. *Screw Loose* was painted on the cab door in large blue letters.

The house looked empty when they pulled up, but as Moscone parked, a woman rounded the corner and stopped on the path to the side door. She pushed an old-fashioned baby carriage. A toddler and a preschooler, both boys, hung on either side.

Moscone jumped from the car. "Excuse me!" he called out, flagging the woman down. Up close, she was gaunt and pale. Her dark blond hair fell limply below her shoulders. There were deep blue circles under her gray eyes. Moscone held out his badge.

"Is he dead?" she asked, her voice barely audible.

"Is who dead?"

"My husband. When I saw you, I thought—"

"Are you Mrs. Pace?"

"Yes, I'm Karen Pace." The pale woman swayed. The toddler clung to her skirt.

Moscone put his arm out to steady her. "We're not here to tell you he's dead."

"He didn't come home last night. I was going to call you, but I wasn't sure—"

"Is it common for him not to come home?" McGrath growled, coming up behind.

The woman flinched. "He's never done it before."

"Mrs. Pace, may we come in?" Moscone asked as gently as he could.

"Sure. We're just getting back from the schoolyard. The house is a mess. I've been so worried about Al, I haven't got much done."

Karen Pace lifted the sleeping baby out of the carriage and entered the house through the side door. Moscone glanced around at the unkempt yard, inhaled deeply and followed her inside. McGrath and the little boys brought up the rear.

They entered a big, old kitchen with a wooden table at its center. The room was tidy and inviting. Apparently for Mrs. Pace, "a mess" meant breakfast dishes soaking in the sink. She offered tea. Moscone accepted for them both. Mrs. Pace moved around the kitchen, working expertly with one hand, holding the sleeping baby against her shoulder with the other.

When they were seated at the table, Moscone ran through the routine questions, McGrath sitting silently by his side. Karen Pace answered quietly. She'd last seen Al when he left in the Screw Loose truck Tuesday morning. She didn't know where he might be. None of his things seemed to be missing and his truck was in its usual position in the yard. That was what alarmed her so. Nothing was different and yet everything was.

The baby, dressed in blue, lay on his back across her lap. He let out a tiny snort and rubbed his nose in sleep.

Moscone leaned forward. "Why didn't you call us, Mrs. Pace?"

Karen Pace sighed deeply, using her free hand to cover her eyes. A tear slid over her cheek. "I thought about it. I was afraid he'd come back and be mad at me." Her voice cracked. "Now I'm afraid he won't come back." She allowed herself one sob, a deep double intake of breath, and then composed herself, wiping her eyes with the side of her hand and glancing nervously toward the little boys in the other room.

Moscone followed her gaze. He was impressed by the woman's strength. In spite of what must have been sickening worry, she got up this morning, made breakfast, and took the children out.

"Has your husband been under any unusual stress lately?"

Karen nodded miserably. The story came out in bits and pieces, but the picture they formed was all too familiar these days. The Paces were in terrible financial trouble. "Al thinks his old boss tricked him into paying too much for Screw Loose. Some months we pay on the house, some months on the business. We're always behind."

The kettle whistled. Karen stood, shifting the baby once again. Moscone felt McGrath beside him, fidgeting with impatience. Moscone pushed back his chair and walked into the next room. The toddler and the preschooler were under the dining table, building with large plastic blocks. Otherwise, the room was spotless. A corner cabinet stood on the far side of the room, covered with framed photographs of four little boys, alone or in groups. They were set-piece shots, the kind taken at the mall around the holidays. In the center of the hutch was the Paces' wedding portrait.

Karen Pace looked much the same—and very different. She was thin, but not yet gaunt; pale, but not yet wan. She wasn't conventionally pretty, but her smile was warm and she glowed in the way all brides should.

Al Pace was something else again. Broad through the shoulders and chest, his muscles bulged under his rented tuxedo. His skin was a dark, honey-colored tan, which set off his piercing green eyes and bright white teeth. A golden mane curled to his collar. Though Moscone didn't consider himself much of a judge of these things, it was indisputable—Al Pace was a stunningly good-looking man. Moscone returned to the kitchen and handed McGrath the photograph.

When they were seated around the table again, Moscone asked, "Have you ever heard of Tracey Kendall?"

"No."

"Fiske & Holden?"

"No."

Moscone nodded. "Mrs. Pace, I think we'd better find your husband. Tracey Kendall died in an automobile accident yesterday, right after Al finished working on her car."

"You're not saying Al had anything to do with it, are you?" Her voice rose in alarm. "Al's a fantastic mechanic. Ask anybody. Around here, they all bring their cars to Al."

"I understand, Mrs. Pace. Right now we don't know what happened. We need to find Al so he can help us figure it out."

Karen Pace didn't respond. Moscone looked around the kitchen again, impressed with its cleanliness and the care taken with each item in it. "You have a beautiful home," he offered, thinking it might be the one observation that could soothe.

"Thank you. It was my grandmother's. I used to come here every day after school and help her clean and make supper. When she passed, Al and I had the chance to buy it from my family. I've always loved this house." Karen Pace smiled. For the first time Moscone caught a glimpse of the woman in the wedding photo. "Are we done? I have to pick up my oldest boy at kindergarten soon."

They stood to go. "If you could just get us a different photograph of Al," Moscone said, indicating the wedding picture. "I wouldn't want to take this one."

When they left the Pace house, McGrath wandered out along the stables, standing on his toes to peer through the high windows of the old doors. The place was cluttered with junk. The contrast between Mrs. Pace's domain in the house and Al's in the stable and yard was striking.

The first four bays of the garage were full. Each held a car in some stage of reconstruction. One had its engine pulled apart. Two were in the throes of major body work. The fourth was up on a portable lift. The fifth bay was empty.

"Hey, hotshot!" McGrath called to Moscone. "Come here and tell me what you see."

Moscone could look through the stable window without standing on his toes. "It's empty."

"What else?"

"There's fresh oil stains on the floor."

"So?"

"So something has been in here recently."

"Moscone, maybe we'll make you a detective yet."

"I've been a detective on the night shift for two—"

"What else do you see?"

This time Moscone wasn't so quick to answer. "He has a license plate collection. There are old plates from all over the place hung up on the walls."

"What else?"

Moscone paused again. "A few plates are missing. There are spaces on the wall where they've been moved."

"Know what this means?"

"It means Al Pace disappeared in an unknown vehicle with three untraceable license plates."

McGrath shook his head. "It means the chief is going to have us running around investigating this bullshit case for days to come, is what it means."

In the basement at headquarters, Ruth requested Tracey Kendall's effects from the property clerk, who was plainly startled to see her in his subterranean domain. Back when the WPA had constructed the building, its lowest level had contained its jail, but today the lack of adequate light or ventilation rendered the cells inhumane by any modern standard. No longer able to use it to secure people, New Derby used the little jail to secure things—the weapons, drugs, money, pornography, and personal artifacts that made up evidence. The old kitchen, processing, and guard rooms had been converted to one large, grated vault lined with storage shelves. The four small cells were left intact, each one furnished with a table used to examine evidence.

Ruth carried the unwieldy box into one of the cells, pulled on latex gloves and removed a leather handbag, briefcase, full gym bag, and the slim silver phone on which Tracey Kendall had her last conversation. Carefully, Ruth removed the contents of the leather handbag—wallet, lipstick, compact, hairbrush, tooth-paste, and a toothbrush in a case. The wallet contained $512.27, a large amount, but not ridiculous. Ruth knew from experience rich people sometimes carried lots of cash.

The briefcase was tailored yet feminine. Ruth popped its lock. Inside, she found a matching pen and pencil, a folder of newsletters and reports, a leather-bound personal organizer, and a notebook computer with a neatly tied electric cord. Ruth flipped the organizer open to the page for Tuesday, the day of the accident. Tracey had noted a 9:30 A.M. conference call. After that, nothing. The back of the organizer contained separate sections including a long series of To Do lists, notes, expenses, and an address book. Ruth was struck by the order Tracey Kendall imposed on the things around her.

Ruth turned on the small computer, groaning when a password box came up. She made a couple of obvious tries, variations on "Carson," "Stephen," "Tracey." Nothing. Ruth also tried to turn on the mobile phone, but either it had been damaged in the crash or its battery had died, and there was no charger among Tracey's effects.

Ruth unzipped the gym bag. The fresh, slightly sweet smell of Tracey Kendall's perfume wafted up from the inside. Ruth wished Moscone were there. He could have told her what it was. The gym bag was full of neatly folded clothes—faded jeans, two turtlenecks, a work shirt, a man's t-shirt, a cardigan, several pairs of socks and underwear, and a pair of tennis shoes. There was an aerobics outfit, leotard and spandex shorts, in a separate zippered compartment. Ruth removed the contents from the bag. The well-worn clothes were an unexpected contrast to the professional edge of the briefcase and pocketbook. Ruth lifted the jeans to her cheek. They were as soft as flannel.

Probing along the inside of the duffel with her gloved hands, Ruth found a small pocket in the lining. She pulled out a felt pouch, emptying it onto the tabletop. There were two pieces of jewelry, a bracelet encircled with diamonds and a locket. Inside the locket were two pictures of the same boy, one taken in babyhood, the other at four or five. Tracey's son Carson, no doubt. He wore the same serious demeanor in each of the pictures.

Ruth held the open locket in her hand. Tracey Kendall's beautiful possessions were now orphans. No one would likely ever love them as she had. The boy, at least, still had a father, but Ruth knew from experience that having one parent was not the same as having two. She had been around Carson Kendall's age when her father had walked off into the night without explanation or good-bye. The hole it left was permanent.

Ruth stepped back and surveyed Tracey Kendall's possessions spread across the tabletop. She couldn't identify the designer of the handbag, briefcase, or wallet, but she could tell they were expensive. Three of New Derby's seven villages were dominated by people like Tracey Kendall, sons and daughters of privilege who had parlayed their head start in life into a rout. Ruth didn't like these people. She didn't like their sense of entitlement or the way they were so often oblivious to the pressures in other people's lives. She didn't like it when they treated her officers like servants, instead of seeing them as enforcers of the law. She didn't need the grief this case would bring with it, especially not now when her appointment was so close at hand.

But when Ruth turned from the expensive leather pieces and looked at the pile of old clothes, her hostility faded. She picked up the cardigan. It was old, even slightly pilled. The essence of Tracey Kendall clung to it. These clothes were not for an emergency change or to be put on after a workout. Ruth recognized them as Tracey's time-worn favorites, packed with care. They were exactly the kind of clothes Ruth would have taken if she'd been forced to select from all her things those that would fit into a single bag.

"Tracey Kendall, where were you going?" Ruth asked the cell walls.

CHAPTER THREE

Ruth was sitting at her desk, eating a solitary lunch, waiting impatiently for McGrath and Moscone to return, when Mayor Rosenfeld knocked twice at the frame of her open door and bounced into her office.

"What's hot?" The mayor started every conversation with the same question. His curiosity about anything that was happening in New Derby was boundless.

"Fatal car wreck."

The mayor nodded, his jowls moving up and down. Rosenfeld's heavy features gave him a mournful look, though he was generally one of the most energetic, optimistic people Ruth knew. "I heard. Willow Road. Terrible accident."

"I don't think it was. An accident, that is."

"Really?" Now Rosenfeld was interested. "What exactly do you think?"

"I'm not sure," Ruth replied honestly. "The mechanic who worked on the woman's car right before the crash has disappeared."

"Negligence?"

"Could be." Ruth kept her tone neutral. "Is that what you came to talk to me about?"

"What? Oh, no. I came to talk about the search firm's report and what we do next."

Ruth smiled expectantly. Finally, the mayor was going to give her the good news. He continued, "We've got big problems."

35

Ruth willed herself to be calm, to remember the mayor's penchant for hyperbole, but she could feel the heat spreading under her uniform. Ruth had learned, in childhood and at work, to stay in control, but there was a traitor living in her body. Heightened emotion—anger, fear, excitement—brought on a deep flush, which started across her chest, then grew, mottled red and dead white, up her neck and finally to her cheeks. She was deeply embarrassed by this outward signal of her feelings, but years of living with it had taught her that the only remedy was to ignore it. "Everyone told me the search firm's report was great," she protested.

"I'm sure it is. They told me over the phone it would be, and why should they lie? I haven't opened it."

"Haven't opened it? Why not?"

"Because once I open it, I have to turn it over to the aldermen. When they get it, they have to vote, and they're not ready to vote. At least not the way we want."

Ruth let her confusion show. "But the aldermen worked hand in glove with the search firm. Why wouldn't they accept the results?"

The mayor trained his sad brown eyes on Ruth. "Because they're not ready," he said as if it was all the explanation required. "I, we, have more work to do."

"But Anna Abbott—"

"As president of the Board of Aldermen, Anna can threaten, wheedle and cajole, but in the end she only gets one vote. Several board members are just not ready to vote your way."

"Why not?"

Mayor Rosenfeld came around to Ruth's side of the desk, leaned his stocky body against it so he was looking down at her and said in a low voice, "Three reasons." He extended a stubby finger. "One, there are those who think your roots in the community aren't deep enough."

Ruth nodded. This was a reference to her transfer from the Boston PD into the New Derby department as a lieutenant ten years earlier. New Derby liked to grow its own officers. It was an objection easily handled. None of the other finalists had any ties to New Derby.

"Two," the mayor waved another fat digit, "there are those who feel your ties to the community run *too* deep."

Ruth understood this as well. Some forty members of her husband Marty's extended family, the Murphy-McDonough clan, lived in New Derby. They taught school, fought fires, delivered mail and owned a variety of businesses, including a dry cleaner's, two liquor stores, and the only cab company. They were not without influence. Ruth's transfer into the department had been the direct result of her father-in-law's intervention. Ruth wasn't worried about this objection either. The search firm's report proved she was qualified for the job.

The mayor pushed his heavy glasses to his forehead and rubbed his eyes. "Both of which could be easily handled, as you know—if it weren't for the big number three—your relationship with District Attorney Baines."

Rosenfeld looked at Ruth expectantly. When she didn't speak, he went on. "Everyone knows you two don't get along. No one knows why." The mayor paused again. Ruth knew he would love for her to tell him why. He was in a business where information, to hold or trade, was a valuable commodity.

But she wasn't telling. "Some tension between us is normal," she pointed out. "Police arrest on probable cause. D.A.s prosecute beyond a reasonable doubt. There's a big gray area for finger-pointing in between."

"Are you saying your relationship with Baines is 'normal'? If I ask the mayors and town managers of the forty-one other communities in the county, will they tell me their police chiefs have the same level of problems with Baines?"

"No," Ruth admitted.

"You're right, because I've already asked them." Rosenfeld softened his tone.

"Why would that come up now?"

The mayor looked at her like she was born yesterday. "Why do you think?"

"Because Baines has been dribbling in people's ears, planting doubts." During the early part of the selection process, Ruth had expected trouble from Baines, but when six months went by without a whiff of him, she'd let her guard down.

"Exactly. I don't know what gives between you two, but he doesn't want you to be chief."

Ruth responded with silence. The mayor threw up his hands. "Look, everyone in the Commonwealth knows Baines is a horse's patootie, but he's the district attorney of this county, and in this state D.A.s generally stay in office until they move up or pass on. I don't see Baines moving up any time soon. It's important for the police chief to be able to work with the district attorney's office. You know that."

"I work fine with his office."

"With the district attorney, then. Chief, it's not an unreasonable thing."

Ruth shifted to look the mayor in the eye. "What would you suggest I do?"

The mayor returned her gaze. "Get back in his good graces?"

Ruth walked to one of the big windows and looked out. She couldn't return to a place she'd never been. The silence stretched again.

The mayor put a pudgy hand on her shoulder. "All right, then." His voice was almost gentle. "This isn't the end of the world. I'll take care of it. Just stay out of Baines's line of fire."

After the mayor left, Ruth sat quietly at her desk. She was rattled by what the mayor had said, and angry at herself for allowing the search firm's positive report to raise her hopes so high. She didn't believe in counting chickens. "It's never done until it's done," she muttered to herself. "You know better."

Ruth hadn't set out to become a police chief or even a police officer. She'd taken the civil service exam at the urging of her in-laws, who never could quite get the distinction between a degree in sociology and one in social work. The test taken, Ruth found herself at a moment in time when the discrimination lawsuits had been settled and the Boston PD needed women, quickly. A window opened and she'd scooted through it, thinking only of paying off her college loans.

She'd turned out to be good at the job, first in Boston and then in New Derby. Police work played to her strengths—her ability to take charge, solve problems, make quick decisions. And, in the early days, being so often the only woman on the shift made virtues of her weaknesses—her difficulty showing her emotions, her minimal need for socializing, and her greater desire for respect than for acceptance. Common wisdom said the women had to work twice as hard as the men to get ahead. Ruth thought a lot of the men didn't work so awfully hard.

Three years ago as captain of the Detective Squad, she'd raised her head up out of the day-to-day long enough to realize she could become chief. The old chief had seen it, too, at about the same time. He'd pushed her onto visible statewide task-forces, taken her to the annual dinners of city volunteer organizations, found reasons for her to make presentations to the mayor and the aldermen. Then, suddenly, the old chief was gone, his wife's cancer scare causing him to retire sooner than either he or Ruth expected.

Now that she was doing the chief's job, Ruth was amazed by how much she loved it, scared by how much she wanted it. The months while the search firm toiled had been agonizing for her, made more and not less so by the people in town who assured her she was a shoo-in. And now, with the goal so close at hand, District Attorney Baines was threatening it. So typical of that odious man.

Ruth took several long breaths to calm herself, closed her eyes, and leaned back in her chair, then straightened herself up and got on with her work.

After lunch, Ruth, Lawry, Moscone, and McGrath sat at the big conference table in Ruth's office and reviewed the events of the morning.

"So this guy sees that he screwed up the Kendall woman's car, freaks out, and takes off," McGrath offered.

"Or," Moscone turned Al Pace's picture over in his hands, "she and Pace were involved and he wanted to get rid of her."

"Involved?" Lawry asked, not challenging, but interested. "You mean romantically? A Derby Hills fund manager and a Derby Mills auto mechanic?"

Wordlessly, Moscone passed Pace's photo to Lawry. "Ah ha," Lawry said when he saw it.

"Why did she have a packed bag in her car?" Ruth wanted to know.

"Maybe they were running away together and something went wrong."

"Oh, for pity's sake." McGrath was having none of this. "Where did you get that?"

"Again, have you seen this guy?" Moscone pushed the photo to McGrath.

"Enough with how good looking he is already. What are you, gay?"

Ruth wasn't so sure about Moscone's affair theory. What she'd glimpsed of Tracey Kendall's hyper-organized life didn't leave much room for that kind of messy social arrangement, and the clothes in the bag had included a comfortable old

T-shirt for sleeping, not lingerie for an affair. But you never knew with people, and this early in the investigation, the goal was to discover any possible connection between the victim and the man who'd disappeared. Ruth vowed to keep an open mind.

"Did Pace have any priors?" she asked Moscone.

"No, but he was in the service, so we can get fingerprints if we need them."

"Are we all agreed this could well be more than an accident?" Ruth asked.

Lawry and Moscone nodded. Ruth stared at McGrath, who pulled a face. "Are we even going to talk about what a stinker this case is?"

"Why is it a stinker?" Moscone asked.

"It's a complicated case," McGrath answered. "Even we started out believing it was a simple accident. A defense attorney will have a field day with that. Plus, we've got a high profile victim, which will attract the press, and not in a good way for the D.A., and a sympathetic defendant. Let's face it, whether he did it deliberately or not, Pace's never been in trouble, he's got a beautiful family—"

"And he's so handsome," Moscone interjected, but this time, before McGrath could say anything, Moscone broke into a wide grin.

"Well, yeah," McGrath had to concede. "Prosecutors hate good-looking defendants, because juries hate convicting them."

"So, what you're saying is we're trying to build a case against a guy the district attorney's office will plead out, absolutely best case."

Ruth was honest. "With a high profile victim, even pleading it out will cause heartburn. McGrath's right. This is the kind of case D.A.s hate, even good ones."

"Which means ours will hate it even more," McGrath finished.

41

Despite Rosenfeld's warning to stay out of Baines's way, Ruth shut the discussion down. "We can't worry about that now. We don't even really know what we're dealing with."

By the end of the meeting, each of them had an assignment. The most important thing was to locate Pace. Lawry would coordinate a search with state and local forces. Following up on Moscone's affair theory, Lawry would also direct visits by local law enforcement, armed with photos of Tracey and Al, to every hotel, motel, and guest house within a half-hour drive of Tracey's office. McGrath would go back to Pace's house to search for connections to Tracey Kendall and talk to any of Pace's friends who might have a guess as to his whereabouts, or at least know what kind of vehicle he'd taken from the empty stable bay. Moscone and the chief were heading to the state garage and then on to the Kendall house.

Sergeant Dan Logan of the Massachusetts State Police Collision Analysis and Reconstruction Section (called, too cutely in Ruth's opinion, C.A.R.S.), met Ruth and Moscone at the door to the state police garage. Logan was short with an upturned nose and cherub cheeks. Only the flecks of gray in his sandy hair and a web of fine wrinkles around his eyes kept him from looking like a twelve-year-old. "You're here about the Kendall car," he said.

"How's it coming?" Ruth asked.

"Slowly. The car was traveling at an extremely high rate of speed when it hit an immovable object, a thick stone wall. No braking occurred. The damage was bound to be extensive."

"Were the brakes working?"

"The entire brake system was destroyed in the crash. We can tell that the brake lights weren't on at impact. Take the speed and lack of skid marks anywhere on the hill and combine it with the fact we know she was alert right before the crash, and

I'd say it's a good bet the brakes were gone."

"Were the brakes tampered with?" Moscone pushed.

"There's no physical evidence left to show they were."

"What about brake fluid? Can't you search the road?"

"Assuming I could find anything, all that would tell me is the brake fluid came out, not how the lines got damaged. We'll download the car's event data recorder in the next day or so."

"The black box?"

"Yup. They were originally put in cars to improve airbag deployment, but now most of them record data continuously on a ten-second loop that stops when a collision occurs. If we're lucky, it'll tell us precisely how fast she was going and whether the brake pedal was pressed down any time before impact."

They were quiet for a moment, absorbing this, then Ruth asked, "Sergeant, does it affect your analysis knowing the last person who touched this car has disappeared?"

"Chief, I can only go with what the car and the scene tell me, and so far neither of them has much to say. Let me do my job, download the data from the black box, rebuild the scene from the photometry."

"How long will that take?"

"Normal course of things, couple of months."

Ruth knew what Logan told her was true. All the new tools, especially the photometric cameras, were focused on clearing the scene faster and getting traffic moving again, but they also supplied miles of data that had to be painstakingly analyzed. Like all the state police labs, C.A.R.S. was overworked and undermanned.

"Are you expecting an insurance problem?" Logan asked.

"Not that I know of. But I've got an unexplained death, one woman's shattered husband, another man's terrified wife, and a total of five grieving children."

Logan peeled back some of his professional detachment. "I'll see if I can move some things around to give it a higher priority." He motioned to the workroom door. "Want to see it?"

Trailed by Moscone, Ruth took a step into the workroom, then stopped abruptly. Tracey's car was up on blocks in the center of the vast concrete floor. Everything that could be removed had been—seats, wheels, doors, fenders. The front end was pushed upward, sideways, then back. The door frames were buckled, the roof concave. In this skeletal form, the SUV's damage looked more explicit and cruel than it had in the photos.

Ruth flashed on Tracey Kendall and the order she imposed on her possessions—the organizer, the contents of her pocketbook, the neatly folded old clothes in the gym bag with Tracey's essence still clinging to them. In spite of it all, chaos had still come roaring in, its violence captured in the twisted frame of the SUV. All of Tracey's efforts to tame life and ride it had been futile. For one horrible moment, standing on the cement floor of the state police garage, Ruth was overcome with such sadness, she thought she might lose control.

Exerting an effort, Ruth pulled herself together. It wouldn't do to burst into noisy sobs in front of Sergeant Logan and Carl Moscone. "I thought these big expensive cars weren't supposed to crumple up like that."

"There's only so much airbags, crumple zones and seat belts can do to protect you from physics," Logan responded. "If this had been a shitbox it would've exploded into a thousand pieces."

Moscone pulled their unmarked car through the gate at the Kendall property and stopped. From the passenger seat, Ruth studied the grounds. An unused guardhouse stood by the gate. In front of them, a wide semi-circular drive of pale, crushed stone surrounded a rich green lawn that rippled seventy-five yards up a hill to the main house. The back and side yards were heavily wooded. There were houses within easy walking distance of the Kendalls', but even on April's second warm day, with the buds just appearing on the trees, the neighbors weren't visible.

To the right of the drive, up near the house, stood a warren of garages, with work or living space above. Further down, to the left of the driveway's other arc, was a three-story structure with huge windows and attic dormers looking out on the lawn. At the center of the arc was the main house, an edifice of weathered shingles and dark trim. Ruth found it more imposing than attractive. On the front lawn stood enough playground equipment for a preschool.

Moscone parked behind the other cars in the drive, a silver sports car and an older model German sedan. The house seemed unusually quiet. Though the days were long past in New Derby when death inevitably brought a flood of neighbors bearing casseroles, the houses of the newly bereaved were still generally filled with family and friends.

The doorbell was answered by a tall, elegant woman in an expensive caftan. She looked at their badges and admitted them into a two-story entrance hall. "I'm Susan Gleason, Stephen's dealer."

Moscone blinked. "Mr. Kendall is an artist," Ruth reminded him, to clear up any confusion.

Susan Gleason nodded. Earrings dangled against her neck. Her long, gray hair was pulled back and anchored with a silver clasp. "An important artist and a good friend." She gave them a smile Ruth knew well. The officer-I-had-a-good-reason-to-run-that-red-light smile. "In fact, if I could impose on you. Mr. Kendall has had a ghastly night. He's recovered a bit, but talking to you could set him back terribly, and no one wants that, so unless this is important—"

Ruth cut her off. "It's important."

Ms. Gleason didn't protest further. She ushered them to the living room and withdrew. Ruth could hear her moving quietly in the entrance hall.

The Kendall living room was lovely, shades of off-white and pale yellow. Everything had been carefully placed, even the books on the shelves and the magazines fanned across the cocktail table. Despite the artifice, Ruth wasn't as put off by the house as she'd expected. There was something warm, almost homey, about it.

A side table held an assortment of photographs in prettily mismatched frames. Most were casual shots memorializing fun times. Tracey Kendall's formal wedding portrait was there as well, in a simple silver frame. Her gown had been chosen to emphasize her height. It tapered from her broad shoulders to her slender waist without a bit of lace or froufrou to distract. Tracey gazed out of the photo with intelligent, hazel eyes. She was a smiling, triumphant bride.

Ruth picked up a photo of a handsome man tossing a toddler in the air. The man and the child were laughing, joyous in the release and sensation of flying, anticipating the catch and inevitable hug. The child was a toddler version of the boy in the locket.

"Chief Murphy, Detective Moscone." The man from the photo entered the living room, right hand outstretched. He was trailed by a fresh-faced woman in her early twenties whom he introduced as the nanny, Hannah Whiteside.

"Please, sit down." Stephen Kendall's voice was striking—deep and resonant. He guided Ruth and Moscone to a pair of upholstered chairs. The chairs were deep and low, clearly all wrong for the kind of conversation they were about to have, but Ruth decided to take what Stephen Kendall offered. He was the newly bereaved spouse, and Ruth thought it was important for him to sit where he was most comfortable.

The nanny sat down on the couch opposite, looking expectant. It was clear she intended to stay. "Is this about Tracey's remains?" she asked. "People keep calling, asking about arrangements and we don't know what to tell them."

Moscone cleared his throat. "Miss Whiteside, yesterday you offered me coffee. I sure would like some now." Hannah hesitated for a moment, visibly disappointed at her dismissal, but then headed toward the kitchen. Moscone stayed in the deep chair next to Ruth's.

Stephen sat on the couch. Ruth moved as far forward as she could in the deep upholstery of the chair and studied Tracey Kendall's husband. He was tall and muscular, but lean, both in body and in face, pale-skinned, but dark-haired and dark-eyed. She judged him to be younger than his wife, mid-thirties at the most.

"Did you come about Tracey's—" As he spoke, Stephen Kendall looked straight into Ruth's eyes, giving her his full attention. The beautiful voice did what looks alone could not. It gave him a magnetic presence. Ruth felt a tug. She shook it off, careful not to be pulled in.

"No, Mr. Kendall, I don't have that information yet. We'll notify you as soon as the medical examiner is through. I came to tell you we're concerned about the circumstances surrounding your wife's death."

If Ruth was looking for a reaction, she got one. Stephen Kendall's jaw dropped open. "What circumstances?"

"Mr. Kendall, do you know a company called Screw Loose?"

Kendall opened his mouth a few times, puffing noisily without forming words. Ruth repeated the question. This time, Kendall's tongue engaged. "They're the people who take care of our cars." His deep voice was shaky.

"Have you ever met Al Pace, the proprietor?"

"No. Never. They do the work at Tracey's office."

"Mr. Pace serviced your wife's car immediately before she died."

"And you think he had something to do with Tracey's death?" Kendall seemed truly astonished.

"Mr. Pace has been missing since your wife's accident," Moscone told him.

"What are you saying?"

"We don't know," Ruth answered truthfully. "It may have been negligence or deliberate tampering. It may have been nothing at all."

"It would help if we understood the relationship between them," Moscone added.

"He fixed her car."

"Yes, but what else?" Moscone pressed. "Pace's wife says he was in financial difficulty. Could Tracey have lent him money?"

"No. She would never do that. We've had our own cash drain lately. The economy has affected Tracey's earnings at the firm and I have a big show coming up—"

"Could Tracey and Pace have been friends?"

"Friends? No."

"You knew all your wife's friends?" Moscone didn't hide his skepticism.

Kendall understood his meaning. "She was not sleeping with this man." He said it slowly, definitely, looking directly at Ruth, not Moscone. "This is my wife. Tracey's no longer here to defend herself, but she cared a great deal how others thought of her. I beg you, please don't turn this horrible accident into something she would be ashamed of." Kendall leaned forward on the couch and touched the arm of Ruth's chair. "Please, Chief Murphy, this is important."

"Halloo!" The call came from the back of the house. Stephen Kendall blinked and looked away. The calls got louder until a woman stood in the vast entrance hall. "Oh, hello," she said, spotting them. "I've brought Carson back."

The woman came to the edge of the living room. She looked

like the perfect suburban matron—expensive, casual clothes and frosted hair done up in a neat 'do. The boy from the photos held onto her left hand. The woman stared at Ruth and Moscone in frank appraisal. "Fran Powell," she said.

Ruth stood, as did Moscone. "Ruth Murphy, Acting Chief of Police. This is Detective Moscone." The boy let go of the woman's hand, ran around Ruth and lunged toward his father.

"Oooh, sorry." Fran backed away, as if noticing Ruth's uniform for the first time. "You want privacy." She retreated across the entrance hall toward the kitchen. Moscone, reading Ruth's face at a glance, followed.

Ruth turned back toward the couch to study Stephen Kendall's reaction to the interruption, but instead saw him angrily shove his son from his lap. "Not now, Carson."

Carson stood glued to the spot, hand to his mouth.

"Go on," Kendall directed. The boy looked uncertain. "I said, go on." Kendall's voice rose. "Hannah! Come get this boy!"

Hannah was through the swinging kitchen door into the center hall in a flash. She bounded across the big living room, knelt and enveloped the boy in her strong arms. "Come on," she whispered. "Daddy's busy."

Carson, clearly confused, allowed himself to be led away, head down, staring at his feet. From the stairway, he looked at his father, eyes wide with hurt.

Ruth, still standing, digested the scene. Stephen Kendall had rejected his half-orphaned son cleanly and completely. And it was atypical. Carson had been stunned. Ruth tried to imagine the swirl of Kendall's mind. Wife newly dead, questions raised. Would that cause someone to push away a child in need of comfort?

"Mr. Kendall," she asked, "where is your family?"

If he thought the question odd, he didn't show it. He leaned forward and spoke directly to Ruth. "Tracey's family is in Southampton. They'll come, of course. They're just waiting to see when we might . . . until plans are more definite. On my side, it's just me and my mother. We haven't spoken for years. She disapproved of my marriage to Tracey. Since yesterday, one of my thoughts has been whether I should I call her in Florida and give her the satisfaction of knowing she finally got her wish—Tracey and I are no longer together. Funny what goes through your head."

"Mr. Kendall, would Tracey have receipts or other records from her interactions with Screw Loose? We'd like to look at them."

"Why?"

"To see if there's anything to help us understand what's happened."

"There won't be. You can't understand a senseless tragedy." Kendall stood to face her. "Besides, don't you need a warrant?"

"Not if you give me permission."

Stephen Kendall shrugged. "You're welcome to look in her study."

Tracey Kendall's study was a small room on the second floor, tucked behind the main staircase. It was neat, yet cozy, a muted mauve color with surprising, lacy curtains on the single window. A few envelopes sat in a rosewood in-box on the desk; otherwise everything was buttoned up tight

Ruth moved to the chair between Tracey Kendall's desk and credenza. Moscone, returned from his conversation with Fran Powell, sat on an upholstered chaise, the only other piece of furniture. The room was too small for two people to search, but Moscone dutifully scanned the built-in bookshelves.

Ruth studied the desk in front of her. A fine film of dust coated the surface. It was easy to tell some items had been recently moved. She opened the drawers of the credenza. They were full of file folders labeled in a neat hand: financial statements, passports, bills for household goods and art supplies. Ruth was struck by the orderliness of the room. In Ruth's experience, every cop was part voyeur. She certainly was— perhaps that was the elusive link between police work and sociology. There was a certain rush to bursting into other peoples' lives so unexpectedly. Yet much of what they saw was so disheveled, the home equivalent of dirty underwear in the emergency room. "How do you know your house was ransacked?" She'd asked that a hundred times.

Ruth removed a file marked "Screw Loose," from the credenza. It held several invoices, all marked "paid."

"What did you get from the neighbor?" she asked Moscone.

"She lives through the woods in the back. Said she was Tracey Kendall's best friend. That was as far as I got with Hannah Whiteside hanging around. Mrs. Powell seems like an odd one. We'll have to go back to her later."

The contents of Tracey's desk drawers were as mundane as the credenza. Ruth stood up and crossed over to the bookshelves. At first, she studied the space between the spines of the books and the edge of the shelves, then she examined the books—*Black Beauty, The Wizard of Oz,* the Bronte sisters, complete sets of the Little House books and Nancy Drew, including some first editions.

"Are we done?" Moscone asked.

"I guess so. You know, this isn't what I expected. Where's the computer? Even if she used the laptop that was in her car, where are the cables, chargers, power strip, something? Where's the phone? Perhaps this room is more a refuge than a place to work. Anyway, the most interesting thing about this room," Ruth concluded, "is that someone searched it before we did."

★ ★ ★ ★ ★

Susan Gleason saw them out.

"Back to headquarters?" Moscone asked.

Ruth didn't hear him. She was staring across the lawn to where Carson Kendall sat alone on the edge of the large sandbox in the center of the play space, temporarily forgotten by an unsettled household.

"Just a minute, Detective."

Ruth approached Carson slowly. He raised his neatly combed head and looked at her steadily. He didn't seem at all afraid.

"I'm Police Chief Murphy." Ruth walked to the edge of the sandbox.

"You're here about my Mom."

Ruth sat down beside Carson, facing the other way, so her feet stayed out of the sand. "I'm sure you miss her." Carson nodded, gazing into the distance. Ruth thought of the silver locket tucked in with Tracey's old clothes. "She loved you very much."

To Ruth's utter surprise, Carson shook his head, no. A tear slid down his nose. "She was very mad at me," he said, and then began to cry in earnest.

Ruth put her arm around him and cradled him to her side, her chest tight with the little boy's misery. She thought about her own children. Just that morning, after their wonderful family drive the night before, Sarah had been late for school and needed a ride. She'd lost her shoes for the umpteenth time that month and was running all over the house searching for them. "Come on," Ruth had yelled, standing by the door. "Put something on your feet, because we are leaving this instant!" Then she'd lectured Sarah for the entirety of the short ride to school about personal responsibility, taking care of her things and respect for other people's time. Sarah had banged out of the car the moment it stopped and stalked off without so much as looking back.

"Parents don't stay mad," Ruth told Carson. "They get over things."

Carson turned his face to hers. "But what if they die before that happens?"

CHAPTER FOUR

Immediately after roll call the next morning, Lieutenant Lawry appeared in Ruth's doorway, a cup of coffee in each hand. They had their second cup together whenever they could manage it, which worked out to about half the time. It was a ritual they both enjoyed.

"Nothing from the hotels." Lawry sat erect, starched shirt on starched skin. He was the only person on the force, Ruth reflected, who could be described as looking dapper in a New Derby PD uniform.

"I saw." Ruth indicated the pile of reports on her desk.

"We may have to go public with the Pace disappearance." Lawry advanced the idea tentatively.

"I know." Ruth dreaded bringing the press into any investigation. Witnesses reacted by clamming up or talking too much. Hours were devoted to following false leads. Most of all, a measure of control was ceded. However, in a missing persons case, the media could be helpful. "Maybe we'll get lucky and a state trooper somewhere will stop Pace for speeding, run his plate, and discover it's forty years old," Ruth said, thinking of the blank spaces McGrath had described on the stable walls.

"Maybe." Lawry was loyal, but not to the point of fooling himself—or her. He wasn't buying into the fantasy.

"I'll let you know about the press by midday."

"You're the boss." Lawry smiled. "Thank goodness."

★ ★ ★ ★ ★

"What does this company do?" Ruth asked as she and Moscone sped toward Fiske & Holden at Moscone's usual maniacal speed. In Derby Center, the sidewalks flying by were crowded with pedestrians enjoying the warm sunshine, aware their liberation from nasty weather might be short-lived. In New England, spring is a discrete event like Indian summer, sandwiched between bouts of chilly rain.

"It's a small cap mutual fund. They take chunks of money from individuals, trusts, and groups and invest it in smaller public companies."

Outside the Center, the crowds disappeared quickly. By the time Ruth and Moscone reached the office parks at the edge of town, no one was around. The modern buildings sat alone on rolling campuses surrounded by vacant cars. Ruth hoped the buildings enjoyed their parks, since people never seemed to use them. She wondered how glass and concrete could be used in so many variations of ugly.

Fiske & Holden's offices were in the ugliest building of all. The last one in the Truman Executive Park, it was a squat square perched on the side of a steep hill. A seamless expanse of tinted windows was sandwiched between large sills of heavy masonry. Despite the glass, the building had an oppressive feel, as if its concrete lid was pushing it into the ground. A parking lot with a dozen spaces led up to the front entrance. Moscone pulled Ruth's official car into one of the two slots marked "Visitor."

Fiske & Holden was the building's only tenant. The reception area was sleek and modern, decorated in black and dark gray. Brenda O'Reilly's marble workstation faced the big glass window and front door. She had a clear view of the parking lot, though the bar-height counter at the front of her workspace blocked her view when she was on the phones. The open door behind her console led into a windowless break room. A large table stood at its center, a refrigerator and sink on the periphery.

"Jack is in Boston. He'll be here soon," Brenda told them when Moscone explained their mission. "I think you should start with Ellie Berger, our office manager. She's been here the longest and does all the personnel stuff."

Brenda punched some numbers and talked into her headpiece. Ellie Berger appeared and led Ruth and Moscone away.

Ellie Berger had a friendly face framed by light brown curls. She was a maternal woman somewhere in the long journey of middle age, short, and while not plump, soft and rounded. Her office was smallish, second in the row of three on the north side of the building. From the window, views of the parking lot and the accident site were obscured, but the hills of Waltham and Weston were visible beyond the stretch of Willow Road in the foreground.

Ellie closed her door and pointed her visitors to two serviceable office chairs facing her wooden desk. "This is about Tracey's accident, I'm sure." Ellie's big eyes brimmed with tears. "I'm sorry. This is a difficult time."

Ruth gave the woman a moment to compose herself. "I'm sure it is, Mrs. Berger. Brenda said you'd known Tracey the longest."

Ellie Berger closed her eyes. "Jack Holden and I are the only ones still here who go back to when Tracey arrived. The place was drying up. Tracey came in like a breath of fresh air. She was only twenty-eight, a whiz kid, young and beautiful. She was so energetic; she swept you up in her enthusiasm. She and Jack took his father's musty old investment firm and reinvented it in less than a year. Those early days were the most fun I've ever had in my working life. As time went by, I watched Tracey fall in love, get married, have her baby." Ellie Berger blew her nose.

Ruth looked out the window at the black ribbon of Willow Road, beginning its steep descent outside Ellie Berger's office. "How did you find out about the accident?"

"Brenda, Kevin, Jane, and I always bring food from home and eat in the break room. As we were getting back to our desks, we heard the sirens. I stood at this window," Ellie Berger gestured toward her view, "and watched the emergency vehicles go by—police, ambulance, fire. I couldn't see where they stopped, so I ran into Jack's office. You can see down the hill from there. Then, Kevin, Jane, and Brenda burst in. Poor Jack was at his desk trying to eat a sandwich and read the paper. We stood around gawking. Of course, we had no idea it was Tracey. You couldn't tell what type of vehicle it was from up here and she'd left half an hour earlier. Hannah Whiteside called us at about 4:30 with the news." Ellie exhaled noisily, fighting for composure.

Ruth counted—Brenda, Kevin, Jane, and Ellie were in the break room, Jack was eating in his office and Tracey, of course, was in the mangled SUV at the bottom of the hill. Brenda had told Moscone there were seven employees. Someone was missing.

"Adam Bender, our trader," Ellie answered when asked. "I don't think he was here. Adam always walks a half-mile up Willow Road in the other direction to the Deli-Cater at lunchtime, gets a turkey on rye and an apple juice and walks back. You can set your watch by him. He eats at his desk. He isn't sociable."

"Who else in the office used Screw Loose?" Moscone asked. "Did you?"

"No. My husband is handy with cars. He does the routine stuff. As for who else used him, Brenda would know better than I. She keeps track of the appointments and the keys." Ellie sniffed into a tissue. "I never understood why Tracey let that man take care of those expensive cars. She said he was good. But he wasn't, and now his carelessness has killed her."

Ruth leaned forward. "Mrs. Berger, do you know that Al Pace's carelessness killed Tracey Kendall?"

Ellie pulled a tissue from her top desk drawer. "It's the only thing that makes sense. Al broke Tracey's car." She wiped her eyes.

"How well did Mrs. Kendall know Mr. Pace?" Moscone asked.

Ellie looked confused. "How well do you know your mechanic, your dry cleaner, your dog groomer?"

Ruth knew her dry cleaners intimately. They were Marty's parents.

Moscone tried again. "Mrs. Berger, did you ever have any indication Al Pace was more to Tracey Kendall than a man who took care of her cars?"

Ellie's open face closed down. "Excuse me? Did he tell you something? Because if he told you he was more to Tracey than a friendly soul with business problems, he's a dirty liar. All she ever did was give him advice from time to time."

"Tracey confided in you?"

"No, she wasn't one to open up about her personal life, but I knew her for eleven years. There are some things I'm sure about."

Ruth assessed Ellie's answer and her vehemence. Would this soft, motherly woman lie? She might, Ruth concluded, to protect a child or someone she related to as one of her children.

"Mrs. Berger, we need to see Tracey's office and talk to the other employees."

Ellie hesitated before responding, her mouth set in a grim line. "Fine. You look at the office while I set up the interviews. We'll start with Jane Parker and Kevin Chun, our analysts." Without waiting for a reply she picked up the phone, then paused. "Are you going to be asking the staff questions like that?"

"Like what?"

"About Tracey and Al Pace."

"Yes."

Ellie Berger studied her desk blotter. "That doesn't make me happy."

Tracey Kendall's office was behind a closed door off the reception area. Large and sleekly modern, it was as different from her study at home as it could be. Two walls of floor-to-ceiling windows framed a full view of the parking lot and partial view of Willow Road. The third wall was hung with two abstract paintings, splashes of color and texture that caused the rest of the room to recede. The desk and conference table were made of sheets of glass supported by clear Plexiglas. On the desk, Tracey's phone and the docking station for her laptop appeared to hover in midair.

Ruth opened the bank of closet doors behind the conference table. The closet was half filled with file cabinets. On a rod on the other side of the closet hung a gray suit, a white blouse still in the cleaner's wrap, and a laundry bag containing a bra, half-slip, panties, and a couple of extra pairs of hose. A pair of black pumps sat on the floor.

"What were these for?" Moscone asked. "Does this support the idea she was getting ready to take off?"

Ruth felt the fine wool of the jacket. "No. These are here for emergencies, like if she spilled something on herself at lunch, or lost a button."

Moscone began opening file drawers. Ruth bent to examine the pockets of the suit.

Ellie Berger knocked on the doorframe. "Ready?"

Ruth glanced at Moscone, who nodded slightly. Nothing

obvious here—and unlike Tracey's study at home, this room hadn't been searched.

"Yes, Mrs. Berger, thank you." Ellie led them from the room.

Kevin Chun and Jane Parker shared an office on the south side of the building. They were good looking, in their mid- to late twenties, wearing expensive business casual clothes. Ruth realized with a start that they were around the same age Tracey Kendall had been when she and Jack Holden transformed this company. These kids looked bright, but Ruth couldn't imagine anyone giving them millions of dollars to invest.

Kevin and Jane stood to shake hands and then pulled four rolling desk chairs together at the center of the room. Jane was the first to speak. "Is it true that guy from Screw Loose had something to do with Tracey's accident?"

"That's what we're trying to find out," Moscone answered.

Jane nodded, taking this in. "It's a terrible loss. We saw Tracey every day, worked with her, traveled with her. Tracey is, was, the person I most admired in my life. I wanted to be just like her."

"What was it you admired?" Ruth asked.

"Tracey knew how to work. She showed us what it is to love your work. She thought this was the best job in the world."

"Our clients give us their money to pool and invest." Kevin Chun explained. "Our job is to find small companies that will grow big. Tracey loved to get up every morning and test her wits against the market. She said some days might be awful, but it would never, ever be dull."

"Was she good at it?" Ruth asked.

"She was great at it." Jane answered without hesitation.

"What made Mrs. Kendall so good?"

Kevin Chun answered. "Tracey could look at a business, meet with its management, and decide quickly if it could be a winner. I read all the plans and reports and did the research and Jane crunched the numbers. Tracey would pore over our analyses, but what she really had was the ability to understand who was telling the truth, who was lying, and who was fooling themselves. She never fooled herself. She never hung onto an investment in a company out of affection for its product, its management, or its history."

Jane Parker continued. "Tracey said that all these companies were like stories and she was getting paid, very well paid, to read them. Every one has a plot and characters and we look at them and wonder, 'How will it turn out?' "

"With the market in the state it's in, I would think it's been more difficult lately," Ruth observed.

"For sure," Kevin answered, "for everybody. We've taken some hits, but given everything, we've done better than most. Our clients are pretty satisfied."

"What will happen now?" Moscone asked Kevin.

"Jack's trying to reassure the clients and convince them not to leave the fund. We'll lose some, for sure. Once things stabilize, I don't know what will happen. He'll look for another partner, I suppose. The clients have the right to pull out if the management of the firm changes, but they'd be crazy to in this market. Hopefully, Jack can persuade them to stay."

"Do you two also work for Mr. Holden?"

"Technically, but Tracey researched and picked the investments. Jack focused more on bringing in the clients. He doesn't involve us much."

Moscone shifted the subject. "Did either of you use Screw Loose?"

Jane shook her head, but Kevin answered, "Yes."

"Did you ever have any trouble with Al Pace?"

"No. As a matter of fact, he's quite competent."

"Did you ever have the feeling," Moscone asked, "that there was more to Mrs. Kendall's relationship with Al Pace than customer–mechanic?"

"Certainly not!" Jane Parker's face flushed. "When I said Tracey Kendall was the person I most admired, I didn't mean just from a business perspective. I meant as a mother and a wife, as well."

"You and Mrs. Kendall were close then, on a personal level?" Ruth asked.

Jane's chin quivered. Her voice broke. "There are just things you know about a person." Jane could hold back her tears no longer. She put her hands to her face. Kevin Chun looked on, concerned.

Ruth waited until Jane's crying subsided. "We'd like to see Tracey's schedule. Mrs. Berger said you could show us."

Jane pulled her head up and wiped her nose. "Sure." She scooted her chair to the computer and pressed a button on the keyboard. The screen transformed itself. Jane typed a few letters and Tracey Kendall's schedule for the previous Monday came up. "She had a conference call at 9:30, then she's all X'd out from 11:00 on." Jane pointed to the grid on the screen.

Moscone asked, "What does that mean?"

"Some people keep their appointments on this schedule, but most of us just use it for internal communication. Our coworkers call this up to find out if we're available for meetings, conference calls, and so on. If you have a time period when you don't want anything to be scheduled, you just "X" it.

"She told the nanny she was busy all afternoon," Moscone said.

"You can't tell from this. You'd have to check her personal appointment book. She carried it with her all the time." Jane pressed another key and the monitor repainted itself to reflect a longer view of Tracey's schedule. Ruth scanned the screen, looking for indications of a regular appointment that might be covering an affair, but the notations were too cryptic to understand. There were blocks of time marked out for staff meetings, receptions, business trips, and chiropractor appointments going out several months, events Tracey would never attend. All those unmeetable obligations made Ruth sad.

"What's going on?" A large man barreled through the doorway, followed by concerned-looking Ellie Berger. He stopped two feet from Ruth.

Ruth stood and extended her hand. "You must be Jack Holden."

He nodded, acknowledging he must be, but didn't offer his own hand. "I'm afraid Mrs. Berger has made a mistake. Kevin, Jane, excuse us." Ruth, Holden, and Moscone moved into the corridor.

Ruth looked straight into Holden's eyes. They were a most amazing blue. Meticulously dressed and groomed, he was a good-looking man, though overweight around the middle and currently flushed red in the face. "Mr. Holden," she began, "as I told Mrs. Berger, I don't believe Tracey Kendall's death was an accident."

"I know my employees have an unnatural obsession with Mr. Pace and his role in Tracey's accident," Holden replied. "The staff is upset right now. So are the clients. In fact, I have nervous, unhappy clients arriving in fifteen minutes. A lot of thought has gone into what to say to them. If my clients find you here, they'll get even more nervous and I may never be able to bring them around. So you have to go. Immediately. If you want to talk to me or anyone on my staff, make an appointment."

Ruth watched the man, considering what he'd said. In her years in command of the detective force, she'd learned to pick her fights. "Fine," she answered, "that's what we'll do. Do you want to schedule a meeting now?"

"Brenda will take care of it." Holden's tone softened. "Did

you find Tracey's briefcase and her laptop?" he asked. "They belong to this firm, so please don't give them to Kendall. They're not his property."

CHAPTER FIVE

"Where to now, Chief?" Moscone asked when they were back in the car. "Headquarters?"

Ruth didn't want to go back to headquarters. She didn't want to do any of the tasks that awaited her there, chief among them calling District Attorney Bob Baines. "Let's go see how McGrath's doing. Maybe we can dig him out for lunch."

When they pulled up in front of Al Pace's garage, McGrath was visible through the windows at the office end of the stable, a hunched figure in a threadbare sports coat.

"Find anything?" Ruth asked as she and Moscone crowded into the small space.

"He overcharged for some used parts here and there," McGrath grumbled.

"Related to this case?"

McGrath pointed to several piles of invoices stacked precariously by the desk chair. They looked like copies of the ones Ruth had found at the Kendall house. "I haven't finished going through those yet."

"Anything else?" Ruth asked.

"Like what?"

"Motel receipts, restaurant tabs, florist bills, that sort of thing," Moscone interjected.

"Oh, please," McGrath boomed. "If the Kendall woman and this guy were going at it, it's a safe bet he wasn't picking up the check."

"Quiet," Ruth hissed. Karen Pace had silently materialized in the doorway. Her appearance was appalling. The heavy, dark circles under her eyes were a striking contrast to her pale, almost translucent skin. Ruth moved forward quickly and introduced herself.

"Did you find something about Al?" Karen asked in her quiet voice.

"No, Mrs. Pace," Ruth answered. "We're working on it."

"Oh. When I saw you, I just thought—"

"I'm sorry, no. Soon, I hope."

"My boys keep asking." Karen's eyes clouded with tears. Damn it, Ruth thought, no matter what this investigation turned up, it would probably add to this woman's pain. Karen Pace choked back a sob.

"I'm starving," McGrath announced, moving toward the door. Moscone followed. Ruth glowered at the two of them as they walked away.

"Mrs. Pace," Ruth put a reassuring hand on Karen's forearm, "if we don't hear something in the next few hours, I'm going to notify the media that your husband is missing. If there's anyone important you haven't told about Al's disappearance—friends, parents, siblings—do it now."

"Should I tell my boys?"

Ruth took time with her answer. "The oldest is in kindergarten, isn't he? The parents of his classmates will talk. Kids will overhear. It's best to tell them, Mrs. Pace."

"Nice goin'," Moscone chided McGrath as they got into the car.

"You were pretty smooth yourself," Ruth added in Moscone's direction.

"What did I do?"

Ruth growled.

"Sheesh," McGrath said. "Easy." He leaned forward from the back seat. "There's a little place just down the road here."

"McGrath, do you know every joint in New Derby?" Moscone teased.

"Walk enough beats long enough in this town and you do. Not that either one of you would know."

The sentiment was pure McGrath, grumpy sour grapes, but the tone was light, bantering. Ruth was quietly pleased. Something about this investigation was turning McGrath around, engaging him as he hadn't been in months. Ruth realized how much she had missed this—being out of the office, joking with the guys.

There was, indeed, a joint up the road, a hole-in-the-wall with a high counter, two tables, and two booths. It was doing a brisk lunchtime, take-out trade. A menu board offered the usual array of subs and pizzas. Ruth and McGrath placed their orders quickly, then sat in the corner booth. Moscone peppered the poor counterman with questions. Where did they buy their ham? Their produce? What grade of olive oil did they use?

"Jeezus," McGrath called. "It's a sub shop. Just order something and get over here."

Moscone finally ordered a Greek salad, no olives, no feta, no dressing and joined them. This time, McGrath scanned the room for listening ears. "This guy, Pace," he paused for emphasis, "is in way over his head—mortgage overdue, business loans overdue, utilities writing threatening letters, Visa, Mobil, Home Depot. He has dunning notices tucked in every corner of that room."

"What else?" Ruth leaned forward, too.

"Not much else. I talked to some of the neighbors early this morning before they left for work. Pace was a pretty popular guy. On the weekends, friends would show up with their cars and they'd pull them apart, put them together, hang out, and drink beer."

"Does anyone know what kind of car he might be driving?"

"Navy blue Saab, eight or nine years old. He told his buddies he was fixing it up to sell. I called it in to Lawry."

"And the license plates?"

"No one has any idea which ones are missing. There'd always been a bunch in that old barn, and Pace added to the collection after he bought the place, but nobody took any note of it."

"Anything about his love life?" Moscone wanted to know.

"His buddies hinted there might be something. He's got the looks for it. And the job. If he disappears for an hour or so, who'd ever notice? But I wouldn't say his friends were anything more than suspicious. I'll say this about the guy, he doesn't kiss and tell."

"Anything else?" Ruth asked McGrath.

"Yeah. They said he was a real good mechanic."

Moscone stayed at the garage to help McGrath, and Ruth started back to headquarters alone. She knew it was time for her to do the thing she had been putting off. She had to call Bob Baines. She usually avoided Baines and did her day-in, day-out business with the real prosecutors who ran the D.A.'s office, but this was different. If she went public with the Pace disappearance and Baines saw her on television talking about a case he knew nothing about, he'd go ballistic and he'd be justified in doing so.

So, she had to call Baines. Personally. Ruth pulled to the side of the road, reluctantly selected Baines's number from her cell phone contact list and punched Send. The call would be complicated by one overriding factor. She hated Bob Baines. And Bob Baines hated her.

Ruth sighed into the headset. Normally, she dealt with the grudges, jealousies, and factions that fueled the criminal justice community like a circulatory system by politely avoiding them. She just didn't get it. Why did people waste time with that sort of nonsense? Her relationships with law enforcement types beyond the New Derby PD were professional and productive.

Except with Bob Baines.

Because Baines had done something he shouldn't have. And Ruth knew it.

Because Ruth hadn't done something she should have. And Baines knew it.

Because the only other person who knew the whole story, Detective Arthur Pezzoli, had been dead for seven years, leaving Ruth feeling like she and Baines were locked in a macabre dance, each with a loaded pistol cocked and pointed at the other's head.

Baines's assistant picked up. Ruth explained that she needed to talk to the D.A. himself. Baines kept her waiting a good, long time.

"Mrs. Murphy. What can I do for you?" His tone was patronizing with a hint of suspicion.

"It's about a case."

"Ah, a case." Baines's voice changed. He must've thought she'd called about his "chats" with New Derby's aldermen sandbagging her appointment. Was he relieved or disappointed?

"I have a missing person. His name is Albert Pace, a mechanic. He hasn't been home for two days. I'm telling you this because I plan to go to the press."

"Where's the mechanic from?"

"Derby Mills."

"And he's been gone for approximately forty-eight hours?"

"Yes."

"And you're going to the media with this story?" Baines all but guffawed. Guys like Pace disappeared from Derby Mills all the time and Baines had the child support backlog to prove it.

"Yes. So, I'm informing you and asking if you want to participate."

Baines paused fractionally to show his contempt. "No, dear. I think you can handle this one. Let me know when the guy turns up."

"Fine." Ruth felt the color in her face and neck rise, as it always did after a few minutes' exposure to Baines. She squelched the instinct to take the bait and ended the call as quickly as she could.

Ruth began to second-guess herself the moment she hung up. Sure, she had alerted Baines that she was going public with Al Pace's disappearance, but she hadn't told him about Pace's connection to Tracey Kendall's death. She hadn't told him, because she knew the information would complicate things. She agreed with McGrath. Baines would dislike the Kendall case intensely, and while he couldn't actually order her not to go to the press, he could insist on being involved, drag his feet, and control the message when they finally did get it out. Ruth knew every day that ticked by without finding Pace diminished their chances of finding the answers they were looking for in Tracey Kendall's death.

This evening, when Ruth talked to the press, she would have to make a choice. If she didn't connect the mechanic's disappearance with the beautiful, wealthy woman's accident, the media would show as much interest in Pace's whereabouts as Baines just had. But if Ruth did say they were looking for Al Pace in connection with Tracey Kendall's death, Baines would go nuts—and so much for Mayor Rosenfeld's directive to stay out of Baines's way.

Sitting by the side of the road, Ruth thought about her family. They'd all made sacrifices so she could have this chance to be chief. James and Sarah had cooperatively, if not always cheerfully, done their homework beside her at the kitchen table while she completed her master's degree in Criminal Justice. They had only occasionally grumbled about the city meetings, seminars, and task forces that kept her out at night as she and the old chief worked to build the network she would need.

And Marty. He had sacrificed not just time with her, but money and his own career, toiling on their side porch, turning down all cases connected to the New Derby PD, taking time from building his practice to fill all the parenting holes her job created. If Ruth didn't become chief, there wouldn't be the raise they were counting on. She might not even have a job, depending on how things fell. No new chief would want his almost-predecessor haunting the headquarters building.

Yet here she was. Baiting Baines. Doing the one thing Mayor Rosenfeld had asked her not to do.

Ruth's cell phone trilled in the silent car. It was Lawry. The medical examiner was ready to release Tracey Kendall's remains.

"I'll go tell Kendall myself," Ruth responded. "Did the M.E. assign a cause of death?"

"No, still waiting for tox screens."

"Good." For the first time ever, Ruth was grateful for the chronically overburdened, slow-moving state lab.

CHAPTER SIX

The Kendall house looked deserted. Ruth could hear the deep pong of the doorbell as it echoed through the rooms. No answer. She turned and looked across the sweep of lawn. There was movement by the smaller house on the left arc of the drive. Ruth set off on foot.

It was hard to tell what purpose the building had originally served. It was a three-story building with a dormered roof, built in the same era as the main house. Had it been a gardener's cottage? A guest house? The door was ajar. Ruth pushed it open and walked through. What she saw stopped her dead in her tracks.

The house had been gutted and refitted so its interior space comprised a single room—extending out to the walls and up to the rafters that had hung in the original attic. The walls and sloping ceilings were painted a glaring white. Skylights supplemented the light streaming in from three stories of windows. The floor was an expanse of polished oak.

But it wasn't the architecture that seized Ruth's attention. Rising from the floor, in some cases almost to the ceiling, were five pieces of sculpture. Ruth wasn't much for modern art, but her response was immediate, visceral. She felt as if she had been punched in the chest. The twisted hulks were abstract, and yet were unmistakably dinosaurs. Their frozen postures were so real; the immense beasts seemed about to break free and resume lives interrupted long ago. Each piece displayed an intense emotion. Ruth clearly understood their rage, terror, hunger, even the strutting self-satisfaction of the crested duckbill. The vitality of the sculptures was stunning, especially as Stephen Kendall portrayed it, shot through with decay. The dinosaurs' gleaming outer skins melted away in spots, revealing torn canvas, jumbled wires, and quick glimpses of jutting metal frames. Even as the beasts ruled the earth, rot was in them, on them, the specter of extinction already present.

Ruth stood rooted to the spot where she had entered.

There was a noise in the rear of the building and Susan Gleason appeared. Tall, cool, dressed with the same bohemian elegance as yesterday, she made her way across the studio floor.

"Amazing, aren't they?" Susan asked, husky-voiced.

Ruth groped for speech. "He does these?"

"Yes. This is what he does. At least, this is what he's doing now."

"Here?"

"Um-humm. The design work takes place over there." Gleason pointed to the open shed addition at the back from which she'd emerged. "Everything else is done in this room. The sculptures are so large that they have to be disassembled to be moved and reassembled at the site."

Ruth noted that the wall of the studio facing away from the main house held a gigantic double barn door. "He sells well?"

Susan Gleason didn't answer right away. "He could. He will. He got a lot of favorable response to his work when he was quite young. His earlier work looked nothing like this. But he refused to capitalize on his success. His whole career can be summed up that way. Every time he achieves acclaim, he immediately sets off in a new direction." She shook her head. "Stephen has a horror of repeating himself. He never follows the easy route. Take these pieces, for example. They're too large for private collectors. That leaves museums and public commissions. Many museums don't have the space, either. That's why the show coming up at the end of May is so important." A shadow of regret crossed her face. "I've recently had to change my gallery space. I just took possession of a wonderful old warehouse. The workmen are gutting it as we speak. Before the walls and floors go back in, there'll be a brief period, three weeks only, when we can show all these pieces together, indoors, in New York."

Ruth looked at the sculptures and then at the space they occupied. The dinosaurs' expressions and postures played off one another. They'd be more compelling grouped together. And, being closed in with them heightened the sensation of being trapped with enormous, dangerous hulks. They would be interesting, even beautiful, displayed outdoors or singly, but in this room their power was enhanced by the interplay of form and space.

"The problem," Susan continued, "is that Stephen isn't ready for the show. He has one more piece planned and he refuses to show without it. And he won't get any help. Other sculptors would have this place crawling with assistants and apprentices doing the scutwork, but Stephen does everything himself—design, welding, sanding." Gleason's hands fluttered outward toward the dinosaurs and then rested on her chest. "There's just this tiny span of time when it's possible to do this show. Then comes summer. No one will be in New York. Besides, I need the three months before fall to get the finish work done on my space. I can't afford to have it empty for a longer period. And now this. He worked a little this morning, but when I came from the house, I discovered he was gone. He must get back to work."

Ruth felt her hostility rise. Was this show more important than a dead wife, a grieving child?

If Susan sensed the animosity, she gave no sign. "People in

New York have been waiting more than five years for Stephen Kendall's next show. This show will launch him finally, definitively, lucratively." She regarded the behemoths reverently for another moment, then turned to Ruth. "You didn't say why you came."

"I was so absorbed by the sculptures, I forgot," Ruth said. "I'm looking for Mr. Kendall. Do you know where he is?"

"No. I ate lunch in my room and when I came downstairs, the house was empty. Whenever I'm staying here, I try to leave the family some privacy. I work here in the studio, in the design area at the back, and try to take some meals in my room and retire early at night. Right now, I'm being especially careful."

"Well, perhaps this will help a little. The medical examiner is ready to release Mrs. Kendall's remains. He'll need instructions. I came to let Mr. Kendall know."

"I'll tell him."

"Thanks. Oh, and one other thing, Ms. Gleason. Were you and Tracey Kendall close?"

Susan hesitated before she answered. "No. We weren't. I've stayed here about three days a month for years. You'd think we'd be friends, but the truth is, she was a very private person."

Ruth had no trouble believing this. She wondered if anyone could be intimate with a creature as monomaniacal as Susan Gleason, a woman who stood here unself-consciously complaining about her client's lack of productivity when his dead wife was not yet in the ground.

They moved toward the door. Susan gazed back at the studio space and its occupants. "You know, I envy you today," she said to Ruth. "You only get to see them for the first time, once."

Ruth left the Kendalls' by way of the service road in the back. Immediately opposite the Kendall house was a mailbox labeled *Powell*. Ruth turned into the driveway, which rose steeply, angling back from the street and then widening in front of the house itself, a modern pile. Ruth ascended a long set of steps that brought her up to an undistinguished entranceway. She found the doorbell. Inside, a television droned.

Fran Powell came to the door looking much less put together than she had the day before. Her high-maintenance hairdo was in disarray and though her slacks and matching sweater were sleek and expensive, she was wearing an improbable pair of bunny slippers.

"Oh," was all she said when she saw Ruth.

"Mrs. Powell, I'd like to talk to you about Tracey Kendall."

Fran hesitated, but only for a moment. "Sure, c'mon in." She turned her back on Ruth and moved unsteadily into the hallway. Ruth's practiced eye assessed her drunkenness at the midpoint between life-of-the-party and unconscious.

Fran led the way into an enormous, antiseptic living room with giant windows framing a spectacular view of Derby Center off in the distance. She sat on the white leather sectional that dominated the room and motioned for Ruth to do the same. In another room, the TV still played. A chubby boy entered with a disk in his hand. "Mommy," his voice was grave, "the DVD is broken."

Mommy sighed loudly. "Did you press 'PLAY'?" she asked.

"Yes."

"Is the TV on channel three?"

"Yes." His expression said, *Do you think I'm an idiot?*

"Excuse me," Fran said to Ruth, "but we seem to have an emergency on our hands." Fran got up off the couch and moved carefully out of the room.

Ruth watched her go. The drunken Fran seemed like an improbable friend for the organized, ambitious Tracey Kendall. Then again, what is an appropriate response to your best friend's death? *Maybe you'd react in the same way,* Ruth admonished herself, knowing full well she wouldn't. She left alone the question of who, besides Marty, her best friend might be.

Fran returned. "Problem solved. Now how can I help you?" The question was solicitous, but Fran Powell still seemed guarded.

"You told Detective Moscone you were Tracey Kendall's best friend."

"Yes. She discovered me here when she was home on maternity leave. She'd wander across the driveway for refreshments and conversation. Later, when the boys got older, we'd stand in the road out here on summer evenings and monitor the tricycle races."

That got Ruth past the troubling question of what Tracey Kendall and Fran Powell might possibly have in common. Ruth knew from experience when one has young children, proximity is a powerful incentive to friendship.

Fran leaned forward. "Stephen said something about you thinking that man, the mechanic, had something to do with Tracey's accident."

"We know he serviced Tracey's car right before the crash. And we know he's disappeared."

"And that makes you suspect . . . what?"

"It's not clear. Did you know the mechanic, Al Pace?"

"No."

"Did Tracey ever mention him?"

Fran Powell stared at the ceiling. "No."

"You're sure? Take a moment to think about it. Pace's friends suspect he was having an affair. We'll find out with whom sooner or later." Ruth still wasn't entirely sold on Moscone's affair theory, but Fran Powell's hesitation made her push harder. "Mrs. Powell, you say Tracey Kendall was your best friend. I know you think you're protecting her, but if you know anything that would help us understand what happened to Tracey, you owe it to her to tell me. I'm asking you again. Did Tracey ever mention Al Pace?"

Fran Powell held her head in her hands. "Yes," she said, so quietly Ruth strained to hear.

"What did Tracey say about him?"

"They were sleeping together. She was having an affair." Fran pulled her head up. "Is this really necessary? Does Stephen have to know?"

After the interview, Ruth sat for a moment, car idling in the drive. She was surprised by Fran's revelation about Tracey and Al Pace. She just couldn't make sense of the two of them as a couple, and there was something she distrusted about the drunken Mrs. Powell. But in twenty years, Ruth had seen all kinds of unaccountable behavior. A rich lady sleeping with her handsome auto mechanic was the least of it. And they finally had confirmation of a relationship between Tracey and Pace that could be a motive for murder.

Ruth glanced at her watch. She could return to headquarters, but for the third time that day, she resisted. The press briefing on Al Pace's disappearance was in less than two hours and she didn't want to use the time between now and then to jump into the other things, the non–Tracey Kendall, non–Al Pace things that would come at her if she returned to her office. Lawry would call if there was something important, as would Mayor Rosenfeld or Marty.

Ruth pulled out of Fran Powell's driveway and steered her car not toward Derby Center, but toward Anna Abbott's house, less than a half-mile away.

Anna Abbott's house, a well-constructed 1920s copy of a Federalist mansion, was two blocks from the Kendall house in

Derby Hills. When Ruth pulled into the circular drive, she saw that all the first-floor windows were opened wide. Ruth yoo-hooed at the unlocked front door and walked in. Three rooms were visible from the impressive center hall and in every one the rugs had been rolled up, the heavy drapes pulled down, and the furniture moved to the center of the room. By next week, these rooms would be sporting "summer" rugs, slipcovers, and curtains. At eighty-one, Anna Abbot spring-cleaned in the manner of her Victorian grandmother.

Ruth followed a series of bumps and thuds through the massive living room into the library beyond. There she found Mrs. Abbott, and her "helper," Mrs. O'Shea, busily rolling up a wine-colored Oriental carpet. They were both decked out in work dresses, aprons, and colorful kerchiefs. From the back, it was difficult to tell which woman was which, although Ruth's suspicion, quickly confirmed, was that Bridget O'Shea was the one who had traded in her sturdy work shoes for cross-trainers.

"Hallo," Mrs. Abbott said, pulling herself upright. "Mrs. O'Shea, we have company."

"Chief Murphy," Bridget O'Shea cried, "just in time for tea."

Anna Abbott looked over her shoulder at the library clock. "Ah, indeed it is."

Mrs. Abbott was an impressive woman, though at this point in life, her presence was more chemical than physical. She was Old Boston through and through, the daughter of a Brahmin, widow of a Brahmin and mother of a gaggle of Brahmin. She was also president of the New Derby Board of Aldermen, chair of the Police Chief Search Committee and one of Ruth's greatest fans. When the old chief had started bringing Ruth around, making introductions, Mrs. Abbott took to her immediately. It amused Ruth that both Anna Abbott and Mayor Rosenfeld viewed her as their own creation. They argued over who had seen her first, like parents bickering about which side of the family contributed a child's best feature.

Mrs. Abbott led Ruth through the living room, the central hall, and the paneled dining room to the bright, windowed breakfast room off the kitchen. Somehow, Bridget O'Shea had beaten them there and set the glass table for two. Mrs. Abbott excused herself to wash up and Mrs. O'Shea appeared immediately with a tray that held the tea things and a plate of butter cookies. Unexpected guests were always received graciously at Anna Abbott's house (though there might be some spirited commentary about the breach afterward), and tea was served in china cups even on spring-cleaning days.

While Mrs. Abbott was out of the room, Ruth considered her approach to the conversation. Her promotion was the topic she really wanted to talk about, but in Mrs. Abbott's world you didn't dive right in. First you made an offering, and nothing made a better offering than a tidbit about something that was going on in town that Mrs. Abbott, with her vast store of knowledge and her extensive network, didn't already know. So Ruth led with the other topic that was so much on her mind these days.

"Did you know Tracey Kendall?" she asked when Mrs. Abbott reappeared.

"The woman from that terrible accident? I read about it in the paper."

"Right now it's looking like it was more than a simple accident."

Mrs. Abbott's eyes lit up. "Intriguing. I do know her husband, Stephen Kendall. When the New Derby Arts Council discovered we had yet another famous, or should I say semi-famous, artist living in town, we approached him about an exhibition. None of us had seen his work. Of course, when we did, we realized we could never show it. We couldn't afford to move it, much less mount it. It's quite affecting, though."

"What's your impression of him?"

"Charming, helpful, and such a deep, beautiful voice. He did suggest some artists to us and from time to time helped us out with contacts in New York. Truth be told, I think all the old ladies were in love with him, and, it being the Arts Council, so were half the young men."

"Mrs. Abbott!" Ruth teased.

"Oh, pish. I will never understand why you young people get yourselves so worked up about the facts of life."

"And Tracey?"

"Never met her. I guess she wasn't much for town things."

Ruth knew this was the worst thing Mrs. Abbott could say about a person. To her way of thinking, not being community-minded was as unthinkable as not bathing. But Tracey had a demanding job, a small child, and the social obligations required to support Stephen's art career. Ruth understood that Tracey Kendall wouldn't have had time for "town things." For Ruth, "town things" were "work things," or she wouldn't have had much time for them either.

Mrs. O'Shea poked her head in through the door that led to the kitchen. "Do you two have everything you need?" she called out.

"Yes. Thank you, Mrs. O'Shea." Mrs. Abbott answered.

Like everyone who knew them, Ruth was fascinated by the relationship between the women. Anna Abbott had been widowed early, a single parent before the phrase was coined. Alone with four children, she saw to their schooling, ran the household and half the town while reading her way through Virgil in the original. Through it all, Bridget O'Shea had arrived by bus every day, done the housework, the cooking, and some of the child rearing, and returned by bus every night to her house-painter husband and her own four children. Now, with the children all in their fifties and her husband dead, Bridget lived in a lovely, large apartment fashioned out of the mansion's servants' wing. In the summer, Mrs. O'Shea went to her daughter on Cape Cod, while Mrs. Abbott vacationed, surrounded by family, in the big house on the island off Marblehead. But October through June, every weekday, Mrs. O'Shea made her way to the main part of the house and went to work.

Anna Abbott picked another cookie off the plate and ate it with relish. Eighty-one years had not dimmed her appetite. "You're quite taken with this Tracey Kendall thing." It was a statement, not a question.

Ruth didn't answer right away. "Yes, I'm taken with it. I don't know why."

"Really," Mrs. Abbott's eyes twinkled. "You don't?"

Ruth knew the question was intended to provoke reflection, not an answer. She did identify with Tracey. She'd felt Tracey's presence as a woman in the old clothes in the gym bag, felt her presence as a mother when Carson sobbed because his mother told him she was angry in the conversation neither of them knew would be their last. Now that Ruth was deeper in Tracey Kendall's life, she saw other parallels. They both were driven to bring order to forces—be they financial markets or crime—others found unpredictable and punishing. Their methods were similar, too: analysis and organization, understanding of stories, and the ability not to fool themselves and to tell when others were lying.

Yet with all her ambition and intelligence, Tracey's skills had failed her. She'd gotten herself into something terrible, something Ruth was sure was responsible for her death. Ruth had to admit part of her motivation for pushing this case forward, in spite of all she was risking, was that she needed to know what happened.

She changed the subject to the one that actually had brought her there. "The mayor mentioned the aldermen have some concerns about my appointment."

"Ah, the Baines business? It's no secret you and District Attorney Baines have an antagonistic relationship. I don't pretend to know why." Mrs. Abbott paused for quite a few seconds. "Fine. Don't tell me. All Baines is saying is, he needs a chief he can work with. It isn't so unreasonable. Aside from the fact that the criminal justice system has to function unimpeded, the D.A.'s endorsement is required for a lot of grant money your department depends on to balance its budget—state money, Department of Justice money and Homeland Security money. If Bob Baines chooses to direct those funds to other cities and towns in the county, you're going to have big problems."

Ruth's exasperation broke through her normally cool exterior. "Why does anyone listen to him? He's just such an awful man. Do you know he calls me, 'dear' and 'Mrs. Murphy'?"

Mrs. Abbott chortled appreciatively. "And you think he does it because he is a male chauvinist? I'm sure he is, but he does it to keep you off balance, to get you to doubt yourself and what you want. If you weren't a woman, he would come at you some other way—your family, your ancestry, even some physical characteristic. Anything he can find to get to you."

The sounds of aggressive dishwashing clattered from the kitchen. Evidently, Bridget O'Shea had decided it was time to stop fooling around and get back to spring cleaning. Ruth stood to go, thanking her hostess.

"You mustn't let Baines undermine your confidence, Ruth," Anna Abbott said at the front door. "If you act like the chief of police, you will be the chief of police."

Ruth took Anna's blue-veined hand carefully in her own and thanked her for the tea and advice, though she wasn't sure it was quite that simple.

CHAPTER SEVEN

As Ruth turned onto Main Street heading back to headquarters, she could see a half-dozen satellite trucks gathered for the news conference, a surprising turnout. The press had been given the barest details. It must be a slow news day. Ruth's stomach clenched at the sight of the trucks, but there was no point in raking back over her conflicted feelings. If the goal was to generate publicity to find Al Pace, then the more interest the better.

She steered past the trucks carefully. They were parked and double-parked in a checkerboard pattern along the street. Hulking, long-necked, metallic, they seemed oddly familiar. *Ah, yes,* Ruth thought, *Stephen Kendall's dinosaurs.*

Ruth met with the media in the roll call room, its usual haphazard arrangement of chairs placed in neat rows by Lieutenant Lawry. She read the prepared statement carefully. Al Pace, auto mechanic, resident of Derby Mills, missing forty-eight hours. She held Pace's photo up for the cameras as Lawry passed it out to the group. They nodded politely and looked hopeful.

The moment of truth. Ruth took a breath and pushed the rest out. "Mr. Pace was last seen in the parking lot of Fiske & Holden, an investment firm in Truman Executive Park. In addition to his missing status, the New Derby Police Department believes he may have been a witness to the motor vehicle crash that took the life of Tracey Kendall. As you know, Mrs. Kendall died two days ago."

That got their attention. Hands shot up.

"Was Tracey Kendall's death not an accident?"

"Was foul play involved?"

"Is Mr. Pace a suspect?"

"Is he a person of interest?"

"You identified Mr. Pace as an auto mechanic. Did he work on Tracey Kendall's car immediately prior to the crash?"

"Is Mrs. Kendall's death being investigated as a homicide?"

Ruth skated around the answers as best she could. Without characterizing the cause of Tracey Kendall's death, she reiterated that Al Pace was a potential witness, nothing more. "Mr. Pace is a husband and father. His family is concerned and needs to hear from him." Ruth repeated the toll-free number and encouraged, "anyone who has seen Mr. Pace in the last two days or has knowledge of his whereabouts," to call.

Then she thanked the gathered media and retreated to her office while Lawry waited for equipment to be packed and cleared the room.

By the time Ruth left headquarters, Lieutenant Lawry was gone. Lieutenant Carse sat at the front desk, bent over, focused on paperwork. In profile, Carse's short brown hair emphasized the elegant angularity of her face. Ruth smiled at the sight. A lieutenant at thirty, officer-in-charge of the night shift at thirty-two, Carse's career was off to a great start.

Ruth wondered to what degree Carse appreciated this. Did she ever feel amazed simply by being here as Ruth did? Ruth thought of herself as a member of a second generation. The first generation of women, who filed the lawsuits, fought the unions and held fast through the years of litigation, had largely been too old or too long in the narrow disciplines of juvenile officer, dispatcher or meter maid to benefit from their own hard work.

Ruth's generation had reaped those rewards, but their tests had come in the station house. They worked without role models to point the way and scrutinized each brother officer to determine his degree of hostility. Now the women Carse's age took the jobs, the assignments, and promotions as their right and acted accordingly. Police work was still a male domain. Measured against an ideal, there was a long way to go, but measured against where they'd started, the progress was head-spinning.

"I'm going home," Ruth called to Carse. "If anyone is looking for me, call me there."

"Sure, Chief." Carse grinned.

At 10:15 P.M., Ruth sat in her usual spot on the hand-me-down, pea-green couch she and Marty both hated but couldn't afford to replace. Marty, in his big blue chair, clicked the remote through the stations that had ten o'clock news broadcasts.

"Where's Baines?" Marty asked. "It's unlike him to give up a chance to have his mug on the news."

"I ran it by him," Ruth answered. "He didn't seem to think the disappearance of an auto mechanic added up to much."

"Even one connected to Tracey Kendall?"

"I didn't tell him about that, exactly."

"Are you kidding, Ruthie? He's going to blow a gasket when he sees this." Marty's brow settled into a worried frown.

At eleven, two other stations replayed the footage shot earlier at the New Derby police station. The third station, the one Ruth called the "Walk and Talk News," had taken its cameras to the accident scene. There, in pitch darkness, a young reporter walked along the road and despite references to "the alleged car," "the alleged victim," and "the alleged stone wall," made it perfectly clear that Al Pace had murdered Tracey Kendall.

"Ugh," Ruth said to the TV.

As soon as the segment was over, the telephone rang. Ruth's

86

hopes rose. Could the broadcast have turned up Pace so quickly?

Marty answered the phone. "Your sister," he mouthed. Ruth groaned and Marty responded with a warning look, pressing his hand to the receiver.

"What does she want?"

"Well," Marty offered, "if history is any indication, she wants to tell you that she had a gigantic fight with a) her employer, b) her boyfriend, c) her roommate, or d) your mother."

"Right now, actually, there is no employer, boyfriend, or roommate, and Mother is in San Francisco on a seniors' tour."

"Then I have absolutely no idea."

Ruth laughed and felt her tension recede a little, just enough to handle talking to her sister. Thank God for Marty. He was so good with her mother and sister, so charming with the irresponsible women who were her only family. Marty handed Ruth the portable phone.

"Hi, Helen."

"Ruthie? I saw the thing on the news about Tracey Kendall. It's so terrible."

"You knew Tracey Kendall?"

"Stephen and Tracey. Actually, the person I'm really close to is Stephen's first wife, Rosie. Stephen was an instructor and Rosie was a student when I was in art school. Rosie and Stephen were still married, but Tracey was on the scene. In fact, we were all friends then. Rosie confided in me a lot because—"

As Helen talked, Ruth cast her mind back over the last twenty years thinking—art school? Art school? When was that? After modeling school? Before film school? Between engagements number one and two, or two and three? She tried to reconstruct the tangle of her sister's life, but failed. How embarrassing. Her sister knew James and Sarah's ages, birth dates, and clothing sizes. Helen even sent Ruth a happy little card every year on the anniversary of her last promotion. Ruth was always momentarily confused by the cards, because even she never remembered. Finally, Ruth had to ask, "When was all this?"

"Oh," Helen answered, "you know, when I was in art school? Nine? Ten years ago?"

Ruth sighed. "Is this first wife still around?"

"Sure. Her studio's in one of those loft buildings in the old mills. She's pretty well known, at least around here. She's gone back to her maiden name, Rosie Boyagian."

"Are you still in touch with her?"

"I am. I'm going to call her first thing in the morning. I know she's still friendly with Stephen and Tracey. This must be terrible for her."

"Thanks." Ruth felt suddenly tired. "It may be helpful."

"It's just so sad about Tracey. I know you're used to this stuff. It doesn't get to you anymore."

Ruth's mind flashed to the way her heart had felt like it would break as she held Carson Kendall in his sandbox, and to her reaction when she saw the stripped SUV. It did still get to her. Some of it, anyway. She'd just become adept at hiding it. But she said none of this to her sister. Instead they indulged in some idle gossip about their feckless mother, who had gone off to San Francisco without telling a soul.

"Honestly, she is too much," Helen laughed. Then she asked after Marty and the children. It was almost midnight when Ruth got her to hang up.

The phone rang again immediately. Carse was on the other end. "He's been spotted! Pace has been seen by several people in New Hampshire—Salton Beach. We're working with their state and local guys to get the word out now."

Ruth hung up after this call with a sense of satisfaction. Her gamble had paid off. Pace was in their sights. And, Fran Powell had confirmed his relationship with Tracey Kendall. Maybe once they had Pace, he would confess and her problems would be solved. Ruth went to bed and fell into a deep and dreamless sleep.

CHAPTER EIGHT

Baines was on Ruth's cell phone in the morning before she even reached her office. "What the hell do you think you're doing?" he demanded.

Ruth pulled her car to the side of the road. "I'm looking for a missing man." There was silence from the other end, until Ruth added, "And trying to find out how and why a woman died."

"She died because her speeding car crashed into a stone wall," Baines replied in an exasperated tone. "Why didn't you tell me you were going to link this Pace guy's disappearance to the Kendall woman's death?"

Ruth took a steadying breath. "Because I knew you'd react exactly as you're reacting now, and I need to find Al Pace and I'm going to find out what happened to Tracey Kendall."

"What's the husband's position on all of this?"

"Mr. Kendall believes his wife's death was a tragic accident."

"As do I," Baines concluded. "But now you've got everyone who watched the evening news last night believing this mechanic killed her. From what I understand, you have no idea where the mechanic is, no forensics, no proof of any kind."

"That's not true. After the broadcast last night, we got several calls from people who've seen Pace in Salton Beach."

"Great. Let's draw another jurisdiction into this mess." Baines took a breath and continued his tirade. "I'm not sure you realize how out of control this is. Since yesterday, I've had calls from Jack Holden, a Susan Gleason who says she is, 'speaking for the Kendall family,' and some swill named Alexander Powell, Sr., who says you're harassing his daughter-in-law."

"I've had one conversation with her."

"That's the way it goes at this level. If you had more experience with cases like this, you'd know. How many actual murders have you had in New Derby in the last five years?"

"Six," Ruth answered, "as you well know because your office prosecuted every one of them."

"Let's see if I remember—domestic, domestic, mob hit, domestic, domestic, and a john who kills a prostitute at a hotel just inside your city limits, neither of them from New Derby."

"And those murders don't count?"

"Do any of your victims profile even close to Tracey Kendall or her friends? Do any of them have that kind of money and reach? That kind of appeal to the public and press? Believe me, if you've never been involved in a case like this before, you have no idea the amount of crap that's going to rain down on you. Why are you bothering the Kendall woman's friends, anyway? According to your theory, your man Pace murdered her because they were lovers."

Ruth was silent.

"Make this go away," Baines commanded.

"Or what?"

"Do I really need to spell it out?" There was a click and Baines was gone.

At headquarters, Ruth sat in her parking space for several minutes, breathing deeply and waiting for the bright red splotches of color on her cheeks and neck to fade before she went inside. Baines was always infuriating and never more so than when he made threats. He was probably on the phone with Mayor Rosenfeld right now, complaining about her. She would have to deal with the mayor as well.

When Ruth's cheeks stopped burning, she glanced in the rearview mirror, decided she was fine, and got out of the car. When she reached the big front doors, she squared her shoulders and put a smile on her face.

Lieutenant Lawry was standing behind the front desk managing a second visit from Mrs. Thurmond Bentley, by now known throughout the station as "the dog poop lady." She was obviously perturbed, and Lawry's high color indicated he wasn't happy either.

"Mrs. Bentley, I didn't tell you my officer would do anything this time," Lawry explained. "I said he would confirm what you reported and we would take it from there."

"And did he confirm it?" the old lady asked.

"Just a minute." Lawry bent to pick up the phone, waggled his neat, white eyebrows at Ruth, punched a button on the console, and spoke. "Is Officer Cable back? Would you be kind enough to send him to me?"

Young Cable reported promptly. At six foot four, he towered over both Mrs. Bentley and his lieutenant. "Did you go out to Maple Drive this morning?" Lawry asked him.

"Why, of course he did," the little woman exclaimed. "I could see him parked right across the street!"

"And what did you observe, Officer?" Lawry continued, as if Cable had answered the question.

"A white male, late thirties/early forties, came out of Number 296," Cable replied, glancing at his notebook. "He was accompanied by a large canine."

"A Great Dane the size of a horse, you mean," Mrs. Bentley muttered.

"A very large dog," Cable concurred.

"On a leash?" Lawry asked.

"No, sir."

"Then what happened?"

"The man and the dog proceeded to Number 306 Maple Drive."

"What time was this?"

"Eight A.M. exactly, sir."

"Go on."

"The dog walked into a patch of dead ivy—"

"Pachysandra," Mrs. Bentley corrected.

"—where the dog took a huge—"

"Ahem," Lawry interjected, reddening.

"Moved his—"

"Ahem."

"Defecated," blurted Cable, by now as red as Lawry. They both exhaled heavily.

"All of that is true," the old lady confirmed, "and I only have one question. WHY DIDN'T YOU ARREST HIM WHEN YOU HAD THE CHANCE?"

"Mrs. Bentley," Lawry answered, recovering, "it is not, in general, New Derby practice to arrest people for violating leash laws. In fact, it is not even our practice to fine people the first time they are caught."

"The first time!"

"They are caught," Lawry reiterated. "Officer Cable, tomorrow would you—"

"I'm not on again until Monday."

"Ah, right. Monday, then, would you proceed to Maple Drive at eight o'clock, and if you observe this behavior again, would you issue a warning to the owner?"

There was a fractional pause while the three of them looked at each other.

"Fine," said Mrs. Bentley, "do it your way. But I'll tell you now, it will not work." With that, she turned and marched away, with Cable bobbing and weaving around her, trying to beat her

93

to the heavy door to open it for her. Lawry put his head in his hands.

Ruth regarded her lieutenant sympathetically. Perhaps Baines was right. This was what policing in New Derby was all about—Citizens with Too Much Free Time and dog poop. Had she overreached herself by insisting on pursuing the Kendall case with its high-profile victim, lack of evidence, and flimsy connections? Was she in the process of demonstrating at the worst possible moment that she couldn't handle the chief's job? Ruth remembered Mrs. Abbott's advice—"If you act like the chief, you will be the chief,"—and beat the doubts back down.

"Any sign of Pace this morning?" she asked her lieutenant.

"Nothing yet," Lawry replied. "It's early."

At eleven o'clock, when Ruth and Moscone arrived for their appointment with Jack Holden, Brenda O'Reilly gave them one of her wonderful smiles. "Jack wasn't sure if you'd be coming," she said. "I'll tell Ellie you're here."

Ellie Berger appeared instantly and whisked them out of the reception area. "Jack's on a conference call. He'll just be a minute. You can wait in my office," Ellie stammered as she rushed them down the hall.

Ruth and Moscone sat in the same chairs they had used the day before. Ellie Berger was at her desk, playing with a string of paper clips. Her fidgeting had a contagious effect on Moscone, who tapped his fingers on the chair arm and upped the ante by jiggling his extended right foot at warp speed. Ellie, as if responding, began shifting rhythmically on her haunches. Ruth sat quietly until she couldn't stand the collective effects of the paper-clip clinking, bottom shifting, finger-tapping, and foot-gyrating a moment longer.

"Mrs. Berger, you seem nervous," Ruth remarked.

Ellie smiled apologetically. "Does it show? Jack's on a call and he didn't give me any instructions. I don't think he was expecting you to come after he talked to District Attorney Baines this morning. The district attorney assured him—"

"Yes, I know, I spoke to the D.A. myself this morning," Ruth interrupted, controlling her irritation. "I'm sure he didn't mean to imply that we wouldn't be thorough in investigating Mrs. Kendall's death."

"Well, yes, I'm sure," Ellie answered, though she didn't seem so sure. "Anyway, I hope bringing you in here was what Jack wanted. I don't think he'd want you waiting in the reception area. I've been making so many mistakes lately I'm not sure of myself. It's so unlike me, really."

"Mistakes?" Moscone asked.

"Well, he wasn't happy I let you talk to Kevin and Jane. And he was even angrier yesterday afternoon when Stephen Kendall came by and I let him—"

"Stephen Kendall was here?"

Ellie Berger nodded. "He came to get Tracey's personal things, you know, from her office. He had some boxes. I didn't see how I could say no, even though it did seem awfully soon, so I let him. Jack was furious. He went on and on about the partnership, confidential information, proper procedures." The office manager shrugged her soft, round shoulders.

"What did Kendall take?"

"I didn't look in the boxes. I wasn't going to make a fuss. Proper procedures! As long as I've been here, this place has been run as a family business. I'm not going to change now."

"Did Stephen Kendall say anything to you?"

"Well, sure. What you'd expect. 'Thank you for your kind thoughts,' 'We'll let you know about the arrangements.' That sort of thing. And they did. That nanny called back later to say the funeral is at two P.M. tomorrow at Second Unitarian."

Barbara Ross

★　★　★　★　★

Jack Holden's office was lush—leather club chairs, Oriental carpets, and antiques. In a photo on the desk, Holden gazed out, flanked by a smiling wife and three adolescents. A heavy cabinet held a TV silently flashing pictures while stock market numbers crawled across the bottom of the screen. At the windows, open drapes revealed Willow Road from where it emerged along the side of the building, down the steep hill, and past the sharp curve at the accident site, until it disappeared into the underpass under the railroad.

Holden came out from behind the massive desk, smiling, right hand extended. "Ah, there you are," he said. "Sorry to keep you waiting." After shaking only Ruth's hand, he moved them to a cherry conference table and offered seats. "Did Ellie get you coffee? Tea?"

"Coffee would be great," Ruth answered. Holden opened the door and called to Ellie Berger to bring in coffee and then settled himself at the head of the conference table. Ruth studied him. What she saw confirmed her impression of the day before—a good-looking man fighting a losing battle with middle age. His facial skin was as red in repose as it had been in anger, and it contrasted eerily with the blue, blue of his eyes. His suit was well cut, but couldn't quite disguise the heft of his midsection. He had a football player's build that would run easily to fat. Ruth imagined it was a constant struggle to hold the line.

"Before we begin, I must apologize for yesterday," Holden said. "I've been under a lot of strain since Tracey died, as you might guess. I'm worried about the business, the clients, employees—" He waved his hand toward his closed office door, indicating everything beyond it.

Ruth weighed the information. Certainly, the unexpected death of your business partner, the concerns of your clients, and needs of your employees could create a pressure-cooker

96

environment that might cause you to lash out. But somehow, the yelling Jack Holden felt more real than the polite, contained man offering them coffee now.

Ellie Berger came in carrying three full Fiske & Holden mugs and coffee paraphernalia on a tray. When she put it down, Holden thanked her politely and asked her to close the door on the way out.

"You know, I wasn't sure if you were coming." Holden spoke only to Ruth, ignoring Moscone. "I called my friend Bob Baines this morning. He didn't seem to think the investigation would amount to much."

"How did you and Tracey Kendall meet?" Ruth asked, deliberately not responding.

"Oh." Holden shifted in his chair, appeared to consider, and then answered. "She came to me about a job. She was Tracey Noonan then. I don't know how she heard about me. For a long time I was under the impression she'd known my sister at boarding school, but it turns out they'd just missed each other. Hildy graduated before Tracey started. In any case, I liked her, and I knew immediately I could use her." Holden leaned forward in his chair, warming to the story. He put his elbows on the table. Ruth noted the starched crispness of his French cuffs fastened by gold cufflinks emblazoned with a school crest. She couldn't make out the name. Prep, college, or business school, she wondered.

"We weren't in these offices then. My father owned that little colonial building on Wembly Street in Derby Center, just off Main. The office was four blocks from the house I grew up in. He ran Fiske & Holden as a suburban branch of a national brokerage house. In those days, your friends were your clients and your clients were your friends. They'd stop by the office every Saturday morning to smoke cigars and talk about how the markets performed that week. In the early years of the business, if one of Dad's customers met with an untimely demise, he had almost certainly named two of Dad's other customers as trustees, and the circle was unbroken. They continued to funnel the investment business through Dad.

"By the time I joined the firm, the handwriting was on the wall. Dad's friends and customers were dying off. Their sons, my generation, didn't need a suburban brokerage office. Nobody had time for cigars on Saturday morning. And the widows—forget tying up their money in trusts. They were on the Internet wheeling and dealing on their own." Holden paused, frowning slightly. He continued to focus on Ruth, not glancing at Moscone.

"Still, I'd worked with Dad long enough to understand what he had—autonomy, conviviality, convenience, an enviable quality of life, as we would say now. I wanted the same things for myself. But how to make it pay? I came up with a plan to sell a few of our sizable remaining family trusts on a mutual fund, run by me and using their initial investment as leverage to get the fund up and running.

"When Tracey arrived, I knew I could make my dream come true. She was the inside person I'd been looking for. She really knew her stocks. I made her an offer she couldn't refuse, and the rest, as they say, is history."

Ruth noted that Jack Holden's history of the firm's glory days was shaded differently from Ellie Berger's. Ellie had placed Tracey Kendall at center stage in the rebirth of Fiske & Holden. For Jack, Tracey was a player in his master plan.

"What was Tracey like around the office?"

"I used to call her the Queen Bee, all the little drones buzzing around her. You won't get an objective opinion about her from anybody in the place. Dad loved her, couldn't be around her enough. One of the things I'm proudest of is that Dad lived to see our success." Holden gestured to the wall behind him, which was covered with framed testimonials and articles. "The Hottest Couple in Funds," one headline proclaimed over a photograph of a beaming Tracey and Jack.

"I provided my father with a place to go to work every day until he died three years ago at the age of eighty-six," Holden continued. "After he passed away, I sold the little building downtown, and we moved up here. We were crammed in like sardines by then, and nobody walks to the office anymore. We needed the parking."

"Did you see Mrs. Kendall's accident?" Moscone asked, nodding toward the windows.

Holden's eyes didn't follow Moscone's gaze. His only acknowledgment of the question was to stop talking, as though a noisy jet had passed overhead. The two men sat stony-faced for a few seconds.

"Detective Moscone wants to know if you saw the accident," Ruth repeated, since Holden didn't seem to see or hear Moscone.

"Me? No. I was here eating at my desk and reading the *Wall Street Journal* when siren after siren went by outside. Then most of my employees came running in here like lemmings." He paused. "We didn't know it was Tracey, of course. It's too far away to see." Holden continued to face Ruth.

Ruth asked, "Did Al Pace ever work on your car?"

"No."

"Do you know him?"

Holden shrugged his large shoulders elaborately. "We all know him, so to speak. He's in and out of the office all the time."

"Can you think of any reason Al Pace would have for deliberately killing Tracey Kendall?"

Holden shrugged again. "No." He hesitated a few seconds, then added, "The news reports implied Tracey had some sort of relationship with him."

"Did she?"

"I don't know. I was her business partner, not her baby-sitter."

"So you think it's possible?"

"I suppose anything is possible."

"Was Tracey happily married?"

"That was my impression, but you never really know, do you?"

"What happens to the business if a partner dies?" Ruth asked. It wasn't clear how long Holden would remain in this co-operative mood and she wanted to get right to it.

Holden cleared his throat. "Well, the partnership agreement states that should either Tracey or I die or become permanently disabled, the remaining partner selects a successor who must be approved by our clients, who are in reality limited partners."

"Kevin Chun told us the limited partners can remove their funds if there's a change in management."

"I don't see how that's relevant, but it's true."

"I understand Stephen Kendall was here yesterday."

Jack Holden smiled and scowled simultaneously. "Poor Ellie," he said. "She's well-meaning, but her judgment is less than desirable sometimes. Imagine letting Stephen Kendall walk off with whatever he wanted."

"So, you don't know what he walked off with?"

"That's just it. I was in Boston, or it never would have happened. Nobody checked his boxes. Ellie thought it would be quote, rude, unquote. I tried to explain to Ellie that most of the materials in Tracey's office belong to the partnership and are not personal effects in any sense. Ellie doesn't know what's what, and Kendall's a goddamned artiste. I can't imagine how he could make the distinction."

"Have you looked through Mrs. Kendall's office to discover

what was taken?"

"Briefly. I really couldn't say—clothes, photographs, her paintings, things like that. I don't know for sure, and I won't until I've really had a chance to look. Speaking about Tracey's personal effects, do you people still have her briefcase?"

Moscone spoke up, a glutton for punishment. "It's in the property room at the station."

Holden didn't even look his way. "But why?" he asked Ruth. "What do you need it for?"

"The briefcase was in the car at the time of the accident," Ruth answered. "It may be evidence."

"Evidence? What kind of evidence? How long will you keep it? There are things in there we need."

"After we find Mr. Pace, we'll determine whether it's material."

"Well, be sure to give it back to me and not Kendall." Holden's voice grew louder. "That's Fiske & Holden property."

The friendly, nostalgic Jack Holden was gone, the angry twin from yesterday back in his place. The telephone rang on the desk behind him and he turned to answer it.

On the phone, Holden's voice was abrupt, "No, Ellie, you were right to interrupt. Hold on just a second. I'll find out if I can take it."

Ruth gestured for him to go ahead and take the call. Nothing more productive was going to happen with Jack Holden today, and nothing would be gained by antagonizing him. He would undoubtedly be on the phone to Baines as soon as they left. She rose and held out her hand. "That's all for now, I think. We'll be back."

"Fine, fine, any time." Holden waved toward the door. "You know the way." He returned to his call.

Moscone fell into step with Ruth as they exited across the parking lot. "Well, that was pointless. What a jerk. And that smell!"

"I didn't notice any smell."

"Are you kidding? He smells like he sleeps at the bus station. And he never acknowledged me. Never made eye contact or answered my questions."

"He figured I had the power in the room and he didn't want to waste time with you. I've seen it before." Though the last time she'd seen it, she hadn't been the one in the power position. She'd been in Moscone's shoes.

"Jerk," Moscone reiterated.

"Pretty full of himself," Ruth agreed.

"Full of himself and without any feelings for his partner of twelve years, recently deceased."

"Maybe. He has a lot of responsibility, to the clients, the employees. He may just be trying to keep it all together."

"Yeah, sure. He wouldn't confirm the affair, either."

"I don't think Tracey was the type to make a confidant of anyone at work."

Moscone turned around to face the ugly office building. "If anyone in there knows about Tracey Kendall and Al Pace, it's Brenda O'Reilly. Receptionists know everything. We need to get her out of the office where Holden and Berger won't be watching her and she'll be more relaxed. I'm going to go back in and ask her to have lunch with me."

"Lunch?" Ruth asked aloud to Moscone's retreating back. "Do you really think that's a good idea?"

Moscone emerged from the building a few minutes later. "She doesn't want to be seen leaving with me. Drop me at the Suds 'n' Spuds up on the corner. She's meeting me there in ten minutes."

Ruth dropped Moscone off as requested, then turned around and drove back down Willow Road toward the Fiske & Holden building. She was surprised Brenda had agreed to lunch so easily, though she guessed Moscone's handsome face, lean body, and well-cut suit might have something to do with it.

A lone figure walked along the side of the road, tall and thin, his head hunched forward. Adam Bender, Fiske & Holden's trader, returning from his daily pilgrimage to the Deli-Cater. Ruth pulled alongside him. Despite the warm spring weather, he wore both his suit jacket and a dark raincoat. He clutched his bag lunch in his hand. Ruth opened her window and stuck out her badge. "Adam Bender? I'd like to talk to you."

"Here?" He pressed his glasses to his nose. She gestured to the Fiske & Holden parking lot. Adam Bender went to his car and waited, setting his lunch on its trunk. Ruth parked her car and got out.

"Sorry we missed you the other day." Ruth offered her hand. "We've met everyone else at Fiske & Holden." Bender returned the handshake mutely. Ruth continued, "You're one of the people who used Al Pace's services?"

"Yes. I had an appointment with him that day, the day Tracey, er . . ."

"Was your car actually serviced?"

"No. It was the oddest thing. On my way to lunch, I found my keys sitting next to Brenda O'Reilly's on the trunk of her car."

"What did you do then?"

"I put them in my pocket."

"Both sets?"

Bender looked baffled. "No, just mine."

"Did you tell Ms. O'Reilly that her keys were out in the parking lot in plain view?"

"Oh, I see what you mean. No. I must have forgotten by the time I got back."

"What time did you find the keys?"

Bender cast his eyes heavenward, then pressed his glasses to his nose again. "Around twelve-thirty."

"I'm sorry, Mr. Bender," Ruth went on, "but were you going to get lunch or returning at twelve-thirty? Ellie Berger told us you left at noon on the dot every day."

"I normally do. I live in an uncontrollable universe. It goes up, it goes down, it's a slow day, it's a heavy day," he said, evidently referring to the stock market. "There's not one thing I can do about it. So I keep the rest of my life as regular as possible. Eat at the same time, same bedtime, regular exercise. I don't like my routine to be thrown off."

"But your routine was disturbed on the day Tracey Kendall died," Ruth prompted.

"Yes. I got an e-mail from Tracey. She wanted to talk about a buy and asked me to wait."

"Was that unusual?"

"Ellie already told you. I go to lunch at—"

"No, I meant were e-mails like that unusual?"

"Well, no. Generally, I prefer written communication. That's how I'm used to working."

"Eventually, you went to lunch."

"Yes. I waited about twenty-five minutes. Then I went and found Brenda O'Reilly in the lunch room. She said Tracey had already left. So I left."

"Was the e-mail from Tracey's computer?"

Both of Adam Bender's hands fidgeted toward his face, where they pushed back his glasses one more time. "Well," he said, "you can't tell if it's from her machine. You only know it's from her mailbox. Anybody could call up Tracey's mailbox on any machine. If they knew her password."

CHAPTER NINE

Moscone smelled Brenda O'Reilly before he saw her. A hint of "Obsession" wafted over the top of one of Suds 'n' Spuds' high-backed booths and then she came into view.

They made small talk through the ordering process. He realized she was excited, happy to be unshackled from the phone console. Lunch out was a rare treat for her. He watched her from across the booth as she chattered. She had clear, clean skin with an attractive sprinkle of freckles across the nose, dark brown hair, and blue-green eyes. It was an arresting combination.

Their waitress deposited lunch in front of them—a plate of greasy, cheesy potato skins topped with bacon and sour cream for her, a mineral water and undressed salad for him.

Brenda gave Moscone her best, professional receptionist smile. "So what do you want to know?" she asked.

Moscone hesitated for a moment, then returned her grin. "Well, Ms. O'Reilly—"

"Brenda."

"Brenda, in my experience, receptionists, particularly receptionists like you who screen every incoming call, know more about what goes on in an office than anybody. Am I right?"

Brenda nodded. "You're right."

"That must be interesting."

"I think so."

"Brenda, I'm going to ask you questions about Tracey

Kendall and Fiske & Holden. Please be completely frank. The important thing is finding out what happened to Mrs. Kendall, not protecting reputations. Are you with me?"

Brenda's eyes widened. "Shoot."

"You saw Al Pace in the parking lot on the day Mrs. Kendall died."

"In the parking lot and in our offices. He was there."

"Did you talk to him?"

"Of course. He's scheduled to come by every month. There's a sign-up sheet in our break room. I post the date he's coming a couple of weeks in advance and the employees who want service leave their names. On the day Al's scheduled to come in, the employees leave their keys with me. That way, they don't have to worry about being interrupted during a meeting or conference call. When Al arrives, he picks up the keys and gets to work."

"How did Al seem the day Tracey died?"

Brenda gazed at the faux Victorian lamp above the booth. "Nervous."

"Nervous?"

"I've thought and thought about it." Brenda squinted into the lamp's light. "I keep worrying I'm imagining it, because Tracey died that day. But I'm not. He was nervous."

"Did he say anything unusual?"

"No, but he was rushed. Jumpy." She turned her palms upward. "Nervous."

"Brenda, did you actually see Al Pace working on Mrs. Kendall's car?"

"Not exactly. Al's truck was in the first slot, the one marked 'Visitor'. His truck blocked my view of Tracey's car, which was in her usual slot next to it."

"You have assigned parking spaces?"

"Well, no. But there are, were, only seven of us. We use the same spaces every day. You know, like you always sit at the same place at the dinner table when you go back to your parents' house?" Moscone nodded to indicate he understood. "Anyway, I saw Al come out from between his truck and Tracey's car wiping his hands."

"So he might not have been under Tracey's car. He could have been coming from his truck?"

"He could have been, but I don't think so."

Moscone groaned inwardly. McGrath was right. This case would be hell to prosecute. There was no evidence in what was left of the car and now no witness to place Pace under it. "You said he wasn't scheduled to work on Tracey's car. Whose car was he supposed to work on?"

"Mine," Brenda answered, "and Adam Bender's."

"What was he doing for you?"

"Changing the oil."

"Did he do it?"

Brenda shook her head. "I don't think so. That day got so crazy, to tell the truth, I completely forgot about it. But when I left, my keys were sitting on my trunk. He hadn't updated my oil sticker or put an invoice on my dash. So I assume he didn't change it."

"Where was your car?"

"At the far end of the lot. Last space facing the road."

"How often did Mr. Pace service Mrs. Kendall's car?"

"There were two cars, Tracey's SUV and Stephen's sports car. The Kendalls were pretty meticulous about oil changes, things like that. So, I'd say at least every other month for the two cars, one car every four months."

Brenda applied herself to the congealing potato skins. Moscone gave her a moment to eat before he asked the next question. "Did you ever see any indication there were problems in Mrs. Kendall's marriage?"

107

Brenda thought for a long time. "Detective—what should I call you?"

"Carl is fine."

"Carl, Tracey wasn't the type to tell you stuff like that. She's the last person in the world who'd walk into the office and say, 'You'll never believe what the moron said last night.' But I do remember one time when things must have been bad. Tracey was in the office and Stephen kept calling, which was odd by itself. He hardly ever calls. They always used e-mail for routine stuff and there was something peculiar in his voice. It was shaky. Each time I tried to put him through, Tracey dodged him. 'Tell him I went to lunch.' 'Tell him I'm in a meeting.' This went on for two days. Finally, she got really exasperated. 'Tell him to go to hell!' she said. Of course, I didn't. I told him she was in the bathroom."

Moscone asked, "Was this recent?"

"A while ago." Brenda shook her head. "You get used to lying in this job. I don't even think of it as lying anymore, more as acting, with me saying my lines in the great business drama that is Fiske & Holden." She smiled and took a breath. "I see all kinds of stuff between people, but this thing between Tracey and her husband was a one-time thing. Tracey always took calls from home. In fact, I had orders to track her down whenever Stephen or Hannah called, because Tracey always wanted to know if something happened to Carson."

"You know Hannah Whiteside?" It had never occurred to Moscone that she would.

"Sure. Hannah's one of my phone buddies. I have lots of them, people that I've never seen, but talk to almost every day. If Hannah called and Tracey couldn't take it right away, Hannah and I would chat." Brenda put one hand over her eyes. "Let me guess. I'm pretty good at this. Wheat blond hair. Pretty face. Big boobs. Figure flaw: kind of a broad back."

"Amazing."

Brenda beamed.

"What did Hannah say to you during these conversations?"

"She was bored, stuck up there with just a kid and Tracey's husband. She had a boyfriend, but she didn't want Tracey to know. She complained he wasn't around enough. Of course, you can ask her yourself." Brenda looked concerned for the first time. "What does this have to do with Tracey's car?"

"Nothing, just interested. This fight between Mr. and Mrs. Kendall, when was that?"

"I don't know." Brenda still looked worried. "Wintertime."

"February?"

"Earlier. December, I think. I remember because Tracey had bandages on her leg. She had a terrible accident on the escalator at the mall while she was Christmas shopping. The fight with Stephen came right after."

Moscone looked up sharply. "Mrs. Kendall had an earlier accident?"

Brenda nodded, missing his meaning. "Uh-huh. She was embarrassed about it. Her arms were full of parcels and she slipped. Her leg was chewed up pretty badly."

Moscone made a mental note to look into the accident. If it were real, there would be insurance documents, a mall cop report, a safety report to the state. He looked at the remnants of the salad on his plate and then glanced at his watch.

Brenda noticed the watch-glancing. "Do we have time for dessert?" she asked. "I hardly ever get out. I always just put the phone on forward and scuttle into the break room. Ellie's covering for me today. I want to stretch this out as long as possible."

When the waitress returned to their table, Brenda ordered a gooey, chocolaty confection. *How in the world can she eat like that,* Moscone wondered, *and still keep that beautiful complexion?*

He smiled at her. "Were Tracey Kendall and Al Pace having an affair?"

Brenda didn't seem shocked or angered as Ellie Berger and Jane Parker had been. She narrowed her eyes as if thinking back through conversations or scenes that might change meaning if viewed with a different set of assumptions. "I never thought of an affair, though I know you asked Ellie and Jane about it," she finally said. "I thought they were pals. He'd been ripped off when he bought his business. She was helping him out. He'd call her up sometimes, like when the bank harassed him, and ask her advice." Brenda hesitated, trying to say something in just the right way. "I never thought of Tracey and Al as a couple, but something about Tracey was hidden. Not just that she was reserved, didn't disclose personal details. It was like she had a secret."

"Was she always like that?"

"To some degree, but I sensed it more recently." Brenda sighed. "I do know one secret she had."

"What was that?"

"She disappeared one time. I'm the only one who knows. She told the office she was on vacation, and she told home she was on a business trip. She called the office every day to check on her messages, saying what a great time she was having. She called home every night to say good night to Carson. At least that's what Hannah told me. That's how I figured it out. Hannah called to chat while Tracey was away and mentioned Tracey being on a business trip."

"So she could have been off with a man?"

Brenda shrugged. "I guess."

Moscone wasn't all that excited by the information. It was hard to imagine what excuse Al Pace could have given for going off for a few days, and Karen Pace claimed he had come home every night, until now. "Was this around the time of Tracey's fight with her husband?"

"No, later. Just after the holidays, early January."

"Did Mrs. Kendall fight with anyone else recently, besides this thing with her husband?"

Brenda spooned the melting dessert onto her tongue and closed her eyes with pleasure. When she opened them, she said, "Oh yeah. Tracey had a doozey with that horrible Ms. Gleason."

"Susan Gleason?"

"I guess so. She didn't call often, but she was always all snotty. 'Inform Mrs. Kendall that Ms. Gleason is on the line.' Some of the people who have money in our fund are richer than God, but they don't talk to me like that Gleason woman did. Anyway, this time she just said, 'I don't care what she's doing, I need to speak to her right now!' So Tracey left an important meeting and went into her office and there was lots of yelling."

"Did you happen to hear what was said?"

"Not much, but Tracey's voice was kind of loud. I remember she said, 'Absolutely we can, legally,' and 'Susan this doesn't have anything to do with the past. This is about the future.' "

"When was this?"

"Maybe late January?"

"Did they talk after that?"

"Several times, but no yelling." Brenda scraped the last of the chocolate from the parfait glass.

"Did Fran Powell call the office often?" Moscone continued.

"Never heard of her."

"She told us she was Tracey's best friend."

Brenda pushed the glass away. "Maybe. I couldn't say she wasn't, but Tracey wasn't one to get personal calls at the office beyond Stephen and Hannah."

Moscone thought back through their conversation. Had he

asked her everything? He didn't want to pull out his notebook, because it would spoil the illusion of an informal lunch, but he didn't want to forget anything either. "Brenda," he said, "here's a challenge. Tell me something about Fiske & Holden that will truly surprise me."

Brenda closed her eyes and squinted, concentrating. "Okay, I've been dying to tell someone, but you have to absolutely swear not to tell anyone else."

"I swear."

"Jane Parker is madly in love with Kevin Chun, and Kevin Chun is madly in love with Jane Parker, and neither one will do a single thing about it! He won't ask her out because he's too shy, and he doesn't believe she likes him. She won't make a move on him because she thinks its 'inappropriate' to be involved with someone you work with. Isn't that stupid? His lack of courage and her silly scruples are standing in the way of their major happiness. So they sit in that back office. Some days you can cut the sexual tension with a knife."

"Really?" Moscone didn't see what this could remotely have to do with Tracey Kendall's death, but as he thought about the time he and the chief had spent with Parker and Chun, Brenda's revelation resonated. There had been something heated and tense in that room. Moscone laughed.

"Yeah, isn't it funny?" Brenda O'Reilly stood to go. "Funny and sad."

CHAPTER TEN

John McGrath lingered in the hallway outside Chief Murphy's office. She was sitting at her desk eating lunch. His feelings were as mixed about his mission as they were about Murphy herself these days. Her promotion three years ago to head of the detective force hadn't mattered to him. All she got that he could see was a desk in the corner and more miserable administrative work. She'd been good at the job—thorough, fair-minded, open to other people's ideas. He'd give her that. But since her elevation to acting chief, she was indisputably the boss. She'd gone over to the other side. And he, McGrath, had been the only one who hadn't seen it coming.

Still, she was showing some guts on this investigation, bucking Baines just at the moment when politics dictated she should be making nice, and yesterday's lunch reminded him of the good old days when he and Murphy traded barbs at every chance.

"A word, Chief?" he ventured, stepping over the threshold.

"Sure," she answered, continuing to eat.

"I've been wondering," McGrath ventured, "what's our theory of this case, exactly?"

"That Al Pace killed Tracey Kendall by tampering with her car."

"Yeah, but why?"

"Because they were having an affair. Fran Powell confirmed it and Moscone is talking to Brenda O'Reilly right now trying to get another confirmation."

"They were having an affair and what? If everybody who was having an affair killed somebody, we'd spend all our time picking up bodies."

"They were having an affair and she wanted to break it off, or he wanted to break it off and she wasn't going quietly, or she wouldn't leave her husband, or she threatened to tell his wife or she had money and she wouldn't give him any. Aren't these things fairly predictable?"

"Yeah, they are. But in this case, there's a little more." McGrath opened the manila folder he carried in his hands. "I went to Al Pace's bank today. On Tuesday, sometime after Mrs. Kendall was killed, Pace came in and made four months' back payment on his mortgage. That's almost five thousand dollars. The bank found this in their records." He handed her a copy of the deposit slip. "They're looking for the videotape now."

The boss looked confused. "Don't people usually withdraw money when they bolt, not deposit it?" McGrath waited while the meaning of his words sunk in. Bingo. Murphy put her head in her hands. "Oh, my God."

"Uh-huh." He nodded. One thing you had to say about Murphy. She was smart.

The chief sat back in her chair. "So you're telling me we've spent the last two days establishing a connection between Tracey Kendall and Al Pace, and now we have to get back out and establish a connection between somebody else and Al Pace?"

"And somebody else and Tracey Kendall. Somebody who wanted her dead."

"He was paid to commit this murder." Murphy sure looked unhappy. "We have to re-interview everybody."

McGrath stared down past his wrinkled shirt and bagging trousers to his scuffed shoes. "It's up to you, of course," he answered. "You're the boss. You can count on Pace to spill it all, but the more we know when we bring him in, the easier it's going to be to get him to talk."

Murphy threw the remnants of her lunch into the bin. "Boy, Baines is going to love this."

Her obvious misery got under McGrath's normally thick skin and made him feel lousy. "You were right, it was murder," he offered, hoping it would help.

She looked him in the eye. "Thank you, Detective," she said evenly. "You're doing great work on this case."

As McGrath left her office, he had to admit to himself it was nice to hear. And it was especially nice to hear it from her.

After McGrath left, Ruth closed her eyes and leaned her head back against her desk chair, trying desperately to order her jumbled thoughts into a coherent picture.

Baines already hated the case against Al Pace and he was going to hate this new turn of events even more. Convicting someone who hired a killer, someone who had never touched the weapon or the body, was extraordinarily difficult. Doing it in the media circus this case could become was even more so. In the course of the investigation, the New Derby police would be knocking on the doors of a lot of prominent people— Kendall, Gleason, Powell, Holden, maybe even Fiske & Holden's clients. This was the kind of case that lost D.A.s their jobs.

"What a mess," Ruth muttered. Baines already opposed her appointment to chief. The mayor had told her to stay out of the D.A.'s way. Instead, she had told Baines a half-truth and then ambushed him on television, creating interest in a high-profile case in which a conviction might be impossible. Every step in the chain had seemed like the right one, but now it was all going totally wrong.

Ruth longed for someone to talk to. She briefly considered calling the old chief, but she knew that what she really wanted was someone who would tell her what to do. And no one could tell her what to do. All the decisions going forward rested solely with her. It was the first time she had felt the enormity of that. And it was galling but somehow inevitable that the source of so many of her current problems was Baines.

Baines. Ruth didn't have to wonder how things had gone so wrong with him. She knew.

It had been Marty's idea to move the family to New Derby. He'd enjoyed their time in Boston, but when the children came, he'd begun agitating to move back to the town he'd grown up in where his parents, uncles and aunts, two of his five brothers, and several cousins still lived. He'd harangued at length about Ruth's safety on the job, how he couldn't sleep at night while she worked. He pointed out the well-known deficiencies of the city schools.

Ruth wasn't fooled by any of this. She knew Marty would be concerned about her safety no matter where she worked, and they'd find a way to educate their children wherever they lived. Marty wanted to go home. He was being pulled by fatherhood back to his own happy childhood. And since Marty was a man who asked for little, but who cared deeply about the few things for which he asked, Ruth agreed to go. It wouldn't be so bad, she'd thought. New Derby was close to Boston and hardly small, a dense and varied suburb. Besides, Marty's career sacrifice would be the greater. He'd leave the Suffolk County district at-torney's office to set out his shingle in New Derby. The extended clan of Murphy relatives and neighbors would have to pay for the advice they'd gotten free these last nine years.

The Murphy family's New Derby connections made it pos-sible for Ruth to transfer as a lieutenant directly into a day shift detective job. It was an unusual move, at a time of declining force size and in a town that preferred to bring its officers up through the ranks. Ruth knew some price would be exacted by her colleagues, and she was right. For training, they paired her with Detective First Class Arthur Pezzoli.

Pezzoli didn't like female officers and he didn't approve of transfers. Of course, he also didn't like Protestants or Jews, Blacks or Hispanics, the upper crust or the poor. Ruth saw her time with him as something to be endured. She knew she was being watched closely by the entire New Derby force.

One afternoon in the sixth week of her "training," Pezzoli hurried Ruth into his unmarked car. "I heard some things," he answered vaguely, when Ruth asked where they were going.

On a narrow street, two blocks from New Derby High School, Pezzoli slowed to a crawl and pointed to the supermarket across the way. A boy in his mid-teens was collecting carts in the parking lot. He wore black pants, a white shirt, and a white cotton jacket identifying him as an employee of the store. He pushed the carts together and strolled back across the parking lot.

As Ruth and Pezzoli watched, another boy sauntered into view from the direction of the high school. He was a slight figure in a ratty windbreaker and tattered jeans. Long blond hair scrawled out from under a baseball cap.

The two boys greeted each other. Ruth pegged the newcomer as younger, perhaps fifteen to the other boy's sixteen or seventeen. The boys stood chatting at the parking lot fence. The younger one lit a cigarette.

"What are we doing here?" Ruth asked.

"Wait a minute, wait a minute," Pezzoli responded.

Sure enough, moments later, a third boy arrived. He approached the older, bigger boy directly.

"Here we go," Pezzoli cautioned.

The transaction occurred in a flash of hands. Pezzoli was out of the car, yelling, "Police officers!" while the cash was still in transit. The bigger boy jerked his hand back as though bitten by a snake. Green bills floated to the ground.

The boys prepared to scatter, but Ruth and Pezzoli were too close. Only the third boy, the buyer, got away. Ruth tackled the big kid from behind as he started to run. When she turned, the ground was covered with plastic packets of white powder and Pezzoli had the slight, blond boy in a headlock.

The boys were Russian immigrants. Both spoke with slight accents, Eastern Europe breaking through more in intonation than pronunciation. The big one was Kvitnitsky, the smaller one Goubanov. Kvitnitsky was angry, bordering on belligerent, but Goubanov looked scared and sick at heart.

At the station, they were printed and booked. The big one had eight hundred dollars in his pocket—and two prior convictions. "I got you," Pezzoli snarled. "You little turds. Teach you to bring your Rusky ways into my town."

Ruth followed Pezzoli back to the roll call room. "Write it up now?" she asked, heading for the stairs.

"Nah," he answered. "Let's go next door and dig up Baines." Baines was an Assistant D.A. then, but with ambitions.

"You've got this first kid—Kvitnitsky," Baines said, "hand-to-hand sale, less than a thousand feet from a school, over 128 grams, third offense. We're talking minimum mandatories here. This kid is going away for a long time." Baines paused. "But I'm not sure about this other kid, Goubanov."

"Whaddya talkin' about?" Pezzoli was incensed. "We've got him on joint enterprise."

Baines looked interested. "You're sure he was involved? Maybe he was the lookout?"

"Lookout, hell, he was the one who had the dope on him."

"You're sure."

"I found it at his feet."

"Not enough," Baines replied. Ruth wasn't surprised. She didn't see how they had the Goubanov kid, either.

Then the D.A. had leaned toward them. "Now, if you'd seen

something, then maybe we could move this ahead."

Pezzoli sat back. "What if I saw Goubanov throwing the dope on the ground?" he asked.

"Then we'd have him," Baines responded.

A look of mock astonishment crossed Pezzoli's face. "That's amazing," he said. "That's exactly what I saw."

Ruth's heart sank.

Baines looked at her. "Did you see the same thing?"

She took a deep breath. "No. And I don't believe Detective Pezzoli did, either."

Baines squared his shoulders. "Here in the 'burbs, we don't let these people sell to high school kids. We like to get them off the street."

In the silence that followed, Ruth's world closed in on her. She thought about the young man. She didn't know the town and she didn't know its streets. He might be guilty as hell, morally, but nothing she had seen or heard could prove it legally. *Damn you Marty,* she'd thought, *where have you brought me?*

A knock on the doorframe interrupted the memory. McGrath and Lawry were standing outside her open door. "We thought you'd probably want to have a conversation about next steps in the Kendall case," Lawry said politely.

Ruth pushed the scene with Baines and Pezzoli out of her mind and waved Lawry and McGrath into her office.

"Pace's car was found in Salton Beach about fifteen minutes ago with a thirty-year-old New Jersey license plate on it," Lawry said when they were settled at Ruth's big conference table. "No sign of the man himself."

McGrath tapped his folders with his pen. "Were the other missing plates from his garage found in the car?"

"No."

"So he could be anywhere by now."

"Perhaps," Lawry answered, "but there've been no vehicles reported stolen from Seabrook to Rye."

"A resort area like that, some folks are bound to have left cars stored over the winter," Ruth pointed out.

"I'll get the New Hampshire guys to check for garage breaks."

McGrath pulled out his reading glasses and opened his first folder. "As you both know, Pace brought his mortgage up to date on his way out of town. Five thousand dollars. I've gone through Pace's finances with a fine-toothed comb. This guy is in big trouble, and has been since he bought Screw Loose three years ago. They also took out a big mortgage, at least for their income, when they bought that house from Karen Pace's family. I've waded through piles of warnings, shut-off notices, threats of liens by suppliers. You name it. Anyway, all the time I'm doing this, something is bugging me. I finally figured out what. In the last six months or so, he never went over the edge. Not once. Nothing ever got shut off or repossessed. At the last possible moment, the bills always got paid."

"That's the way those guys operate," Lawry pointed out. "They pay the squeaky wheel—"

"Yeah, but this was too neat. For one thing, there was never any jump in his business. The takings were pretty steady from month to month. How did he do it? Or, if he had the money coming in, why didn't he pay his bills in the first place?"

"He's robbing Peter to pay Paul," Lawry countered. "The minute he pays off one guy, the meter starts running on some other poor schmo. Now the second guy has to wait until he threatens a shut-off or a lien until he gets paid."

"That's what I thought, but I couldn't find enough information around Pace's office to prove it, so I called his creditors and got his records faxed over here."

"And?"

"He was definitely doing some shifting around. That was part of it. But what really struck me is since late November, every single one of these last-minute payments was made in cash. There isn't a check drawn on his account for even one of them."

"Could this be underground economy stuff?" Ruth asked. "We already know he fixes his buddies' cars. He gets strapped, he pulls some cars in, works 'round the clock and collects his fees in cash."

"Could be," McGrath nodded, "but it doesn't feel like that to me."

"Do we think these payments have anything to do with the five thousand dollars?" Lawry asked.

"Impossible to know. Certainly none of the bills paid were anywhere close to that amount. It was dribs and drabs. Hundreds, not thousands, of dollars at a time."

"Different amounts, different patterns. Therefore probably a different source," Ruth said. "The person making these small, irregularly timed payments was not the person who paid him the lump sum five thousand dollars the day Tracey Kendall died."

"It could be he was blackmailing someone," Lawry offered. "That's what it smells like to me. He taps the source when he's the most desperate."

"Or it could be his rich lover was giving him cash to cover his debts," McGrath said.

"Back to 'the affair.' " Ruth sighed. "Returning to the five thousand dollars, it's a lot of money to Al Pace, but it isn't a lot of money to some of the people we're dealing with. If we follow the money, it could take forever."

"That's true. Maybe this will help." McGrath opened the manila folder again and pulled out a sheaf of invoices. "I finished going through Pace's invoice file. As expected, I found invoices for Brenda O'Reilly, Kevin Chun, and Adam Bender. I also found invoices for Fran Powell and Susan Gleason, the latter at the Kendalls' Derby Hills address."

"You're saying Al Pace did work at the Kendall house?" Ruth was surprised. "Because that's definitely not what Stephen Kendall led me to believe."

"Looks that way," McGrath confirmed.

"Okay. Detective McGrath, you stay on the paper trail. Moscone's on his way back from the Suds 'n' Spuds. He must've done well with Brenda O'Reilly. He was there a long time. Lieutenant Lawry, send a uniform to pick Moscone up, then catch him up on what's going on and have him meet me at the Kendall house."

CHAPTER ELEVEN

Ruth pulled up behind a gray van with "Mo's Cleaning Services," stenciled on its sides. All the windows of the Kendall house were open and the mournful drone of a heavy-duty vacuum cleaner emanated from inside. Ruth sighed. This was not the ritual spring cleaning that had been going on at Anna Abbott's—cleaning that affirmed the certainty of the seasons and the continuity of life. This cleaning was all about death—hasty preparation for Tracey Kendall's funeral.

Ruth had to bang and hallo at the front door for some time to be heard over the din. Hannah Whiteside finally appeared, looking exhausted and uneasy. "Stephen's in his studio." She pointed down the lawn.

At the studio, Susan Gleason opened the door. Her face was flushed, her mouth set in a grim line. "Do you really have to bother him?" she asked in a more clipped version of her cool tones. "He just got back to work early this morning." Ruth assured her that she did and stepped into the huge studio space.

The dinosaurs loomed in front of her. Susan Gleason was right, Ruth reflected. The first impression was the most powerful. Not that the second look was uninteresting. Ruth stood for a moment and enjoyed the interplay of their facial expressions and body language.

A network of steel pipes, the beginnings of a new sculpture, rose from a plywood stand near the center of the room. Ruth couldn't tell what it would be. A rolling scaffold stood beside it.

Ruth looked up and noticed the elaborate system of ropes and pulleys hanging from the ceiling three stories above. So this was how a single man could move the heavy materials.

Ruth followed Susan Gleason through the maze of sculptures to the office at the back of the converted cottage. The space had been created from a one-story shed. It was small relative to the soaring studio space, but artfully arranged. Despite the presence of several large pieces—a desk, drawing table, two computer workstations and filing cabinets of several sizes—the room wasn't crowded or disorganized.

Stephen Kendall stood up from his computer as they approached. "Chief," he said, "what brings you here?" Susan Gleason stood off to the side of the room. There was tension in the air, and Ruth was sure she and Kendall had been arguing.

"We're still working on the matter of your wife's death. We have more questions."

Stephen turned to Susan. "Give us a minute, okay?"

The air crackled with tension. Susan looked like she was about to protest, but then seemed to think better of it and began noisily gathering her things from in front of the second computer. Ruth noticed that Susan carefully shut down the computer itself, erasing from the screen something that seemed very reminiscent of the program Tracey Kendall had used to manage her schedule.

"I didn't think we would see you again," Gleason addressed Ruth. "Your district attorney assured me that your investigation was routine and you wouldn't be bothering Stephen anymore. He is a very busy man." Giving Kendall a last malevolent look, she said, "I'll be in my room."

Ruth waited as Gleason's footsteps clicked across the studio floor, followed by the bang of the solid front door. She scrutinized Kendall carefully. He didn't seem angry as Susan Gleason had. He seemed somehow diminished. His eyes were red with fatigue and his body curved inward on itself, as if he was protecting an injury to his chest or abdomen. He no longer radiated the energetic charisma Ruth had felt in their first meeting.

Kendall indicated a chair next to his desk. "Sit down, Chief, please. Did you catch the guy, the mechanic?"

"No, he's still missing." Ruth kept her eyes on the sculptor. Did this information make him more tense or less? One brief exhalation was perceptively greater than the rest. Less tense, she decided. "Mr. Kendall, yesterday you told us that you didn't know Al Pace. Since then, we've learned that Pace worked on a car here at the house at least once. Does that help you remember whether you've met?"

"Why would it? I don't know when this was, but I was probably here at the studio or off somewhere. I don't mean to be snobbish, but I have no interest in car mechanics, or in cars for that matter."

"Would you say it's unusual for someone who has no interest in cars to own a high-performance sports car?"

Stephen Kendall shrugged. "The car was a gift from Tracey. Truly, I don't care about it. Tracey took care of the cars. That's why she had this 'arrangement' you seem to find so suspicious with Mr. Pace at her office. I will say again, I never met the man."

"Mr. Kendall, you went—"

"Holy shit!" Detective Moscone's voice echoed through the studio. Evidently, Kendall's sculptures affected him as well. Ruth waited while Moscone came through to the design space, pulled up a stool, and opened his notebook.

"Mr. Kendall," Ruth continued, "you went to your wife's office yesterday and removed some items. What did you take?"

"Just things, you know, personal items, paintings, photos . . ."

"It seems an odd thing to do so soon after your wife's death.

What are you looking for, Mr. Kendall?"

Stephen Kendall looked away. "I don't know what you're talking about."

"The first time we came here and went through Tracey's study, the room had already been searched. What are you looking for?"

Blank stare. No answer.

"We'd like to see what you took from Fiske & Holden."

Kendall sighed. "Certainly. It's all in the closet over there."

Moscone opened the closet and pulled out three boxes. He began removing items while Ruth continued the interview.

"What is your financial situation, Mr. Kendall?" she asked. "Who makes the money? Who spends it? Who benefits from your wife's death?"

The questions clearly upset Kendall. "My wife was worth much more alive than dead," he snapped. "Tracey's job generated a great deal of income both from fees and from the firm's investments, and that income has been used strategically for my art, yes, so I don't have to teach or spend time applying for meaningless grants. For materials, and yes, so that we could move in circles with people who have the money to buy art." Kendall gestured broadly with his hand, indicating the studio, the house, the lawns. "Tracey saw to all of it. She was brilliant with money. But it wasn't a one-way street. Tracey and I viewed my career as an investment. Tracey was only thirty-nine. She didn't see herself as a partner at Fiske & Holden for the rest of her life. As soon as my work brought in real money, Tracey planned to leave and build her own fund." At this, Kendall's voice caught. "And we were close. So, so close."

Ruth glanced over at Moscone, who was making a list of the boxes' contents. He was listening carefully.

"What were the terms of Tracey's will?" Ruth asked.

Kendall composed himself. "Standard, I guess. She leaves

everything to me. There's some life insurance that goes into a trust for Carson's education. You won't find Tracey left any money to this Pace character, if that's what you're thinking."

"We'd like you to call your attorney and give permission to verify the terms of your wife's will."

Kendall shrugged. "Sure."

Moscone began to repack the boxes. Ruth glanced at him again. He rolled his shoulders. Nothing.

Ruth thought about Tracey Kendall. Southampton, the Madeira School, Princeton, Harvard Business School. "What about the family money?" Ruth asked, turning back to Kendall. "Who gets that?"

"Why don't you ask the family?" Stephen's face wore an expression Ruth couldn't read. "They'll be here later this afternoon."

Ruth and Moscone walked back up the lawn to the main house. The cleaning crew was still busily at work. In the background their industrial vacuum ground away noisily. Just as Ruth raised her hand to knock on the door, the vacuum cut out and the sound of raised voices echoed down the back stairs.

"My God, you stupid cow," Susan Gleason's angry yell vibrated through the open windows. "Whatever were you thinking? The police are at the studio now. Everyone knows they always suspect the husband. Yet, neither of you can show any more restraint than a couple of horny teenagers!" Her voice died abruptly, as if she'd just realized the covering sound of the vacuum had halted.

There was a moment of silence followed by the sound of Hannah Whiteside's great, gasping sobs.

Ruth and Moscone pushed through the unlocked door and followed the escalating sounds of crying up the stairs to a closed door on the second floor. When they burst into the room, Hannah Whiteside looked terrified. Susan Gleason cursed under her breath. Without speaking, Ruth and Moscone moved in unison to separate the women, leaving them no time to calm down or confer.

Moscone looked around. He and Hannah were in a library or den. The room was lined with books. A television sat in a fancy cupboard built into the shelves. Hannah sank into a leather couch.

Moscone was angry with himself. When he'd originally interviewed Hannah, his tone had been big-brotherly. At the time, it had seemed the best tack to take with a young woman who'd just heard her employer killed over the phone. Now, all he had to show for his two earlier conversations was a detailed account of Tracey Kendall's last words, an account he must now consider suspect.

"It's illegal to hinder a police investigation," he snarled, letting her know they weren't pals anymore.

More sobs. Louder sobs.

"You lied to me about the circumstances of Tracey Kendall's death, didn't you?"

Noisy sobs, then a little voice, "No."

"Didn't you? It seems like you left something important out. You're screwing the dead woman's husband."

He was shouting now. She answered with a crescendo of wails.

Moscone sat down opposite the sofa. "Hannah, Hannah, Hannah," he sneered at her, "the nanny and the 'marster.' Such an old story. Was it in your job description?"

Hannah rested her forehead in her right hand. She looked up at Moscone through spread fingers. "It wasn't like that."

"What was it like, then?"

Hannah snuffled louder, looked around, and then wiped her streaming nose on the back of her hand. "We didn't mean for it to happen. It just did. Tracey traveled so much. Stephen and I were alone. Day after day, caring for Carson together—"

"Did Tracey know?"

Hannah shook her head miserably. "No."

"You're sure of that? Could anyone have told her? What about the boy? Could he have said something inadvertently? Answered the phone and said, 'Hannah can't talk now, Mom. She and Daddy are taking a nap?' "

Hannah looked horrified. "No! It was never like that. We were discreet. We only—saw each other—at night after Carson was in bed, when Tracey was away."

"In her bed, Hannah? Did you do it in the woman's own bed?"

Hannah Whiteside's face was a map of guilt. "Never. Not even in the house. In the guest suite over the garages."

"Evidently you weren't so discreet last night. Susan Gleason found out."

"I don't know what happened. Stephen came up to my room. He was crying. He just wanted me to hold him. That's all. We didn't go to the guest suite. It seemed unnecessary. The door flew open. It was Susan. Raging. Screaming at Stephen. 'You stupid, stupid fool!' Why was she prowling on the third floor at three A.M.? Her room is on the second."

Moscone didn't respond.

"It wasn't supposed to be like this," Hannah said quietly.

Moscone took out his notebook and led her step by step through the day Tracey Kendall died. Three times. Her story never changed.

After the third time through, he put his notebook away and crept out into the hall. Someone was still vacuuming in a far-off room. Moscone knocked at the closed door to Tracey Kendall's study. The door opened. Inside, he could see Susan Gleason on the chaise, sitting erect.

"The nanny admits she was sleeping with the husband," Moscone whispered to the chief. "Ms. Gleason surprised them last night in Ms. Whiteside's room on the third floor, in flagrante, as it were."

The chief nodded, hands on hips. "How could she deny it after what we overheard? What did she say about Al Pace working here?"

Moscone swore quietly and hurried back into the library.

Susan Gleason sat rigid throughout the conversation in the doorway. Ruth thought it must take enormous discipline not to even glance at the whisperers. Susan had made it clear that small town civil servants didn't impress her. She had grudgingly admitted Al Pace had fixed her car once when it had failed to start in the Kendall driveway, but she pooh-poohed the event's significance. "Oh, was that his name?" she asked. "All I knew was, it was late Thursday afternoon and I had to get back to New York. Tracey said she knew someone who could help out." No, she didn't remember if Stephen or Hannah had been home during Al Pace's house call.

"Ms. Gleason, you were here when I visited on Wednesday. Did you come to be with your client immediately after you heard about the accident?"

For the first time during the interview, Susan looked uneasy. "As a matter of fact, no. I was already in the area."

"When did you arrive?"

"I left New York early Tuesday morning. I stopped in Connecticut to visit another client, a painter, and then I came on toward Boston."

"Did you come straight to the Kendalls'?"

"No. I checked in at some galleries on Newbury Street and then treated myself to a late lunch. The Kendalls were expecting me in the early evening, but Hannah called around four o'clock to say that Tracey had been in an accident. Naturally, I came straight here after that call."

"You seemed very angry with Hannah just now. You came up from the studio and immediately got into a loud argument."

"I am angry. My God, the man's wife hasn't even been buried. You'd think the girl would have more sense."

"You might think the widower, who is more than fifteen years older, would have some sense." *Or some decency,* Ruth thought.

"Stephen's addled by grief. He doesn't know what he's doing. I'm angry at him, but I'm furious with her."

Furious, Ruth wondered, *on Tracey's behalf or your own?*

CHAPTER TWELVE

"Now what?" Moscone asked as they walked back toward Ruth's car in the Kendall drive.

Ruth checked her watch. Tracey's family wouldn't arrive until late afternoon and Ruth wanted to give them a little time to get settled before she spoke with them. "I've been thinking we need to know more about Tracey and Stephen's relationship. Let's cast the net a little wider, shall we? Let's pay a visit to the ex-wife."

Rosie Boyagian, Stephen Kendall's ex-wife, lived in a warehouse converted into artists' lofts in Derby Mills. She buzzed them into her building as soon as they explained who they were. She answered her door wiping her hands on a brightly colored rag. The large features of her face contrasted prettily with the petiteness of her frame. Her sunny studio was lined with canvases painted in a style Ruth recognized instantly.

"Police, huh?" Ms. Boyagian said. "I bet I know what this is about."

"Tracey Kendall," Ruth confirmed. "Ms. Boyagian, we have some questions for you."

"I thought she was killed by her mechanic. It's been on the news."

"We don't know yet what happened," Ruth answered. "At this point we're just gathering information."

Rosie frowned. "I'm not sure if I can help, but I'll tell you what I can. That poor, poor little boy. And Stephen, too, of course." The artist treated them to a sweet smile. "I practically mainline caffeine," she said. "May I offer you some coffee?"

Ruth accepted, even though she knew drinking coffee this late in the day would lead to trouble sleeping. Moscone waved the offer away. Rosie brought out a pair of beautiful, hand-thrown mugs. "A potter friend gave them to me in trade," she said when she saw Ruth examining them. She motioned them to the plastic porch furniture in her spare living area. "What can I tell you?"

"You were married to Stephen Kendall," Ruth stated.

"Sure was. We were married twelve years ago in June and divorced two years later in August. The decree was final three days before his wedding to Tracey."

"You were angry."

"I was angry. I was hurt. I knew Stephen enjoyed women, of course, but I didn't think he would do that to me. I was the one he married, after all. And with Tracey. That made it worse."

"You knew Tracey, too?"

"Stephen and I were together when we met her. It was at a gallery opening. We were there to support a friend. She was there with some money people. I saw the sparks fly the minute they shook hands. My stomach literally heaved. I knew. But then nothing seemed to happen. Tracey came around a lot, but the three of us always did things together. Or, at least, I thought we did. I convinced myself I had been wrong. So by the time they told me, I was blindsided. I was the proverbial last to know."

"What happened?"

"I cried. I begged. I humiliated myself in ways I don't care to think about now. I lost. She won. At least I thought so then."

"But now you don't feel that way."

"No. Art circles in Boston are very small. There was no way to avoid them and within a few years all three of us moved past that awful point. We weren't close friends, but I would say we were fond acquaintances, happy to run into each other at openings and parties. The truth is, eventually I came to feel grateful to Tracey. She saved Stephen and me from a life of abject poverty, from a life of teaching and grants and grinding. My little paintings don't take much to support, but Stephen's sculpture is expensive." Rosie Boyagian spread her paint-stained fingers in front of her. "And she saved me from spending my life with a man who would never be faithful to me."

"There were other 'other women'?"

"A parade. I didn't find out until later, of course. Between the time he left me and the time the divorce was final, people came out of the woodwork to tell me. They seemed to think it would make me feel better. All the time we were dating, engaged, and married, there was always someone. Always one at a time. My friend Helen says Stephen is a 'serially monogamous philanderer.' " Rosie Boyagian laughed while Ruth, momentarily distracted by the mention of her sister's name, reflected that Helen's insights about men were limited to those with whom she wasn't personally involved. "Stephen's thing is falling in love," Rosie continued. "He feeds on the energy of it. He thinks he needs it for his art, so he's always looking for that sensation of falling." She shook her head.

"So you wouldn't be surprised that he was cheating on Tracey in the same way he cheated on you?"

Rosie hesitated. "For years after his marriage to Tracey, Stephen had a reputation as a bad boy tamed. Some even said she'd ruined him. He hasn't had a major show since Carson's birth. But then, this new show for Susan came up. Stephen's under a lot of pressure to create, just as he was during his wunderkind days when he was with me. If he was going to roam, now would be the time."

"Was Susan Gleason one of your husband's lovers?"

"The physical part of Stephen and Susan's relationship was

over before he and I met. Susan and her husband, Mortimer, 'discovered' Stephen when he was a student. Mort declared Stephen a prodigy, gave him his first show. So much early promise. But Stephen was not an easy investment. Whenever the Gleasons would get buyers excited about a direction Stephen was taking, he'd turn and start going somewhere else. The Gleasons believed in Stephen's talent and eventual ability to command high prices, but toward the end, Mort was getting impatient. Only Susan's pleading kept him going."

"Toward the end?"

"The Gleasons had a famously open marriage. Two years ago, Mort ran off with their secretary, Jean-Paul. It took eighteen months for the courts to unravel their business and professional relationships. You'd think Susan as the wronged party would have come out of it well, but Mort knew Susan would do anything to hang onto Stephen. His lawyers got her to give up the gallery, the co-op, and contracts with several reliably productive artists."

Ruth sipped coffee from the elaborate cup, pondering this new information. Did it mean anything in relation to Tracey Kendall's death? If Susan Gleason had given up so much to retain Stephen Kendall, then the success of his upcoming show would be critical to her. Surely, she wouldn't have done anything to jeopardize it. Or maybe it should be looked at another way. She wouldn't allow anyone to get in her way.

"Would Stephen and Tracey have returned Ms. Gleason's loyalty?"

"Tracey's only loyalty was to Stephen's career. Without Mort, Susan is weaker, financially and influentially. Tracey would have been concerned."

"And Stephen? Would he have left Ms. Gleason if his wife advised it?"

"He would have resisted. It's ironic for me to say it, but he is loyal, in his way."

"And if Tracey persisted?"

"I can only tell you this. Stephen's mother objected to his divorce from me and his marriage to Tracey. He chose Tracey. He hasn't spoken to his mother since the day he and Tracey married. If you want to be in Stephen's life, you don't, you didn't, align yourself against Tracey."

Ruth looked the small woman directly in the eyes. "Rosie," she said, "you were married to him. Did you ever think he might be capable of having his wife killed?"

The artist was plainly startled by the question, but she pulled herself together, answering carefully. "I don't know. I hope not. You see, you're asking the wrong woman. I have a proven blind spot when it comes to Stephen Kendall."

Moscone shut his notebook. Ruth agreed there wasn't much point to continuing. She thanked Rosie and stood to go.

"I'm sorry that I couldn't be more help," the artist responded. "When all was said and done, I liked Tracey. There was a lot to admire about her. In fact, I gave her two of my paintings. They were titled, 'Be Careful What You Wish For,' and, 'You Might Get It.' "

"I know," Ruth responded. "They were hanging in her office when she died."

"More background?" Moscone asked as they plowed out of the parking lot at his usual breakneck speed.

"More background," Ruth confirmed and gave him directions to their next stop.

The Holden house stood on a couple of acres along School Street, which ran from Derby Four Corners to Upper Derby. Ruth had driven by it many times and always considered it a monstrosity. Built ten years earlier, it towered above the ground, a brick colonial with a thyroid condition. Wings hung off either side. One wing housed a three-car garage. Ruth was willing to bet the other held a "great room."

Margot Holden opened the door immediately, as if she had been standing in the front hall. "You're here about Tracey Kendall," she said when they identified themselves. "I don't know what I can tell you. I didn't know that auto mechanic."

She was a statuesque woman with thick blond hair piled casually on her head. She was cursed with the Brahmin horse-face, but her voice was warm and deep. She was accompanied by a large black Labrador that sniffed at Moscone. Moscone sniffed back. "C'mon in," Mrs. Holden said. "He's just a big old baby." Evidently, she meant the dog.

They followed her through the large, formal, marble foyer, into a large, formal living room decorated in rich tones of aquamarine and contrasting peach. The house wasn't dirty, just disheveled. CDs were piled on the mantel. A suitcase and basket of folded laundry sat in the front hall. Magazines were scattered across the sofa. Ruth thought about her own comfortable, feet-on-the-couch house, where things were always piled up on the steps, waiting to be carried up or down and the front hall was cluttered with backpacks and an assortment of oversized sweat-shirts that never seemed to find their way back to their owners. The mess in this house wasn't much different, but in this formal setting the clutter stuck out sorely, like a woman in a formal suit with her shirttail hanging out.

Margot Holden moved with great energy, picking up and putting things away. "I'd like to help if I can. We weren't close, but I always liked Tracey." In the living room, she turned. "I won't ask you to sit down. I just ran back here after school to pick up a load of laundry and my things. I've got to get out of here."

Mrs. Holden seemed to catch the puzzled look on their faces. "I teach," she explained.

137

"Get out of here?" Ruth clarified.

"Jack didn't tell you about our living arrangements?"

Ruth shook her head. Margot Holden kept moving, straightening as she talked. "When Jack and I separated, this house was only five years old and all three of our kids were still at home. Jack couldn't bear to sell. He was so proud of his School Street address. And I didn't want the kids shuttling back and forth, going somewhere else on the weekend. They had their friends, sleepovers, sports teams. They were more tied down than we were." Margot Holden smiled. "So that turned out to be the solution. The children stayed put. Jack and I do the shuttling.

"I'm here during the week. Jack's in a little condo we bought when they converted the old Abbott School. On Fridays, I move to the condo and Jack comes here after work and stays until Monday morning. The children are, or were, here all the time. The older two are at boarding school now. Johnny's in the sixth grade, so we have a couple more years of this to go." Margot Holden pointed toward the great room.

People truly were astonishing. Sometimes Ruth thought she'd heard everything. "Does this work?"

Margot Holden gave a little laugh. "For the kids, it's been the best solution, though I sometimes worry Johnny and the dog think they own the house because they're the only ones here all the time. Jack and I live out of the trunks of our cars."

Ruth shot Moscone a look, remembering his objection to the smell of exhaust fumes on Holden's suit.

Margot Holden continued, "We both got what we wanted. I got a permanent home for my kids. Jack gets to pretend he's still married and living his life the way he imagined it would be."

Ruth thought about the photo of the happy family on Holden's desk and all it was meant to convey. "How long have you been divorced?"

"Separated five years, divorced for two of those."

"You and your ex-husband share this condo?" Moscone clarified. "Why don't you at least get your own places?"

Margot Holden held her hand up and rubbed her thumb against her fingers. Money.

"I thought your ex-husband made a good deal of money," Moscone responded. "Tracey Kendall did."

Margot shrugged. "It depends. Some years more than others. The last few years have been in the 'other' category, not the 'more than.' "

"Did he and Tracey Kendall take the same amount of money out of the business?"

"No. They had a complex formula based on who brought in the client and who was the lead partner on the stock that I never really understood. Tracey was supposed to be the stock spotter and Jack was in charge of bringing in and managing the clients. Eventually, of course, the clients figured out Tracey was the brains and started coming to her directly. All I know is, as the years went by, Tracey made more and more, Jack less and less. Which is not to say that we're poor. Most people would love to be as poor as we are."

"How did your ex-husband feel about this? Tracey Kendall getting more and more."

"Lately, when his need for money has been greater, he's resented it. Appearances are everything to Jack. He was a boy of moderate means brought up surrounded by rich boys, the sons of his father's customers. He's still trying to prove that he's playing in the right league." Margot Holden glanced at the thin gold watch on her wrist. "I've got to get going. Technically, this place is Jack's as soon as I leave Friday morning." In the front hall she picked up the suitcase. Moscone grabbed the laundry basket. "Bye, Johnny!" she called in the general direction of the great room. "See you Monday, after school."

Ruth, Moscone, and Mrs. Holden left together, pausing while Mrs. Holden unlocked her car. On the front steps, Ruth looked around. The Holden property rolled off in both directions. She caught sight of another structure behind a knoll below the house. Long and low, the building was not visible from the road. It was a garage, four bays in length. With a three-car garage attached to the house, what did they need this other building for? "What's that?" She pointed down the hill.

"A second garage. Jack drives and restores vintage cars." Ruth raised her eyebrows at Moscone, who nodded back.

Margot Holden and Moscone loaded her possessions into her car. As Moscone stepped away, she backed out of the drive at full speed, gave a little wave, and accelerated away.

"We better go, too," Moscone prodded. "We still need to get back to the Kendalls'."

Ruth was opening her mouth to respond when Jack Holden pulled his coupe down the driveway.

"You!" he barked. "What are you doing here?"

"We had some questions for your ex-wife."

"My wife! What could she possibly have to do with anything? Bob Baines assured me this afternoon that you'd tracked this Pace guy to Salton Beach. I thought I'd seen the last of you, and frankly, the thought made me pretty happy."

Ruth ignored the diatribe. "You're home early," she remarked.

"I had some stuff to take care of. It's been a helluva week. Even you can understand that."

CHAPTER THIRTEEN

The cleaning company truck was gone when Ruth and Moscone arrived back at the Kendall house, but the driveway was crowded with other vehicles—a green minivan, a pickup truck, a plain gray sedan, and a catering company van were crowded at the top of the circular drive. Stephen Kendall's sports car and Susan Gleason's elderly German sedan weren't visible.

The oak front door was open for the caterers, who were unloading tables and serving dishes into the dining room. Ruth called out and knocked and called again before she and Moscone entered the big front hall.

"My daughter would want a priest there!" The voice—female, loud, insistent—came from the direction of the kitchen. Ruth glanced through the doorway. A gray-haired woman sat at the head of the kitchen table, kneading a rumpled tissue. An older man stood behind her, hands on her shoulders in a soothing gesture. On one side of the table were two men who looked more alike than any adults Ruth had ever seen. At the end of the table, a short woman in a maternity smock stood, toddler on her hip. Tracey Kendall's family.

"Now, Ma," one of the men was saying. "Tracey wasn't into that stuff. She hasn't been in church since her confirmation. She wasn't even married in the Church."

"That wasn't her choice." Tracey's mother shot a look in the direction of Kendall's studio. "I don't hold with this Unitarian stuff. Your sister didn't even go to that church."

"Stephen didn't want a church at all," the other man said. "He's trying to compromise. Give him a little credit."

"And there'll be no casket?" the mother continued. "Your sister won't be there with us?"

"Well, I can't agree with that," the twin who'd spoken before said. "Tracey was never one to miss her own party."

"Oh, for God's sake!" the other responded. "She died in a terrible car crash. It's not like we could have an open—if she can't look good—" his voice broke. He couldn't go on, but he'd made his point. The others nodded sadly, except for Tracey's mother.

"This is my baby," she said quietly. "I want her there."

"Oh boy," Moscone whispered from behind Ruth. "This is going to be awful."

Ruth moved toward the kitchen. "Let's get it over with."

Ruth and Moscone interviewed Thomas and May Noonan in the Kendall living room. Ruth would have preferred the straight-backed chairs in the dining room, but she wanted the older couple to be as comfortable as possible. The Noonans sat together on the couch. Ruth and Moscone sat again in the chairs that were too deep and low for this purpose. Ruth perched on the edge of hers. Her thigh muscles ached from the effort required to stay balanced.

Mrs. Noonan continued to knead her rumpled tissue. She had on a shapeless dark dress, her short gray hair uncombed. She looked much older than Ruth expected. Ruth wondered whether this was her normal state, or if she had been a vigorous, well-dressed sixty-something only four days before, until she'd been told about her daughter's death.

Mr. Noonan tried too hard. He offered tea and answered Moscone's routine questions—name, age, address—in a strong voice. He had a full head of white hair and deep gray eyes. Ruth watched him as he talked. These were not the people Ruth had expected.

"I own a little grocery store in Water Mill, New York, on Long Island," Mr. Noonan said.

"Relationship to the victim?" Moscone asked formally.

"May is Tracey's mother. I'm her stepfather."

"You are her father," Mrs. Noonan said forcefully, emphasizing every word. It was the first time she had spoken.

"Now, May, I'm trying to be accurate. These are the police. They don't care how we feel about each other. They want facts." He turned back to face Moscone. "Tracey's father left when she was a baby. Can you imagine? The twins were two, Tracey was a newborn, and he walked out." He paused to let the picture sink in. Ruth thought about the abandoning father, something else she and Tracey had in common, though Tommy Noonan, with his kind eyes, had been a part of Tracey's life almost from its beginning.

"May had some tough times, very tough times, let me tell you," Mr. Noonan continued. "I met her at church two years later. I'd just moved back to town. My father was sick and he needed help at the store. It was love at first sight, but it took me five years to persuade her. She was gun-shy after her first marriage, don't you see? And there were some legal problems with the divorce since we couldn't find her husband. During all the time we courted, May never once let me help her out financially, though things were tight, I can tell you." Tommy Noonan shook his head as if his wife still amazed him. "Anyway, we were married in June the year Tracey was seven."

"And you never formally adopted her?"

"In the family, we say Tracey adopted me. She left first grade as Mary Ann Tracey. The school system skipped her, so she started third grade the next fall. 'Hello,' she said, shaking the teacher's hand just as an adult would, 'My name is Tracey

Noonan.' And so she was, ever after, until she became Tracey Kendall, that is. When Tracey wanted something, she took it upon herself to get it. She wasn't going to wait around for me and May to make a decision." Tommy Noonan smiled at the recollection.

"Had Tracey talked to you about any problems she'd had lately, at home or at work?"

"Tracey didn't have problems," May Noonan answered. "She wasn't the type."

"Or if she did, she certainly never told us," Mr. Noonan said.

"And your son-in-law, Stephen Kendall, how do you get along with him?"

"He's okay," Tommy Noonan answered. "We haven't seen them as much as we'd like. It's hard for us to get away from the store, and they're always busy with their lives."

"I've never liked him." May spoke for the third time. Her voice was loud and clear, its sound as startling as her candor. "But now, I suppose I have to be nice to him, because if I'm not, I could lose Carson, and that would be more than I could bear. I don't think Stephen cares anything about Carson. He hasn't spent five minutes with the boy since we've been here. I wish Carson could come back to Long Island with us." Mrs. Noonan dabbed the crumpled tissue at her eyes, but there was too little of it left to have much effect.

"I think we have everything we need," Ruth said quietly. She wanted to move on. There was little point in putting this woman through any more. Ruth gave the couple on the couch a look of frank assessment.

"We're not what you anticipated," Tommy Noonan offered.

"No."

"We used to say, how come Tracey comes from money and the rest of us don't? We couldn't understand it. The truth is Tracey graduated first in her class from high school. She was accepted at a lot of good schools, with scholarships, which we needed, but Princeton turned her down. That fancy prep school offered to let her repeat her senior year of high school. Something they almost never do, I understand. Tracey saw it as another chance. She could retake the college boards, try again. This is the way our Tracey responded to adversity. She kept trying, looking for another way around. Tracey never gave up. She could bulldog her way through anything."

"Thank you both for your time," Ruth said, taking Tommy Noonan's hand. He smiled a sad smile.

Tracey Kendall's brothers were still in the kitchen. As Ruth and Moscone entered, one of them was standing at the phone while the other sat at the kitchen table, a set of blueprints and a pile of forms in front of him. The brother on the phone shouted to make himself heard over some noise on the other end. "What do you mean the plumber didn't show? Does he know that— Well, call Fred and give him holy hell. Yes, now. And see if you can—"

Ruth and Moscone sat down at the kitchen table. "I'm Phil," the sitting brother said. "That's Brian." Brian wound up his call and sat next to Phil. They were startling to look at. Ruth had seen twins who were dressed and coifed alike in childhood, but in her experience in adulthood, twins tended to look less identical. One stayed lean while the other got fat. One's hair was short, the other long, and so on. But Brian and Philip Tracey looked exactly alike. They had thick, brown mustaches, identically trimmed, the same haircut, even the same length of sideburns, gray sprouting in the same pattern at the temples. Their hands were big and rough from outdoor labor. Ruth wondered if the calluses were in identical spots.

Both men were dressed in jeans and heavy work boots, the same brand, and each wore a plaid flannel shirt. The only difference was that one shirt was blue, the other gray. "Brian, blue," Ruth said to herself three times, but she knew that if she were to see them again dressed in different clothing she would never be able to tell the difference.

"What's this about?" Philip, gray-shirt, asked. "Stephen told us Tracey died in a car accident."

"That's true," Ruth responded, "but some aspects of your sister's accident make me uncomfortable."

"Stephen mentioned something about her mechanic," Brian responded.

"The man who serviced your sister's car has disappeared. His name is Al Pace. Do you know him? Did your sister ever mention him?"

Both men shook their heads. Phil asked, "How can we help?"

"We need to know more about your sister's life."

Phil looked at Brian. "You see more of her than we do."

"My older boy is the same age as Carson," Brian explained. "Tracey liked to get them together. We're Carson's only family. We'd come up and spend the weekend here. Last summer, Carson came and spent a week with us. Anyway, it doesn't matter who saw her last. Tracey never changed."

"It's true," Philip said fondly. "Our sister was a one of a kind. She became the general in our war games when she was still in diapers." His tone was one of fond remembrance, his voice husky with grief.

"She always got what she wanted," Brian continued for his brother. "Phil and I were powerless."

"When did you see her last, exactly?" Moscone asked.

"We were supposed to visit after Christmas, over the school break," Brian answered, "but Tracey telephoned and told us something had come up. So that means I haven't seen her," he counted on his fingers, "since the weekend before Halloween."

"Did Tracey seem upset when she called to cancel your trip?"

Moscone continued. "Was she disturbed about anything?"

"I really didn't think about it. She canceled plans all the time. She traveled a lot in her work."

"Were your wives close to Tracey?" Ruth asked.

Philip shook his head. "No way. Jean was scared to death of her. Tracey was a little intimidating if you didn't know her. My kids are much older, teenagers. We never hung out here the way Brian's family did."

"Maura and Tracey mostly talked about mommy things," Brian filled in. "You know, croup, toilet training. It was pretty superficial. They didn't have a lot in common besides the kids— and me, of course." Brian cleared his throat and looked away.

Neither of these big men was going to break down in front of her, but both were obviously affected by the death of their sister. Ruth wondered why she was bothering these people. They had nothing to do with Al Pace and there was no family money to provide motive for anything. She asked one last question. "If your sister didn't confide in you, I'd like to find a friend or confidant she might have talked to. Do either of you have any idea who that might be?"

Both men looked surprised. "Did you check Fran Powell across the street?" Philip asked. "She and Tracey have known each other since grade school. Mary Frances Kanjorsky she was then. Mary Ann and Mary Fran. They were thick as thieves."

It took a moment for Phil's remark to sink in. Tracey Kendall and Fran Powell childhood friends?

CHAPTER FOURTEEN

Ruth strode up the service road toward the Powell house, Moscone close behind her. She'd had enough of the dissembling Mary Frances Kanjorsky, childhood friend of Tracey Kendall. Indeed.

When Fran Powell opened the door, she was sober, clear-eyed, and well put-together. Definitely a change from the day before.

"May I help you?" Her voice was frosty.

"Yes," Ruth said and went through into the living room. "Sit down."

Fran Powell narrowed her eyes, then moved to the center of the enormous sofa. Moscone drifted into the shadows beside the big picture window.

"My father-in-law called the district attorney and was assured that—"

Ruth interrupted. "Mrs. Powell, the last time we spoke, you lied to me."

"I don't know what you're talking about."

"You told me you met Tracey Kendall a few years ago, when Carson was a newborn."

"I did not. I said that Tracey discovered I was here a few years ago." Fran Powell's tone was terse.

"But that wasn't the whole story."

"No. It wasn't."

"You knew Tracey when you were girls."

"Yes."

"You were best friends."

"Yes."

"And yet, you didn't tell me this."

"I didn't see what possible relevance it could have."

"Then why did you lie about it?"

"I didn't lie," Fran Powell said. "It's a simple story, really. Tracey and I grew up together. We graduated from high school. She went on to that 'post-grad' year at that boarding school. I went out to USC. We lost touch. It happens. After my mother died I had no reason to return to Long Island. I graduated from college. I stayed on the West Coast and got a job. I got married. I got pregnant. My husband didn't want to raise a child out there. His parents owned this land. They built a house here. I never saw the place before the day we moved in. I didn't choose it. I certainly didn't know that Tracey Noonan was living in my front yard."

"And when you found out, you resumed your old friend-ship."

"Yes."

"You know that what you've just told me is wildly improb-able?"

"Then it must be true."

"I hope for your sake that it is. Next lie. You said you didn't know Al Pace."

"I don't."

"Mrs. Powell, how long do you intend to keep this up? We have a copy of an invoice from Al Pace to you."

"What does that prove?"

"Al Pace worked on your car, last October."

"So what if he did? It doesn't mean I met him."

"If he worked on your car, he did it right here, in your driveway."

"Perhaps I wasn't home."

"Al Pace was working on your car. Where would you have gone?" Ruth seethed with impatience, waiting for an answer, but none came, so she continued. "Another thing, you told us Tracey Kendall was having an affair with Al Pace. We haven't found anyone else who can confirm it. Are you sure that was what was happening?"

Fran Powell, up to then defiant, dropped her head. "Yes, I'm sure. Tracey told me herself."

"Give me some details. Where did they meet? When? Were they in love?"

"She never told me those things. Even as a child, Tracey was discreet."

"Think, Mrs. Powell."

Fran raised her head. "There is one thing that I thought was unusual. Tracey said she gave this Al Pace money sometimes. Cash. Maybe that's something you can confirm? From his bank account?"

"Why would she do that?"

"She said she felt sorry for him. And a little guilty, so she wanted to ease things for his family."

Ruth dropped Moscone at his car in the headquarters parking lot. She intended to run into her office, chuck the paperwork that had been piling up all day into her briefcase, and go straight home.

Too much had happened today. Baines's scolding started off the morning, followed by the strange visit with Jack Holden at his office, Adam Bender's information about the lunchtime e-mail, Brenda O'Reilly's disclosure about Tracey's accident at the mall and previous disappearance, the five thousand dollar payment to Al Pace, Stephen Kendall's affair with Hannah Whiteside, and Rosie Boyagian's confirmation of Stephen's many affairs, including a relationship with Susan Gleason. Ruth wasn't sure she believed Fran Powell's story about the money, or anything else the woman said for that matter. But the cash payments were a fact. Ruth was dying for time at home to put everything back together and think it through. But before she could run out the door, Mayor Rosenfeld came through it.

"What the heck is going on around here? I asked you to make up with Baines or at least stay out of his way, and what do you do? Like a bee, you fly straight up his nose!"

Ruth felt the telltale red blush climbing her neck. She resisted the urge to stand up from behind her desk and raise her voice to the same volume as the mayor's. That would just escalate the confrontation. Instead, she remained sitting and asked in a voice much calmer than she felt, "What's Baines saying now?"

"He says there isn't a shred of evidence against this Pace guy and there isn't going to be. He says you're going around bothering citizens and chewing up resources for no good reason."

Ruth let her irritation show. "I disagree."

"Agreeing or disagreeing isn't what matters. You can't bring this or any other case without a D.A."

"So we just walk away from Tracey Kendall, never know what happened? Leave two killers out on the streets?"

"Two?"

"We have evidence Pace was paid to kill her. There's another killer out there."

"Paid to do it? You can't even prove it was murder!" Mayor Rosenfeld dropped into the chair opposite Ruth's desk and lowered his voice to a normal speaking level. "Chief, I think you're losing the forest in the trees. Never mind what you're doing to your career, and to those of us who have always supported you. Think about your troops. Think beyond this case. You can't be at war with your D.A. It hurts every officer, every case." Rosenfeld paused. "I don't want the wheels to come off here. Besides your problems with Baines and the aldermen, I'm hearing rumors of dissension in the ranks, cops wondering what you're doing. Are you going to risk it all for one dead lady? You need to get back in control of the situation."

Ruth drove toward home tired and angry. In a long, upsetting day, the mayor's news about unhappiness in the New Derby PD was the most upsetting thing yet. Ruth hadn't seen or heard it. In fact, she had been basking in McGrath's renewed interest in his job. But if rumors had reached City Hall, things must be bad. Her troops would tolerate a strained relationship with Baines. Some senior officers, like Lawry and McGrath, even knew her problems with Baines went beyond bureaucratic to personal. But the force wouldn't tolerate open warfare with the D.A.'s office. They knew it could make their lives a living hell, from trouble getting warrants to rejected cases and even dropped prosecutions.

She'd only been able to command effectively through these six months as acting chief because her force assumed she'd get the job. With no other internal candidates, she was their preference. But as her problems multiplied with Baines and with some of the aldermen and if, God forbid, she lost the support of the mayor, her troops would split into factions, seriously diluting their effectiveness and her own, and making the job a misery.

Baines. All her problems seemed to come from Baines. And now, for the broader investigation the discovery of the five thousand dollars required, Ruth would need access to resources Baines controlled—C.A.R.S., computer forensics, the medical examiner.

Distracted by the thoughts swirling in her head, Ruth didn't pay attention to where she was driving. Suddenly and quite unexpectedly, she found herself at the intersection of Adams

Street and Willow Road, quiet at the end of the workday. Ruth parked in the empty lot at Fiske & Holden. She picked up the phone and called Dan Logan. He would have gone home from the state garage hours ago, but she had his personal cell number. Maybe Baines hadn't gotten to him yet.

"What can I do for you, Chief?" Logan asked when Ruth found him at home, eating his dinner.

"How's my SUV coming?"

There was a long pause. "I've been instructed not to change any priorities at the garage to accommodate any requests you might make about that car."

"By who?"

"You know who."

"But I need the black box data and I need your reconstruction. I can't wait."

Logan had the decency to sound embarrassed. "Chief, if there was anything I could do—"

"Okay. You've been doing this a long time. Without all the fancy computer-generated info, just based on the damage to the car and what you know about Mrs. Kendall's injuries, how fast do you think she was going when she hit?"

"My best guess, and that's all it would be, is over seventy."

"And how fast would she have to be going on that hill at the time she discovered she didn't have brakes, to hit the wall at seventy?"

"Now you're in territory I couldn't even guess about."

"Try it."

"You'd have to hit fifty at the beginning of the steepest part of the hill to get up that much momentum, assuming you weren't accelerating the whole way, which you'd only see with a suicide."

"We know this wasn't."

"Agreed. Nobody is cold enough to off themselves while chatting with the nanny about what to have for supper."

Ruth hung up and stared through the windshield into the last glow of the setting sun. She'd painted herself into a terrible corner. She'd gone on TV and made herself highly visible at the most vulnerable time in her career, talking about a case that would probably never be solved and would certainly never be prosecuted. She was a fool.

The best thing to do, the wisest course of action, was to let it go and hope it would fade quickly. Perhaps after Tracey's funeral tomorrow the world would lose what little interest Ruth had been able to stir up. Tracey's husband and colleagues at Fiske & Holden would be grateful if that happened.

But even as she considered walking away from the case, Ruth thought about Tracey Kendall and the neat lists of things to do in her personal organizer. She thought about the locket tucked in with Tracey's old clothes, and about Carson crying on the edge of his sandbox. The boy would grow up believing his mother died selfishly, carelessly, speeding down a hill toward her aerobics class, talking on her cell phone.

Ruth was convinced that wasn't what had happened. She was infuriated by the situation and the horrible sliminess of Baines. That Baines would, just to avoid a difficult and public case, deprive a four-year-old of an explanation for his mother's death for the rest of his life, was unconscionable. Tracey deserved more, she deserved better.

It always came back to the odious Baines.

Ruth gunned her car out of the Fiske & Holden lot, driving with the confidence of someone who took the route every day, and turned left on Willow Road. The road descended gently for ten yards, then took a steep downward turn. She kept her foot on the gas pedal, gathering speed. Outside her window in the twilight, a squiggly arrow meaning "dangerous curves" flew by, followed in quick succession by signs saying SLOW, 15 MPH and SLOW again.

Ruth sucked in her breath. Over the dark spiders of the budding trees, she could see the parallel tracks of the railroad running along the steep embankment separating it from Willow Road. Her stomach heaved. She gripped the wheel as tightly as she could.

At the midpoint of the hill, descending wildly, Ruth took her foot off the gas and fought the impulse to brake, focusing on the place ahead where the road jogged sharply to the right. She knew if the car continued to gain speed, she wouldn't be able to make the turn. The grassy verge bordered by the stone wall where Tracey Kendall died appeared in her high beams. Ruth waited until what she judged was the last possible moment, the stone wall growing larger straight ahead, glanced at the speedometer, slammed her foot on the brake and pumped. The car rocketed around twice in an impossibly short stretch of road. Ruth's stomach climbed into her throat. A scream from deep inside her pushed its way through her lips, although there was no one to hear.

The car came to rest with its back wheels on the grass, facing the way it had come. Ruth jumped out and stood looking at the stone wall, shaking and gulping air. The speedometer had never gone over forty.

CHAPTER FIFTEEN

For hours that night, Ruth hung between waking and sleeping. She'd come home in a daze, overwhelmed by what she'd done. No one in the family seemed to notice her quietness, beguiled as they were by the computer, the television, and the incessant beeping of Sarah's cell phone.

Ruth hated impulse. Raised by one impulsive woman, and sister to another, Ruth believed their spontaneity had brought them far more sorrow than joy. Yet tonight, when she was so close to reaching her dream of being chief, she had careened recklessly, dangerously, criminally, down a street in the town whose laws she was sworn to uphold.

At midnight, Ruth went to bed, but not to sleep. Picturing Carson Kendall alone in his sandbox, she thought about what it would do to Sarah and James to have their mother suddenly yanked from their young lives—and worse, through her own stupidity.

Ruth tossed, turned over, and looked at the clock. Two A.M. Three A.M. Four. She needed to be sharp in the morning. Beside her, Marty stirred in reaction to her movement.

At quarter to five, Ruth got up. She was one of the first people in New Derby to know the spell of fine weather was over. A steady rain fell from the night sky. She pulled on a pair of sweats and met the paper deliveryman on the porch, startling him so badly he nearly lost his footing. She went back in the house and put on a pot of coffee.

She briefly considered surprising the family with bacon and eggs on a Saturday, but told herself to get a grip. The greatest kindness she could do her loved ones was to be out of the house before they awoke.

Ruth sat at her desk and dug into the reports she'd thrown into her briefcase the night before but never looked at. The clouds outside colored her office in shades of gray, so she worked in the circle of light provided by a single lamp. The reports, flat words on paper, filled-in spaces, and check marks, gave her the comfort they always had. The frantic misery of her sleepless night began to recede. Two-thirds of the way through the pile, she came upon the inventory of the possessions from Tracey Kendall's car. Ruth tucked it under her arm and headed for the property room.

In the basement, Ruth wasn't pleased to see the young property officer reading *Car and Driver*. She knew the property job was loaded with hours of boredom, especially so early on a weekend morning. She was also sure if she checked, she would find cataloging, filing, and reporting to be done. Ruth made a mental note to speak to his supervisor.

The clerk took Ruth's signature and badge number and buzzed her in. Ruth removed Tracey Kendall's property from its shelf and headed to the farthest of the old cells. Moving to the center table, she carefully arranged the articles that had made Tracey Kendall's final journey.

After Ruth's initial examination, Moscone had searched Tracey Kendall's property meticulously and found nothing. Nothing at all. Yet, too many people in this case were looking for something. Tracey's study had been searched. Stephen Kendall had emptied Tracey's office at Fiske & Holden two days after her death. And both Stephen Kendall and Jack Holden had asked repeatedly about the property in Tracey

Kendall's car. Ruth was sure the objects in front of her would tell a story, if only she knew how to hear it.

Ruth sifted through the clothing in the gym bag, but couldn't change her original assessment. These were comfort clothes. Clothes a wealthy woman, with closets full of suits and drawers of designer underwear, couldn't bear to leave behind. Ruth searched the pockets of the jeans, flannel work shirt, and cardigan, but found exactly what Moscone had—nothing.

She opened the briefcase and looked through the papers. They didn't interest her much. The industry reports and financial newsletters were rapidly becoming obsolete and would soon be as useless to everyone as they were now to Tracey Kendall.

Next, Ruth turned to the laptop. Baines controlled access to the Computer Forensics Lab, so Ruth would get no help from it. Moscone had tried every obvious password they could think of, but now Ruth had new information. She adjusted the cursor on the screen and typed, "MaryAnn," Tracey Kendall's birth name. Ruth was prepared to try every variation on the name, including those for capitalization, and then to try every permutation again with "Noonan" added on the end, but on this first try, the computer whirred and Tracey Kendall's desktop icons appeared.

Ruth scanned the directories on the hard drive, learning nothing. She read the titles of the word-processing files, spot checking them against the documents they represented, and learned Tracey was a precise and articulate labeler. The document appeared to be, in every case, exactly what the title described. Then Ruth checked the folders containing stored e-mails, faxes, and on-line database information. Zip. Zero. Zed.

Finally, she set the screen to the on-line Fiske & Holden schedule. With no one to access and download new information, it remained as it had been at the moment of Tracey

Kendall's death. The real schedule, back at Fiske & Holden, was being updated continuously as the six remaining employees went on with their business lives, but the version on Tracey Kendall's computer was frozen in time.

Ruth turned her attention to the leather personal organizer. She found it to be marvelously methodical. Every meeting on the calendar had a corresponding summary in the Notes section. Each of the action items from the meetings was neatly transferred to the To Do list where it could be checked off as done or delegated with a date assigned. Scheduled outcomes, such as calls or follow-up meetings were transferred back to the calendar. The final section, the directory, had all the names, addresses, phone and fax numbers that would be needed. The To Do list section was a mix of business and family. "Carson—new pants" appeared below "Finalize decision on Belton Ind. w/Jack." Ruth shook her head at the completeness of the system.

Ruth read backwards through the daily calendar. On March fifteenth, she found the notation, "mainten—SUV." By the time she reached the mid-February dates, Ruth had found three Tuesday afternoons that bore the notation, "Susan G. here." with a line traveling through the next two days, confirming Susan Gleason came up every few weeks, as she had said. The calendar noted several rounds of parties, some given, some attended. Those given often had corresponding guest lists and menus in the Notes section which resulted in "to calls" and "to buys" in the To Do's. Ruth searched in vain for a friend's name that popped up frequently enough to imply intimacy, but there was none. Fran Powell's name appeared here and there on a guest or "to call" list, but sometimes weeks went by without it being mentioned.

Ruth stared dejectedly at the items on the table. What wasn't she seeing? She decided there was nothing left to do but compare the on-line schedule to the calendar in the organizer, to see if omissions emerged in one place or the other. She flipped the pages and the screen back to the day of Tracey Kendall's murder and started to work.

McGrath pulled into the headquarters parking lot at eight-thirty. Since his wife had left, he often came to the station at odd hours. He enjoyed the calm rhythms of the detective squad room during the quiet shifts, and the truth was, after he'd eaten his breakfast and thumbed through the paper, there wasn't much else to do.

McGrath stopped on the way upstairs. "Not too busy," he commented to the officer behind the front desk.

The officer nodded. "The hooligans sleep in on the weekend, not like us working stiffs."

"Who's around?" McGrath asked carefully.

"The chief's down in the property room."

This was unexpected. "Just what I need. Whatever you do, don't tell her I'm here."

In the detectives' squad room, McGrath pulled off his seedy sport coat and spread the tangible remains of Al Pace's financial life out on the table. Something was here and McGrath knew it. Somewhere amid the shut-off orders and final notices, there was something. He hadn't looked hard enough, made the right connections. He settled in to work.

Ruth paused and rubbed her eyes. The laptop screen wasn't designed for extended viewing. The fluorescent light hanging over the little cell's table didn't help matters. Ruth had worked back, comparing the on-line schedule to the personal organizer from the day Tracey died in April to mid-February.

The two calendars were indeed different, but so far, those differences had told her nothing. In the electronic version, Tracey accounted for her whereabouts during normal business hours, even if she was using personal time, for example "chiro-pract. appt." She also included meetings conducted outside of business hours, such as dinners with clients or networking breakfasts. The calendar in the organizer was much richer. It duplicated the on-line entries, but also contained more personal information: art world dinner parties in New York, meetings with Carson's preschool teacher, weekend hairdresser appoint-ments.

As Ruth worked through the calendar, she looked for signs of an affair. Now she couldn't imagine Tracey having one without dates for the rendezvous appearing somewhere in her organizer. What had really happened? In the beginning, Ruth had been pulled into Moscone's theory because she needed to establish a connection between Tracey Kendall and Al Pace, and, though she had a hard time admitting this, because Pace was such a handsome man. But no one seemed to have any knowledge of the affair except Fran Powell. Did the affair even matter? If Pace was hired to kill Tracey, he'd used his relationship as her mechanic, not his relationship as her lover, to do her in.

The left-hand pile of calendar pages was growing thinner. Where was the smoking gun, the precipitating event Ruth knew must be here? The kind of murder they were investigating, murder for hire, required planning and timing, but how far could the trigger be from the explosion? Two months was a long time to wait when you wanted to get rid of someone. Of course, it was always possible the event, whatever it was, had been spontaneous, and therefore not on the calendar.

Ruth rubbed her eyes again. When she looked up, John McGrath was standing in the cell doorway, shirt sleeves rolled up and reading glasses perched on his nose.

"This is important," he said, skipping the pleasantries. "In February somebody gave Pace five thousand dollars in cash."

"What?" Ruth's voice was louder than she intended.

"I almost missed it. The money was never deposited, but a bunch of bills were paid, all on the same day. He must have paid them in cash."

Ruth was stunned. "What are you saying? We've been working on the premise that the accident, the original five thousand dollar payment, and Pace's disappearance are all related. If there's another source for the money, we're right back to criminal negligence where we started."

"That's what I thought, too. So I checked. Sure enough, there was an invoice from Screw Loose to Kevin Chun dated February twelfth, the day all these payments were made."

"Pace was at Fiske & Holden that day. Maybe the murder was supposed to take place then?"

"Yeah," McGrath added. "Maybe this five thousand represents the down payment. The balance didn't get paid until Mrs. Kendall finally died."

Excited, Ruth opened Tracey's organizer to February twelfth. No car appointment appeared. On January thirteenth, there was one that said, "mainten—sports car," and Ruth had already seen the entry about the SUV on March fifteenth. "Damn, that's not it."

"Slow down," McGrath cautioned. "Think about it. Was Tracey's car scheduled for maintenance on the day she was killed?"

"No."

"And she wasn't scheduled on February twelfth, either."

Ruth furrowed her brow. "He must have thought it would look less suspicious if he did it on a day when he wasn't scheduled to work on her car."

"Bingo."

"So why didn't Pace kill her in February?"

"Something went wrong. Did Mrs. Kendall pull her disappearing act in February, the one Brenda O'Reilly told Moscone about?"

"No, earlier. January."

McGrath shrugged. "Maybe Tracey was out of town or just away from the office when Pace came."

"In any case," Ruth theorized, "whatever started this chain of events happened before February twelfth." McGrath nodded and started to move away. Ruth held up a hand. "Stay here."

McGrath got a chair from the cell next door and sat at the table next to Ruth. With two people working at it, the comparison of the calendar in the organizer with the on-line schedule went much faster. The pages on the left side of the organizer quickly dwindled to a few.

"Damn it," Ruth cursed when she came to the final two pages of the calendar representing the first week of the new year. Then, suddenly, there it was, in Tracey Kendall's neat handwriting. A morning meeting on January third, a meeting that wasn't in Tracey's electronic schedule.

McGrath shut down the computer and returned Tracey Kendall's property to its box. Ruth picked up the receiver of the phone hanging on the old cell wall and punched in a number.

Ruth felt a fleeting moment of self-consciousness about her sneakers and jeans when she entered the sleek lobby of the Boston office tower that housed the Wilson Brenner law firm. But on a Saturday the lobby was deserted, except for a sleepy-eyed guard at the security desk who waved her in.

When the elevator opened into the reception area on the twenty-third floor, Ruth had the eerie sensation she had traveled not vertically, but through time. In the building's lobby she had caught a final glimpse of the sleek marble and clean lines of the beginning of the twenty-first century. Now, she was standing in a room that would have been comfortable for anyone visiting a solicitor at the end of the nineteenth. Someone had gone to enormous trouble and expense in disassembling, reassembling, and installing the burnished burl walnut paneling and cherry flooring that graced the oversized reception area. Ruth shuddered at the thought of all those billable hours.

The dark wooden doors off the reception area were locked, as Ruth had been told they would be. Following directions, she entered a small alcove, picked up the wall phone, punched in an extension number and waited, yawning. The sleepless night was taking its toll. She hoped she had the edge required for this meeting.

"Ruthie?" Wink Segrue came through one of the doors. He was the lawyer sent by central casting, from the tip of his graying but full head of hair through his broad shoulders and on to the elegantly tapered waist of his casual Italian slacks. He took her trench coat and hung it up. "Great to see you. C'mon back."

Ruth followed him down a long hallway with more rich wood and dead partners hanging on the walls. Segrue's office was in the northeast corner of the building. Its huge windows offered a panorama of a modern Boston harbor, dramatically shattering the illusion of an earlier century so carefully cultivated in the windowless lobby and hallways. Ruth took a moment to appreciate the view, impressive even on a rainy day.

It was hard to believe Wink Segrue had been Marty's best friend in high school. Now Wink was a fixer, a lawyer who handled ugly personal matters for the presidents and board members whose corporations, universities, and hospitals kept Wilson Brenner in antique paneling. Taking in the view, Ruth wondered, did Marty ever regret the choices they'd made that resulted in his cramped office on the converted side porch of their house?

Ignoring the lovely sitting area at the other end of the large office, Segrue seated himself behind his desk and gestured to the guest chair opposite. On the credenza behind him was a picture of his second wife with their two young children, posed casually and smiling for the camera.

Ruth turned her attention to Segrue. "Thanks for seeing me on a Saturday."

"No trouble." He gestured to the deposition open on his desk. "I was here. As you knew I would be. What's this about?"

"Tracey Kendall came to see you in January."

Segrue's smile disappeared. "I can't confirm that."

"Let's say I already know it. What was the nature of her visit?"

"You know that's privileged."

"So you're confirming Tracey Kendall was your client. You're not the Kendall family attorney. You're not the Fiske & Holden corporate attorney. And yet, she came to you."

"No, I'm not confirming it."

"You have no privilege if she wasn't your client."

Segrue's expression remained flat. "Is there a point to this?"

"Tracey Kendall is dead."

"I'm aware of that. And you, no doubt, are aware that as a result of the Charles Stuart case, Massachusetts courts have made it absolutely clear death in no way ends privilege."

"It can be waived."

"Not by me." The attorney settled back in his chair.

"Did Tracey Kendall speak to you about changing her will?"

Segrue's face relaxed. "I certainly would have notified the probate court by now if she had."

"Then did Mrs. Kendall come to see you about a separation?" This time Ruth thought she caught some movement behind the eyes, but Wink Segrue, at the top of his field, had a famous poker face. It was impossible to be sure.

"I'm not willing to sit here and play 'warmer/colder' with you, Ruthie." Segrue's tone was light, but firm. "If Bob Baines were behind you, I suspect you could threaten to eat up great chunks of my expensive time with excruciatingly pointless activity, but since I, like everyone else in the state, know that you don't have the smarmy weasel in your corner, I see no reason to continue this conversation."

Segrue shifted forward in his chair. He was smiling again. "Now, how are Marty and the kids? How come we don't get together more often?"

Ruth drove home from Boston as fast as she dared. When she reached her house, Moscone's unmarked car was already in the driveway. In their big, old kitchen, Marty was assembling lunch and telling Moscone stories. Sarah sat opposite, fixing Moscone with a puppy-dog gaze.

Ruth entered apologizing. "I'm sorry I'm late. Just let me get changed."

Moscone glanced at his watch. "No problem. We've got time. I'll just stay here until you're ready."

Across from him, Sarah sighed a happy sigh.

CHAPTER SIXTEEN

Ruth and Moscone parked behind headquarters and walked the two blocks to the Second Unitarian Church on Main Street. The crowd was large in spite of the bad weather. Out of the corner of her eye, Ruth noticed the young patrolman who had been hired to work the funeral traffic detail lounging against a parked car. Moscone excused himself, went over, and whispered something in the patrolman's ear. The young man shot a look at Ruth, pulled himself erect, and waded into the middle of the street to help the crowd across.

"Thank you," Ruth said to Moscone.

"Funny, I think it's him who should thank me," Moscone answered.

Inside the cavernous church, islands of mourners were visible in the pews. Stephen Kendall sat up front, flanked by Hannah Whiteside and Susan Gleason. Even from the back, he looked shaky. The women talked to him in quiet voices, occasionally patting his upper arm or shoulder.

The Noonan family also sat in front, across the aisle from Stephen Kendall. Brian and Philip wore identical suits, with white shirt collars protruding at the neck. From the back of the church, Ruth wondered about the ties. Same colors, different patterns was her guess. Brian's wife Maura wasn't there. Perhaps she had stayed home with the children. There was no coffin in sight.

The Fiske & Holden delegation was arranged in two rows

167

behind the Noonans. Ruth could make out the bowed heads of Ellie Berger, Brenda O'Reilly, and Jane Parker in the front. Jack Holden, Kevin Chun, and Adam Bender sat in the row behind. As Ruth watched, Margot Holden swept down the aisle toward the Fiske & Holden group. They expressed delight in seeing her and she kissed and embraced each one in turn. Each one, except Jack Holden.

The rest of the church was filling up with clients and neighbors, fellow preschool parents, artists, and dealers. Ruth moved slowly down the center aisle with Moscone. She spotted Fran Powell sitting inconspicuously in the middle of the church, her blond frosting hidden under a dark scarf, her eyes obscured by dark glasses despite the gloomy day. A bloated man Ruth took to be the husband, Sandy Powell, sat to Fran's right. Ruth entered the row and sat down. "Hello, Mrs. Powell," she whispered. Fran Powell moved closer to her husband and took his arm.

The service was led by the Reverend Annie Warner, pastor at Second U. Ruth knew Annie from town youth activities and could imagine how the Kendall/Noonan family's problem of where to hold the funeral had appealed to her big heart. The Reverend Warner worked valiantly, but her efforts only confirmed Ruth's belief that in spite of all the religions, sects, and creeds, there were only two kinds of funerals—the kind where the speaker knew the deceased and the kind where he or she did not. Annie Warner had done her homework, but it showed. She had not known Tracey Kendall in life, just as Ruth had not. They were both here, working, trying in different ways to make some sense out of a stranger's passing.

Evidently, though, Reverend Warner's efforts struck home for many in the church. As Ruth watched, Stephen Kendall's shoulders began to heave. He brought his hands to his face, and the women who flanked him bent forward with concern, laying their arms across his back. Across the aisle, Tracey's original family mourned, too. Mrs. Noonan cried aloud and Tom brushed away tears. Brian and Philip sat hunched forward, heads bowed as if in prayer. In the Fiske & Holden rows, the women cried, Ellie and Jane sobbing. Behind them, the men sat motionless, except when Kevin Chun reached out and patted Jane Parker's shoulder.

When the service ended, the congregants stood and waited respectfully for the most bereaved to make their way from the front of the church. As Stephen Kendall moved slowly up the aisle, Ruth turned and caught a glimpse of his first wife, Rosie Boyagian, wiping away a tear as she exited out the back.

Outside the rain had really started, cold, windswept, and devoid of the promise of May flowers. Ruth shivered and pulled her trench coat closer. The family climbed into the limos. At the close of the service Annie had invited everyone present back to the Kendall home. Ruth had no intention of going. It would move her presence over the line from respectful to intrusive. Besides, she had work to do.

She and Moscone were walking purposefully past the second limo when its tinted window slid open. "My mother wants to invite you both back to the house specifically," Brian or Philip said. "You're the only people in the church besides Fran Powell we recognized."

Ruth leaned over and looked in the open window. "Of course we'll come back, Mrs. Noonan," she said. "We're just going to get our car."

A valet tried to take the unmarked car at the front door, but Moscone waved him away. The Kendalls' front hall was crowded with people shedding wet raincoats. Two young women in black vests, white shirts, and bow ties whisked the coats away. In the corner of the dining room, a bar had been set up and a young man, also dressed in a caterer's uniform, was turning out drinks as quickly as he could. More minions were busy bringing out hot food, placing the platters on the long dining table.

Susan Gleason and Stephen Kendall were seated in the living room, Stephen receiving the condolences of his guests. Up close, he looked awful. Black circles ringed his large eyes. His face was drawn and as he reached out to his guests, his hands shook.

Hannah Whiteside circled nearby. "Hannah, get Stephen a drink, please," Susan purred. "And while you're there, get me one, too." Hannah shot her a withering look, but complied. There was no graceful way to refuse. As soon as Hannah stepped out, Fran Powell moved in. She gave both Stephen and Susan a hug and whispered something about the lovely service. She had removed the head scarf, but not the dark glasses and Ruth wondered what she was hiding. "Susan," Fran said, "I think you're wanted in the kitchen. The caterer has a question." Susan shook her head, as though she might protest, but then thought better of it, got up, and moved off. Fran sat down next to Stephen and took his hand.

That left Fran's husband Sandy standing awkwardly to the side and gave Ruth time to study him. Her impression from the church was confirmed. He was bloated and red-nosed. He was, in fact, one of the most dissipated individuals Ruth had ever seen still functioning in polite society. He had not removed his raincoat and stood clutching a large umbrella. As Ruth watched, he approached his wife, whispered something in her ear, shook Stephen Kendall's hand, then turned and exited through the front door, his funereal obligations fulfilled.

Hannah Whiteside returned with the drinks. She handed a Bloody Mary to Stephen and stood briefly with the other drink, a white wine, looking around for Susan Gleason. When Susan didn't appear, Hannah squeezed her not insubstantial behind between Stephen Kendall and the arm of the sofa and sipped the wine herself. "Mrs. Powell," she said, looking past her employer to Fran, "Maura thinks the children should be fed. Since your little Xander is here, maybe you should help her out."

It was an amateur ploy by an inexperienced player and Fran Powell didn't fall for it. "Whatever for?" she asked. "You're the nanny." Neither woman moved. Stephen stared straight ahead. If he was aware of all the jockeying going on around him, he didn't show it.

Ruth wondered if the implications of this shifting tableau were as obvious to everyone present as they were to someone with her knowledge of Susan and Hannah's claims. Hard to tell. Ruth decided that despite the morbid fascination the women's dance held, nothing could be gained by watching them further. She went in search of Tracey's parents.

The crowded front hall was dominated by the folks from Fiske & Holden. Moscone, his back turned, was in deep conversation with Brenda O'Reilly. As Ruth watched, Brenda smiled with obvious pleasure. Jack Holden stood on the other side of the hall, talking to two men in expensive suits whom Ruth concluded must be clients.

The Noonans had staked out the far corner of the dining room, opposite the bar. May, Tom, Philip, and Brian stood in an awkward clump. Ruth saw that she'd been wrong about the brothers' ties. Same pattern, different colors.

Ruth went to the family and took each hand in turn. She murmured she was sorry, it must be a difficult day. She stood with them, not talking for a while. She found she wanted to show some solidarity with Tracey's family, to make their little group appear less isolated.

Maura entered the dining room with the four children: Carson Kendall, Xander Powell, and her own two, the boy Carson's age and the toddler. The children were dressed formally, though they hadn't been at the church. Xander and Brian's son took the plates Maura offered and moved quickly to the table. They were excited, amazed by the food and sweets. Maura insisted they take some salad as she deftly fixed the toddler's meal. Carson stood well back, staring at the laden table, his plate held at his side like a book. As Ruth watched, the significance of the meal seemed to strike him like a lightning bolt. Ruth felt her throat constrict.

"Dad?" The room was crowded with people balancing plates and making small talk. Ruth wasn't sure anyone else had heard. She took a step forward.

"Dad!" Carson's voice was louder and more desperate. He began to shake.

The guests around the table hushed. "Get Stephen!" someone stage-whispered into the hall.

"Dad! Dad! Dad!" As the crowd watched, Carson fell apart in the obvious way children do, like a ship breaking up in a storm. He dropped the plate and sank to his knees. "Mom!" He was sobbing, tears running freely. "Oh, my Mommy."

Voices called out. "Stephen! Call Kendall!" The crowd in the hall parted, providing a clear view to the couch where Stephen Kendall had sat. He was gone.

"Mommy, Mom-mee!" Carson was prone on the floor, legs kicking, arms flailing.

Hannah Whiteside glanced at the empty spot next to her on the couch, jumped up, and started running, but May Noonan was faster. She knelt beside her grandson, gathering him in her arms. "It's Grandma, Carson. It's Grandma."

Carson jerked back physically, staring at his grandmother as if she were a stranger. For a terrible moment, the crowd held its breath. Would he bellow or bolt? Then, the boy's stiff body softened. He brought his head to his grandmother's chest and allowed himself to be comforted.

Everyone moved at once. Brian Noonan went to Maura, who stood stricken, toddler on one hip, his plate in her other hand. In the hall, Jane Parker cried on Ellie Berger's rounded shoulder. Margot Holden looked at the food on her plate with disgust and deposited it on a side table. Ruth stepped back next to Tom Noonan and put her arm through his in a gesture of support. She felt his weight shift as his knees buckled, then stiffened. He moved toward his wife and grandson.

The crowd broke up. Carson Kendall's raw grief made it impossible to ignore the reason for the gathering. Those who were distant enough to persuade themselves that leaving early was the best response looked for their coats. The group that stayed on chatted nervously.

Tom Noonan picked up Carson and carried him from the room.

Ruth left the house through the kitchen door. The rain had stopped, but the grass was soaked and slippery. She came around front in a broad circle, staying well away from the living-room windows, and headed straight down the lawn. Sixty feet from the house, she stopped and looked back. Moscone was on the verandah with Brenda O'Reilly and Kevin Chun. They were heavily engaged in conversation, Moscone gesticulating wildly. Brenda O'Reilly stood at his side, occasionally opening and closing her mouth, her hands still. Voice alone would be the stock in trade for a receptionist. Kevin Chun leaned against the railing, without regard for the back of his raincoat. He also was rapt, but was listening more than speaking. Ruth wondered what on earth they were talking about.

She knocked at the door of Stephen Kendall's studio, pushed it open, and walked in. Her pace quickened as she walked between the sculptures. The clouds over the skylights hid them in shadow. They were looming, menacing.

At the center of the room, Ruth paused and stared at the new sculpture. Much work had been completed. Its metal skeleton rose to the ceiling and long ropes attached it to the pulley system. Kendall's tools were arrayed across the floor. An old acetylene torch sat on a drop cloth, a tangible reminder of the work in progress.

"Mr. Kendall?" Ruth called.

"Back here."

Ruth followed the sound of Kendall's voice toward the design room. Kendall was sitting in his desk chair, his eyes rimmed in red, his fine nose raw.

"Carson is calling for you."

"Hannah and his grandparents are there."

"He's calling for *you*."

Kendall hung his head, staring into his lap. When he finally looked up, Ruth saw the strain in his face and realized how it had been building over the last four days. She saw a man who wasn't eating or sleeping, a man who looked like he was being eaten away from the inside out. But why? Had he hired Al Pace to kill his wife?

The stress had tempered Kendall's personal magnetism, but not snuffed it out. Ruth still felt its pull. She wanted to tell him his young son desperately needed him and it was up to him, the adult, to move past whatever it was that kept him away and go to his son. But she didn't say it. It wasn't her place. More important, she couldn't see the future. Why push this man to embrace his young son, only to tear them apart later if the man went off to prison for the hired murder of his wife?

"I've been to see Wink Segrue," Ruth said. "I know Tracey consulted him earlier this year. The problem is he's claiming attorney-client privilege. He won't say what they talked about."

"Why tell me?"

"You're Tracey's executor. I want you to release Mr. Segrue

from his privilege."

"I can't do that."

"You can," Ruth countered. "You're the only one who can."

Stephen shook his head. "I won't."

"Your wife met with Wink Segrue in early January. Two days later, she disappeared. She told her office she was on vacation. Hannah believed she was on a business trip. Her meeting with Segrue was important. Don't you want to know who killed your wife?"

"You've told me who killed my wife. Al Pace."

"Don't you want to know why?"

"No. It won't change anything. As soon as I can, I want to forget the end of Tracey's life so I can remember the rest of it. No offense, I like you, but what I want is to never see you again. I want you to return Tracey's things from her car and I want you to go away so I'm not constantly reminded of all this."

"It will go away a lot faster if you release Wink Segrue from privilege."

He didn't respond to her question. He stood and walked over to the new sculpture. Ruth followed, stopping by his side.

The sculpture was crude, a three-dimensional rough draft, but its type, size, and mood were unmistakable. A tyrannosaurus rex, with giant hind legs and tiny front ones, he charged across the room, anger and a desire to kill infesting every part of his body. Except his head. Its line resisted the charge, pulling the great body back ever so slightly.

"What do you think of him?" Stephen asked. The question seemed like an honest one, not a request for praise.

"I like him very much," Ruth answered truthfully. "What's he doing? Why is he charging forward and at the same time pulling back?"

Stephen pointed to the other end of the studio where a completed triceratops stood, head down also readying a charge.

"The T. Rex fights because he must," Stephen explained. "It's his instinct. But somewhere in his tiny brain, he knows this fight could mean oblivion. A portion of him hesitates, questioning, but not enough to prevent the battle. He can't stop himself."

"You make it seem very sad."

"It is."

"What will happen to him now?"

"Once I'm certain every nuance of his position is correct, I'll build up his layers, burlap, canvas, metal mesh, and then cover his surfaces with fiberglass squares impregnated with epoxy resin. It's a tedious and noxious process, but in the end he will be strong, and lighter weight than you would think."

Ruth reflected that Stephen was a natural communicator. Perhaps Tracey's income had not saved him from teaching, but deprived him of it.

"They're fiberglass?"

"Yes. Like the body of a sports car."

Ruth stepped back so she could see the entire piece. "I can't believe I'm getting this much from just the underlying structure."

Stephen Kendall nodded. "The armature is the most important part of the piece. It should be a work of art in and of itself. The piece has to be right at its core. If it isn't, someday, it will all fall down."

CHAPTER SEVENTEEN

The post-funeral gathering was drawing to a close when Ruth returned to it. Moscone offered to drive her home. Ruth sent him on his way. She was exhausted to the point of befuddlement, hungry from a day when her last meal, breakfast, had been hours before. She walked out the Kendall gates onto the sidewalk, but instead of heading toward home, turned and walked the half-mile to Anna Abbott's house.

Mrs. Abbott answered the doorbell herself. Mrs. O'Shea was on the Cape visiting her children. "Why Chief, how nice to see you," Mrs. Abbott said. "You look a little peaky. Everything okay?"

"Fine. Fine. Busy though."

Mrs. Abbott took Ruth by the elbow, exerting a surprising strength, and pulled her through the door. As she performed this maneuver, she squinted westward. "So hard to tell if the sun is over the yardarm when the days are cloudy," she said. "I think it must be. We'll both have a nice sherry."

Mrs. Abbott led Ruth to the upstairs sitting room. A fire blazed in the hearth. A gardening show was on public television. Mrs. Abbott flicked off the TV and went to the little kitchen off the sitting room to get the sherry. Ruth sat by the warm fire, sipped the sherry, and brought Mrs. Abbott up to date on the Kendall investigation.

"Do the two five-thousand dollar payments to Pace help or hurt your case?" Mrs. Abbott asked.

"They bolster the murder theory, but create a whole new pool of suspects," Ruth answered honestly. "Maybe it'll never be unraveled."

Anna Abbott was not impressed by negative thinking. "Of course you'll solve it. How can I help?"

"Tell me about Jack Holden," Ruth ventured.

Mrs. Abbott paused slightly, and then began. "Jack and Hildy are the children of John Holden's second marriage. John Holden was a wonderful man, a friend of my late husband. He had a son and daughter by his first wife. Sadly, she died when the children were young. John was alone for many years, struggling, building a business, bringing up a family. When I was a young widow, we were often paired at dinner parties and the like. He was a delightful fellow."

"Oh really?" Ruth teased. "Was it romantic between you?"

"Oh, no, no. After Mr. Abbott died, I was never really interested. I've always said of husbands, once a woman has broken one in, she should move on to other challenges." Mrs. Abbott winked, and Ruth laughed in appreciation.

"In any case, evidently John Holden didn't feel the same way. After his children went off to school, he was lonely. He married his secretary, settled her in a big house in Derby Center where they produced Jack and Hildy. For a while, everyone was happy. John delighted in his new family. He told me once he felt guilty because he had so much more time to spend with them. He realized what he'd missed with his older children."

Mrs. Abbott took a sip of water from her crystal goblet and gazed out the window. "Then suddenly, it went bad. John had a minor stroke. There was no lasting damage, but I think his wife got scared. For the first time, she realized what it meant to be married to a much older man. She ran off with little Hildy's violin teacher. I suppose John knew where she was, but no one saw or heard from her again. Jack and Hildy stayed in the house with their father. He'd brought up children alone before, and now he had to do it again. Poor man. It took him years to recover."

"Were the Holdens rich?" Tracey asked, remembering what Margot Holden had said about money.

"Another intriguing question. It depends on what you mean by rich. Does he have a nice house in Derby Four Corners and another in Bar Harbor? Yes. Do his children go to the best schools? Yes. Does he have some expensive hobbies? Yes. But is he so wealthy he doesn't have to ask how much things cost? I don't think so. Stockbrokers like John Holden made money because they had rich friends, not because they themselves were rich. He left young Jack the business, so I assume any remaining assets were split among the other three children. And, of course, Jack himself divorced a couple of years ago. That usually adds to the strain. His ex-wife is one of the Dover Brindells. Excellent family. No money whatsoever. I'd say Jack Holden has a comfortable life, but it's financed largely by the income from his business."

"Do you know Fran Powell, the Kendalls' neighbor?" Ruth asked.

Mrs. Abbott harrumphed. "She's married to that fool Sandy Powell, Alex's son. More money than brains in that generation. He went out to Hollywood after working in Daddy's law firm for a few years. He was going to become a big producer. Came back with his tail between his legs and his girlfriend in a family way, as we used to say. Alex and Ginger gave them a big wedding anyway—very tasteless in my opinion. After the baby was born, out of respect for Ginger, I tried to involve Fran in town things, volunteer work, clubs. She never took to it. I called her again after her son went to nursery school, but she made it clear she wasn't interested."

Ruth took the last sip of her sherry. It was sweet and made

her feel warm inside. Mrs. Abbott's fire made her feel warm on the outside. The drink and the heat combined with her sleepless night tugged at her eyelids. Mrs. Abbott took their glasses to the little kitchen and refilled them. Then she went to the fireplace and fussed with the logs.

"Mrs. Abbott, how much trouble is my promotion in?"

Mrs. Abbott straightened up and stood by the mantelpiece. "I was hoping you wouldn't ask. The district attorney has made a lot of trouble for you."

"Is it over?"

"No," Anna Abbott responded resolutely. "Not nearly. You'll be fine. As long as nothing else goes wrong."

At one-thirty in the morning, something else went terribly wrong.

Marty had picked Ruth up at Mrs. Abbott's. The combination of the sleepless night and the sherry had been a powerful one. Marty laughed to see his so-in-control wife made soft by drink. She had even allowed him to baby her a bit, giving her a preventative dose of water and aspirin and tucking her into bed. But neither Marty nor Ruth overestimated the degree of her drunkenness. They both knew if she had been with anyone except Marty, the one person who made her feel so safe and loved, she could have pulled herself together and taken charge in a heartbeat.

Ruth was jolted out of sleep by the telephone. It took a moment to get her bearings in the dark. Lieutenant Lawry was on the other end.

"Lieutenant, what is going on?"

"I'm at headquarters. Someone tried to break into the property room."

Twenty minutes later, Ruth and Lieutenant Lawry were standing in the rain outside the headquarters building watching Detective Albert "Dusty" Miller lift fingerprints. A tarp had been thrown up over the rear basement window that led to the property room and a high-powered light was trained on it. Two of its covering bars had been cut away with an acetylene torch and the pane of glass that had covered one third of the window was broken. Detective Miller worked diligently.

Ruth peered at the window. "Could anyone have been inside? Is the opening big enough?"

Lawry put his hands on his knees and looked closely. "I can't tell. Maybe a small adult or teenager."

"We won't know until I can dust inside," Detective Miller added. "Fingerprints, footprints. Grossly, it doesn't look like anyone was down there, but we can't check too closely, yet. We don't want to mess up the scene."

Ruth closed her eyes and thought about six months of court appearances in which every defense attorney challenged the chain of evidence. She saw cases being thrown out wholesale. "Where was the property clerk?" she asked, keeping her voice even.

"He says he was at his desk, right along, reading," Lawry answered.

"I find that hard to believe. This operation must have taken a while, and made some noise."

"I dunno," Detective Miller said. "The breaking glass certainly would have made noise on the inside, but I'm not so sure he would have heard the rest from where he sits."

"He said he investigated as soon as he heard the glass break," Lawry added. "I think whoever it was accidentally broke the glass. The property clerk must have scared him off. That's why he dropped the torch."

"Anything unusual about the torch?" Ruth asked.

"Nope, standard," Miller answered. "I'll dust it, but any

mechanic or plumber would have one."

"Or sculptor," Ruth muttered.

"Excuse me?"

"Nothing. How are the prints coming?"

"Exactly as you'd expect. Very little on the stone, way too much on the sills around the windows."

"This can't be a common place for people to put their hands, surely."

"When was the last time the city painted this woodwork? There are years' worth of smudged, partial prints here."

"Footprints?"

Miller shook his head. "Whoever did this knelt," he pointed, "here. Maybe there's an expert out there can tell something from these knee prints, the weight of the person or the material of their trousers. We sure don't have that kind of expertise in-house."

Ruth knew he was right. "Detective, we need to know as soon as possible whether anyone's been inside. Lieutenant, when he's done we'll need a complete inventory of the property room to make sure everything's accounted for. I want a full report from the property officer as to everything he did from the minute he came on shift, and I want copies of everything to go to Internal Affairs."

Lawry grimaced. "Is that really necessary?"

"Yes. I want to understand how anyone could have gotten this far."

Mayor Rosenfeld was waiting impatiently in Ruth's office. He was in a track suit, though he certainly wasn't going jogging in the middle of a rainy night. His expression was strained, his movements staccato. He skipped a greeting and went straight to the point. "This is a disaster."

"I know."

"Chief, this is not a good time for a disaster." The mayor's voice rose with each syllable. "First the Kendall mess, now another serious problem."

"It's not another problem. The break-in's related to the Kendall case."

That did it. The mayor started to shout. "There's a half million dollars worth of drugs in there! And evidence from about a hundred pending cases. There are guns, there's jewelry. There's as many reasons to break in as there are boxes of property." The mayor paused. "You're killing me, you know that? Haven't I supported you every step of the way? When people said you were too young, the promotion came too fast, I defended you. And when they made noise about your transfer, I was there. I even spoke up for you on the female thing." The mayor stopped to catch his breath. "You're obsessed with the Kendall woman's death. You're killing your chances to be chief, and you're killing me."

Mayor Rosenfeld picked his wallet and keys up off the conference table and headed toward the door. At the midpoint, he turned. "Make the Kendall case go away. I don't care how you do it. I don't care what you do. End it. Now."

When the mayor left, Ruth stood in the center of her office, the blood in her cheeks and neck pounding in time with the rapid beat of her heart. End it? Even if she wanted to, how could she end it now? She'd set too many wheels in motion.

Her office phone rang. It was Lawry, his voice urgent on the other end.

"It's Pace. They've found him in Salton Beach. He blew his head off."

CHAPTER EIGHTEEN

Ruth moved through the throng in front of the Ocean Vu Motel looking for rank. The Ocean Vu was on the bay side of the spit of land that formed Salton Beach. Like all the buildings in this former combination honky-tonk and working class resort, it was built to maximize a tiny lot. The street in front of the building was crowded with New Hampshire State and Salton Beach police cars. Uniformed and plainclothes personnel, standing well away, formed a wide circle around one of the ground-floor units. A sour-looking man in his fifties emerged from the motel room. He stood on the front walk, sighed deeply, and lit a cigarette. Ruth stepped up to his side.

"Lieutenant Thibodeaux?" she asked, sticking out her hand. "I'm Acting Chief Murphy. We spoke on the phone."

Thibodeaux nodded, skipping the handshake. "Go on in. Not that it will help you much. The sonofabitch put a shotgun in his mouth and pulled the trigger."

"Did he leave a note?"

Thibodeaux shook his head.

"Where'd the shotgun come from?"

"You tell me. He comes from down your way. Did he have it with him?"

"Dunno. We'll check at our end. Have you released the name yet?"

"Nope. The first uniform on the scene got a description from the owner. He realized it might be your guy. You're the only

184

ones we've called. Your D.A.'s here, though."

"Who called him?"

Thibodeaux shrugged. "Not us. Like I said—"

"Thanks."

Ruth entered the unit through its sliding glass door, McGrath behind her. They had driven up together. Moscone, who had followed in his own car, was at their heels. Wherever Moscone had been, he'd arrived at the scene quickly after Lawry tracked him down.

The little motel room was shabby and cold. Even with the door closed, the baseboard heating was no match for a New Hampshire spring. The picture window at the back of the room framed a view of the bulrushes in the bay and the lights on the towers of the Seabrook nuclear power plant beyond. Solitary and enormous, Seabrook loomed like an evil castle against the night sky.

Ruth scanned the room, careful not to touch anything. Two lab guys worked in opposite corners of the outside wall, bright lights trained on their respective sections. Off to one side, Baines stood, his mouth to the ear of the young pathologist from the medical examiner's office in Concord. They were in an intense, whispered conversation. Baines gestured toward the corpse.

Ruth steeled herself and did what she'd been avoiding. Whatever revulsion she felt at seeing Baines, she knew it was nothing compared to what would come next. She looked directly at the corpse. Her swift glance confirmed that reality can be even worse than imagination. The gun's charge had decapitated Pace. His body, covered in blood from the stump of the neck down, sat blown back in the unit's desk chair, palms spread out, facing upward. The gun stood butt-end on the floor between his legs, barrel resting against his left knee. Ruth gulped and looked back at where the men were working, admitting what her psyche had denied the first time. The texture of the wall was a bas-relief of blood and brains and skull fragments. Behind Ruth, Moscone made a strange noise in his throat. McGrath was silent.

"And he was such a handsome man," Ruth said to no one in particular.

She introduced herself to the assistant medical examiner, ignoring Baines. "Got an estimated time of death?"

"Late last night or early, early this morning, but don't hold me to it."

"No one heard the shot?"

"The officers are still checking, but it seems unlikely. He was the only guest registered and the owner lives off premises. The houses on either side are closed up for the season."

Ruth took another look around the room. "Will you do the autopsy soon?"

"It's obviously suicide." Baines spoke full voice for the first time.

"Obviously?"

"Likely," the M.E. corrected. "District Attorney Baines was just explaining this man is a suspect in a homicide."

"I guess he couldn't take the guilt," Baines said sadly.

Outside, Ruth headed back to Lieutenant Thibodeaux, who hadn't moved from the front walk.

"So you like him for a murder," Thibodeaux commented.

"He's a strong suspect in a homicide."

"Think he killed himself out of remorse?"

Ruth shook her head. "I don't know."

Thibodeaux's eyes moved under heavy lids. "Looks that way to me. And to your D.A."

"Was the door locked from the inside?"

"No. Thoughtful type. Probably didn't want the owner to go to all the trouble of kicking it in."

"Not very thoughtful leaving your brains all over the wallboard." Ruth's tone was neutral. "This may be a bit more complicated than you're thinking."

Thibodeaux grunted. "I don't like complicated." He turned and walked away.

Baines approached across the lawn. "A word?" he asked politely. "Over there." He pointed to a place beyond the parked cruisers.

"You got lucky with this one," he said, as soon as they were out of earshot. "Don't pretend you didn't."

"Funny, I don't think Mrs. Pace is going to feel that way."

"Whatever. It's over now. Let's put this one behind us and move on, Chief."

Ruth noted the "Chief" instead of his trademark, "dear." The public nature of their "feud" probably wasn't helping him, either. "We can't put it behind us yet," she responded. "We've found two five-thousand dollar cash payments to Pace, one on the day Tracey Kendall died. Pace wasn't acting alone. Someone paid him to kill her."

"God dammit!" Baines yelled so loud the cops at the crime scene fifty yards away turned to stare. Baines lowered his voice to a hoarse, but menacing whisper. "Are you insane? Prosecuting Pace would have been impossible. The idea of prosecuting someone else, now that Pace is dead, is a joke. A cash payment? You have no witnesses, no paper trail. My God, are you crazy?"

Baines took a moment to catch his breath and then moved back into conciliatory mode. "Chief Murphy. Be smart. This case is terrible for both of us. It ends here. Leave it alone and I'll—"

"And you'll what?"

"And I'll make some calls," was all he said, but Ruth knew what he meant. He would call the mayor and the aldermen he had spoken to and undo the damage he had done to her appointment.

She didn't respond. Baines stuck his hand out, but Ruth

wasn't ready to shake.

"Think about it," Baines urged. "I'm sure you'll see the sense in what I've said." He turned and walked away.

The New Derby contingent stayed in New Hampshire two more hours, listening to Baines spin and respin the suicide tale for the young pathologist and an eager Lieutenant Thibodeaux. "He couldn't handle the guilt," Baines kept saying. "He whacked his girlfriend, but he couldn't stick. He took off, then he killed himself. Your classic murder-suicide, just delayed by a few days."

Ruth listened and said nothing. Beside her, Moscone and McGrath said nothing either, following her lead. Murder-suicide. The mayor would be thrilled, Ruth thought grimly. The case was solved. There would be no trial. It would go away, just as he had ordered.

Ruth returned alone to McGrath's car and sat in the passenger seat watching the diffuse dawn light seep through the clouds over the ocean. Baines was right. The case against Al Pace would've been a difficult one. Now that Pace was dead, it would very likely be impossible to convict his accomplice. Even if Ruth arrested someone, which she couldn't without Baines issuing a warrant, the case would probably never go to trial. Pace's apparent suicide brought the opportunity to close the book on Tracey Kendall's death and move on.

Ruth was still turning this over in her mind when McGrath and Moscone walked over to the cars. Moscone got into his own car and McGrath climbed into the driver's seat next to Ruth. Moscone's car swung out from behind them and sped away, disappearing down Route 1A.

"The Pace house?" McGrath asked. When Ruth nodded yes, McGrath said, "Indeed." He started the car and drove off down the road, the medical examiner's van growing smaller in the rearview mirror.

Riding along in the silent car, Ruth found herself thinking about the moment ten years before when her relationship with Baines had gone sideways. She considered what she could have done to prevent it, how she should have reacted when Pezzoli offered to perjure himself.

At first, she'd stood her ground, insisting, "That's not what I saw."

Baines's gaze met her own. "No one's going to ask you what you saw."

Ruth hadn't replied. It was one thing to refuse to support another cop's lie. It was quite another to call a brother cop a liar. In fact, it was impossible. Ruth was a woman, on a new force where she wasn't known, in a new county where she wouldn't be believed. To make any charge against Pezzoli was to kiss her career good-bye. And each of the three people in the room knew it.

"Good. I'm glad we understand each other." Baines flipped his litigation bag closed, shook Pezzoli's hand, and walked out the door.

Ruth and Pezzoli walked back to headquarters. The boys' parents had arrived. Kvitnitsky's father, bald and bearlike, was angry—angry at the police, angry at this new culture, but mostly angry at his big, dark-haired son with two prior convictions.

Goubanov's mother was bewildered, frightened. She dabbed her glistening eyes with a pale pink hanky. She was an old mother for such a young son, late fifties or better, her hair steel gray. Her English wasn't good enough to keep up with the booking sergeant's. Her son translated the charges for her. When it was done, they wrapped their arms around each other and walked away.

The Goubanov boy might be guilty. He also could be innocent, a lonely boy, ditching school who stopped to get a little taste of home by chatting with a countryman. The charges against him were serious.

Pezzoli went upstairs and typed up their report nice and neat, listing what the charges would be. Ruth took a little comfort in that. A good defense attorney would smell a rat, know they'd been to the D.A. before writing it up. Ruth clung to the idea that the boy could save himself, because she couldn't save him. But what had the chances really been?

Ruth could see now that despite his misconduct, Baines was not the problem. For Baines, it had been a business transaction quickly forgotten. She was the one for whom it was a festering boil. In her eagerness to keep her new job, she had violated her own beliefs. The incident disgusted her. She was disgusted with herself for not standing up to Baines and Pezzoli, not living what she believed in. Then she had turned the hatred outward, blaming Baines, not for what he'd done to the boy, but for what he'd made her do to herself.

"So, murder-suicide," McGrath said neutrally, bringing her back to the problem at hand. "All tied up nice and neat."

Ruth said nothing. They drove a few more miles in the early morning light. Finally, Ruth spoke. "We know it isn't."

McGrath nodded. "The ten thousand dollars."

Ruth closed her eyes and saw the space where Pace's handsome head should have been. "It isn't over," she said quietly.

McGrath kept his eyes trained ahead. "No matter how much you want it to be."

Ruth cradled her forehead in her palm.

"The M. E. seems like an okay guy," McGrath said, "but kinda young, inexperienced."

"Impressionable," Ruth finished for him. She had made her decision. "Turn around, Detective. I need to go back to talk to him. Point out a few things he should be looking for."

When Ruth got back into the car after talking to the young medical examiner, McGrath took off again down Route 1A. On a cloudy Sunday just past dawn, the road was mostly deserted. They passed an occasional diner, fully lit, feeding fishermen their coffee.

Ruth and McGrath said nothing. They had known each other too long to pick apart the meaningful moments in their lives. It'd been their practice not to talk about the important things from the moment they had met, when McGrath had rescued Ruth from Detective First Class Arthur Pezzoli.

Ruth knew there were whispers around the station house about what had happened. Pezzoli had probably told the story himself, playing her up as the fool. The day after the Goubanov boy was arraigned, John McGrath stopped Ruth in the hall. Ruth knew him vaguely. The New Derby detective force was small and she had a passing knowledge of everyone on the shift, but it wasn't her job to hang around the office and she hadn't yet found a place on the grapevine.

"How ya doin', Lieutenant?" McGrath asked, sticking out his hand.

"Fine," Ruth answered, her guard up. She held her breath. McGrath pulled her closer, his grip still tight on her hand. "I've been noticing lately that you seem to know your way around here pretty well." He paused while Ruth wondered what he was getting at. "It seems to me that someone who knows her way around as well as you do, shouldn't really be in training anymore. Is that true?"

"Oh, yes." Ruth felt the color heighten in her face. "I think I'm really ready to assume full duty now."

McGrath let her hand go and looked at his fingernails. "I thought so. Tell you what, I'll have a word with the captain. I need a new partner, you know."

Ruth felt a wave of gratitude that stung behind her eyes, not just because McGrath had rescued her from Pezzoli, but because he'd restored her faith in the place where she worked. McGrath knew the score. He knew she wouldn't be called to testify in the Goubanov case, he probably knew why, and he was offering his support. "Thank you," Ruth said. "I'd like that."

Ruth and McGrath had partnered for seven years until she'd become a captain and the head of the detective force and he'd paired up with old Parsons, who'd retired, making way for Moscone.

The Goubanov boy's court-appointed lawyer had pled him out. Looking at the seriousness of the charges, he'd had the boy cop to simple possession for three years' probation. No one ever asked Ruth why she wasn't involved in the case anymore. No one noticed the too-neat report. At least the boy had avoided juvenile hall, though the guilty plea might have ruined his chances for citizenship. Ruth still thought about the hurt in his mother's eyes. *Welcome to America,* she thought. *It must seem a lot like home.*

"Damn!" McGrath jerked his head around so he could glare at the car behind them. It was tailgating, crowding their back bumper. Miles of empty road around and the two cars rushed on, eighteen inches apart.

Ruth glanced at the speedometer. They were going too fast. When the car crept up behind them, on a two-lane road full of curves with painted double yellow lines that meant no passing, McGrath responded by speeding up, trying to put some distance between them and the other car. The other car stayed right on their tail, adjusting its speed to their own, until finally McGrath, pushed beyond his comfort level, swore and slowed down. The car behind them flashed its high beams, twice. McGrath muttered and pulled to the side of the road. The car sped by, obscured in the morning gloom.

"Jerk," McGrath said and pulled back onto the road. Shortly afterward, they left 1A and crossed to Route 95 without incident. They drove straight to Karen Pace's house.

CHAPTER NINETEEN

The vigil at the Pace house had been building as the days went by. Despite the early hour, parked cars surrounded the corner lot. Outside, a group of men and older boys were standing sheltered by the overhang of the old stable. McGrath seemed to know most of them from his previous visits. He split off and went to talk to the group, greeting many by name.

He's still a good detective, Ruth thought as she continued toward the house—*thorough, straightforward, honest.*

Inside, an assembly line of women made pancakes to feed the crowd. Children of all sizes ran through the rooms or watched cartoons in the living area. A woman at the kitchen table rose when Ruth walked in. She was holding the Pace infant.

"I'm Karen's sister," she said.

"I need to speak to her."

"She's in their bedroom. She's been up all night. She won't see anybody, not even her children. I've tried to tell her they need her now more than ever, but she won't even nurse the baby." Karen Pace's sister shrugged her shoulders at the futility of it all.

"It's urgent."

Karen Pace's sister handed the baby to another woman. "Wait here," she said and started for the stairs.

She returned five minutes later. "Karen wants you to come upstairs." The sister turned again. This time Ruth followed.

At the top of the stairs was a tiny landing framed by three

closed doors. Karen Pace's sister knocked on the one directly ahead.

"Come in." The voice was a whisper.

There were no lights on in the room and the clouds outside prevented natural light from coming through the windows. Karen Pace lay curled up on the bedspread of the double bed. A mass of tiny, pink papers lay beside her. She had been crying. Though there were no tears now, a line of broken blood vessels across her forehead attested to the violence of her sobs. Ruth wondered for a second if she had already heard the news about her husband. No. Not yet. The name hadn't been released.

Ruth crossed the room to look out the window into the backyard below. McGrath was still out there, talking earnestly to the circle of men. Ruth could tell he'd already told them Al Pace was dead. Their heads were bent, the conversation quiet. Ruth didn't have much time.

"Mrs. Pace, I'm here because the news is bad. Your husband is dead."

Ruth expected renewed crying, but Karen was all cried out. When she finally spoke, her voice was thin. "Where?"

"In Salton Beach, in a motel room. Mrs. Pace, there's more—"

"I know." Karen rolled herself up to a sitting position. "I found these in a box in the attic," she said, indicating the papers on the bed. "I wasn't even looking—I just wanted some old clothes for the baby." She handed one of the papers to Ruth. It was a motel receipt for the Hightide Motel in Rockport, one town beyond the New Derby PD's original search. "They're all the same," she went on when Ruth had finished reading. "There are thirty-one of them." Karen began to sniff. Tears oozed from her eyes.

"I'm sorry," Ruth whispered.

Karen tried to wipe the tears away, but the floodgates had

reopened. She doubled over, moaning, head bent to her knees.

Ruth stood at the window and watched the young woman rock and hold her stomach. The worst part was that Ruth wasn't sure enough of anything to tell her what had happened, and wasn't sure, in any case, whether the motive for Al Pace's betrayals would make them any easier for his young wife to endure.

On the bed, the new widow quieted slightly and said in her little voice, "Just tell me, was he alone when he died or was there a woman with him?"

Oh, God, Ruth thought, *how to tell the rest?*

Ruth sat on the bed and explained the circumstances of Al Pace's death in simple sentences. She was as graphic as she thought the media might be, judging it better to say as much as she needed to all at once. Then she called to McGrath, who returned to the car for gloves and an evidence pouch to remove the motel receipts.

In the kitchen, Ruth spoke to Mrs. Pace's sister, suggesting a physician be called and that Karen might bear watching.

Back in the car, McGrath asked, "Why would he keep the receipts? It's hardly likely he paid for the room."

"Think about it," Ruth responded.

Because it was Sunday, McGrath drove through the city and up the coast to Rockport. It would take a little longer, but he preferred the shifting scenery of Routes 1A and 127 to the endless malls and office parks along Route 128. Despite his lack of sleep and the chief's sense of urgency, he was in no hurry. The trip had a feeling of inevitability about it.

The Hightide Motel in Rockport was a string of guest cottages laid out along the rocky shore facing west across Ipswich Bay. In the summer their little porches would be lovely places for tired tourists to sit and watch the sun go down. The rest of the year, they were pretty desolate and depressing. It was an awfully long way for a career woman to go for a midday screw.

McGrath walked across the parking lot and knocked on the office door. The office was in the largest cabin, which also housed the owner's living quarters. A skinny man in khakis and a flannel shirt answered the knock. "You here about a room?"

"You the owner?" McGrath asked.

"Curse God, I am," the man answered. "You interested in buyin'? Make a fine retirement business for someone who had some other income—like a pension." He looked McGrath up and down.

"Not at the moment. I'm not retired. In fact, I'm here on business. New Derby police." McGrath showed his badge. "I've come to ask you about a guest."

"Only have two couples right now," the man answered. "Both out somewhere havin' a fancy Sunday meal."

"A former guest," McGrath clarified. "Last fall, mid-October through December. A man and a woman. They wouldn't have stayed overnight."

"We don't rent to that kind here. This is a nice family place."

"Um-hum. You recognize him?" McGrath showed the picture of Al Pace.

"That's the guy who's been on TV. Missing, he is. If I'd recognized him, I would've called you. I haven't seen him."

McGrath considered this. "You the only one who works here?"

"I wish. This place doesn't pay enough for that. I've had to keep my regular job."

"Who clerks when you're not here?"

"Last couple of years, two sisters who go to Salem State have shared the weekdays. They work it around their class schedules, you know. But they don't rent the place to parties who only want to stay a couple hours. Those are my orders."

McGrath got the names, address, and phone number for the student clerks. The skinny man showed him to the door, opened it, and looked out at the bay. "When I bought this place, it was a real going concern," he said. "Filled up every day all summer and weekends every spring and fall. Then the goddamn Canadian dollar went right down the toilet, and the trade never came back when the dollar did. I got nothin' but empty rooms."

"The land must be worth a lot," McGrath said, gazing at the view, which was currently slate gray water under a slate gray sky, but which held a lot of promise.

The skinny man snorted. "Zoning. Setbacks. Septic permits. You can't build nothin' here. You couldn't even build this place today. Nope, I'm stuck, I am, in a hell that looks like heaven."

McGrath called the motel clerking sisters from his cell phone. One was home studying. She said she'd wait. McGrath edged back onto 127 carefully and, following her detailed directions, arrived at an old house near Salem State that had been divided into apartments. The woman who answered the door was a petite, attractive Filipina. She introduced herself as Christina de las Alas. Her absent sister was Angelica. McGrath noticed the living room had no TV.

Christina agreed to look at the picture. She recognized Al Pace right away. "Oh yes, I remember him because he was so handsome." She aimed her pretty smile at McGrath. "He came lots of times last fall with a lady companion."

"Did they stay the whole night?"

The young woman shrugged. "I don't know. I get off when the owner returns from his job at six-thirty. Most of the guests are out at that time, at the shops or having dinner. I don't know who comes back and who doesn't."

"How did the handsome man pay?" McGrath continued. "Did you give him a receipt each time?"

"The lady secured the room with her credit card. We require a credit card when guests check in. But sometime later, the man would come, give me cash, and watch as I tore up the credit card slip. I don't know why, but I always assumed she'd given him the cash, that she was paying, but she didn't, you know, want it on her credit card bill. Then he'd always ask me for a cash receipt. I never understood that part because I doubted he was there on business." Christina de las Alas laughed a little and smoothed her shining black hair.

McGrath felt suddenly self-conscious in her presence, aware for the first time in months, maybe years, of his shabby old clothes. No wonder the motel owner thought he was retired. "And the lady who was with him, do you remember her name?"

The motel clerk shook her head. "Sorry, I can't remember. I'm no good with names. Besides, I only made the imprint of the card. I never even processed it, because he always came by after with the cash."

"Was this her?" McGrath placed a picture of Tracey Kendall on the coffee table.

The young woman shook her head. "No."

"Can you describe the woman then?" McGrath persisted.

"Oh, yes," Christina de las Alas answered.

Ruth sat in her living room, restlessly turning the pages of the Sunday paper. Baines's face blazed across the television screen. A logo in the right-hand corner marked the telecast as a live feed. Sunday evening was the perfect time to put out news you hoped no one would see. "I am pleased to announce," Baines said in the voice he used for press conferences and political rallies, "that we have found Al Pace, the missing man from Derby Mills." The picture of Al Pace that the New Derby PD had circulated flashed up behind the D.A. "Unfortunately, Mr. Pace was himself found dead this morning in Salton Beach, the victim of a suicide."

"Was he the killer of Tracey Kendall?" a reporter asked.

"We could speculate as to why Mr. Pace might have taken his

life," Baines responded, leaving little room for doubt, "but now we'll never know for sure."

The camera panned away and the Sunday anchor reappeared. "In other news," she read, "New Derby's police headquarters was the target of an attempted burglary last night. That's right, folks, someone trying to break *in* to a police station! More after this."

Ruth moaned.

CHAPTER TWENTY

On Monday morning, as Ruth walked through the door from the parking lot into headquarters, she was greeted by a smell so powerful and so awful that her eyes watered. She hurried to the front desk, where a crowd of officers and civilian employees had gathered, most of them holding hand or handkerchief to nose.

Lieutenant Lawry, looking irritated, stood behind the desk. In front of it was a little man covered from head to foot in something absolutely indescribable. Officer Cable, only slightly less covered, also stood in front of Lawry. Finally, off to one side, looking slightly disheveled, but not so much the worse for wear, stood Mrs. Thurmond Bentley, now known throughout the station house as "the dog poop lady."

It took Lawry, skilled as he was, a little time to get it sorted out. "When the young officer didn't come Saturday—" Mrs. Bentley was saying.

"I said Monday," Cable interrupted. "I was off Saturday."

"You said Saturday," Mrs. Bentley snapped. "Don't give me that."

The gist of it was, when Officer Cable didn't appear, Mrs. Bentley decided to act on her own. On Sunday afternoon, while her neighbors were kept inside by the rain. She carefully removed the pachysandra remaining on her front lawn. Then she hired two high school kids to dig a big pit. While they were digging, she made a trip to Macy's and purchased a dun-colored top sheet especially for the occasion. "It was on sale. I only use

201

white myself," she added to the discussion. That night, under cover of darkness and with some difficulty, Mrs. Bentley filled the pit with the contents of not one, not two, but four plastic garbage barrels filled with dog excrement she had been hoarding and preserving for months, by adding water and a special formula of her own invention. Then she covered the pit with a plastic drop cloth, covered that with the brand new sheet and rearranged the pachysandra.

This morning, right on schedule, the little man, whose name turned out to be Chiarousco, came walking down the street with his Great Dane. The Dane, drawn inexorably to its date with destiny, bounded into Bentley's yard, squatted briefly and dropped out of sight. Mr. Chiarousco, whose brain registered only that his three thousand dollar dog had disappeared, jumped in after it. Only the cushion of Mrs. Bentley's concoction and Mr. Chiarousco's diminutive stature prevented the man or Dane from being seriously hurt.

At this point, Officer Cable had pulled up. "I missed it all by only two seconds, Lieu, I swear!" Cable interjected. Hearing the shouts, and the piteous doggy whining, Cable had run to the edge of the pit to help its occupants out. Mr. Chiarousco, recognizing Cable from his reconnaissance mission three days before, assumed it was the police who set the trap. So, when Officer Cable bent down over the pit, full of concern, and put his hand out, Chiarousco slugged him in the jaw. Cable fell sideways, teetering on the edge, and it was only on account of his superior reflexes that he didn't fall all the way in.

In the end, Cable managed to get the dog and its owner out of the pit. He arrested Mr. Chiarousco for assault and battery on an officer of the law and loaded him and his Dane, aka "Pookie," into the back of the squad car. He brought in Mrs. Bentley as well, though he wasn't sure whether to charge her or exactly what the charge would be. He had contravened all accepted procedure and allowed her to ride in the front with him. "I just couldn't ask her to sit in back," he said.

Lawry examined all three participants in the fracas with a keen distaste. "Where is the canine now?" he asked dryly.

"Still in my patrol car," Cable reported.

"Pookie's an expensive purebred," Mr. Chiarousco added, "and I hold you personally responsible—"

Lieutenant Lawry picked up his desk phone. "Get me Animal Control," was all he said.

An hour later, Lawry appeared in Ruth's doorway, a faint odor of Eau de Pookie still clinging to his crisply starched uniform. "Not that it matters now," he said, "but USC called back. They never heard of Fran Powell, or Mary Frances Kanjorsky, or any other such alias."

Ruth checked her watch. "McGrath and Moscone left half an hour ago. They should be back any minute."

Lawry nodded. "Sounds like this could be it."

Ruth looked through the back of the two-way mirror into the New Derby PD's only interview room. Inside, Moscone and McGrath were just bringing in Fran Powell. Moscone took her raincoat. Chameleon-like, she'd changed again and was dressed now like a successful businesswoman: black suit, green blouse, understated jewelry. Moscone offered her a chair. Both men remained standing.

"Do I need a lawyer?" Mrs. Powell seemed tentative.

Moscone answered. "At this point, you're a witness, not a suspect, Mrs. Powell. You can certainly call a lawyer, but—" Moscone's tone and demeanor indicated that this would be dreadful overkill.

Fran Powell relaxed visibly. "No, thanks. That's okay."

Moscone sat down in the chair across from her. "You're not a suspect, Mrs. Powell," he said quietly, "but it's difficult for us to understand why a witness would need to lie so much."

Her face closed up. "I don't know what you mean."

"Well, let's start with your relationship with Mrs. Kendall. You told us you were neighbors. You met because you lived across the road from one another, had children the same age. But you and Tracey Kendall were childhood friends. Best friends. Why did you hide that from us?"

"As I told your chief," Powell answered, looking straight into Moscone's eyes. "It just seemed needlessly complicated." Her own eyes brimmed with tears. "Tracey and I lost track of each other after high school. She went to college here in the East. I went out to USC—"

"Lie number two!" McGrath boomed from the corner of the room. "USC never heard of you."

Moscone smiled apologetically as if he were embarrassed by his partner's rudeness. "Mrs. Powell, we don't really care about your higher education. It's the pattern that concerns us."

The tears that had been building in Fran Powell's eyes spilled over. "It's true, I never finished—"

Moscone looked saddened. Behind him, McGrath said, "Never started either, never took an evening class or a weekend seminar, according to their records."

There was a moment of silence. Fran Powell patted her eyes with the sleeve of her beautiful, green silk blouse, but the tears continued to flow. Moscone waited, looking sympathetic. McGrath stepped back into the shadows along the wall.

"It wasn't easy being Tracey's friend." Fran Powell's voice was a whisper.

Moscone leaned forward. "What did you say, Mrs. Powell? I didn't get that."

"Imagine what it would be like," she spoke more clearly, "if your best friend, your only friend, really, won every race, was valedictorian, class president, captain of the field hockey team. And your claim to fame, your only claim to fame, was that you were her friend. People want to spend time with you because you are Tracey Noonan's friend."

"It doesn't sound that great," Moscone sympathized.

"It wasn't. Tracey and I loved each other when we were children, but I spent junior and senior high in a state of continuous anxiety. If Tracey dropped me, I had nowhere to go but down, down, down. I couldn't keep up with her, stand at the pinnacle of the class on my own.

"Our senior year was a nightmare. In addition to being accepted to do that post-grad year at that fancy prep school, Tracey got bids from five or six colleges. People actually called her house and asked her to apply, offered scholarships, loans, jobs. She turned them all down, because for her it was Princeton or nothing. I hadn't told Tracey exactly what my grades or my test scores were. She knew they weren't like hers, but I don't think she had any idea how big the difference was."

Fran Powell paused, wiped her eyes again, and looked straight at Moscone. "I used money from my after school job to submit applications to a dozen different colleges, places I thought would command Tracey's respect. I didn't get into any of them. My mother had no idea what was going on with me. She never gave a thought to the future, mine or hers. I told everyone I'd been accepted at USC. That September, when everyone went off to college, I took the five hundred dollars I'd saved from my job, packed up all my clothes, and moved to Los Angeles. Tracey wrote to me a few times, but I was afraid to write back. I didn't know enough about college life to fake news. By two years later, my mother had drunk herself to death and I was relieved of the responsibility of ever facing Southampton, my classmates, or the Noonans again. So you see, that's why I left out the first part of my friendship with Tracey Kendall when I talked to you.

It isn't a happy memory."

Fran Powell stopped talking. The tears stopped as well, but watching from the other side of the glass Ruth felt they weren't far away and could be summoned back if they were needed.

"It must have been quite a shock eighteen years later to find Tracey Noonan living at the end of your driveway," Moscone said quietly.

Fran Powell nodded. "May I have a tissue, please?"

Moscone rose like a gentleman, left the room briefly and returned with a box. Fran Powell selected a single tissue and blew her nose.

"You were saying?" Moscone prompted. Fran looked puzzled, as if she'd lost her place. "You were talking about what happened when you and Tracey Noonan, now Tracey Kendall, met again."

Fran Powell blew her nose and forged on. "When we were children, Tracey's favorite pastime was spinning tales about the future. We'd lie across her bed in the summertime and talk about what our lives would be like when we grew up. Tracey was going to be a successful businesswoman, rich, living in a big, beautiful house. She would describe the house, room by room, the living room, her bedroom, her study. Her husband would be a famous artist, handsome, of course, and caring. They'd have a perfect family. A boy, a talented artist like his father, and a girl, for Tracey to dress and cuddle, and eventually, to do things with and confide in. A replacement for me."

"And when you saw Tracey again?" Moscone pressed, just a little.

"I wasn't prepared for what it did to me. When I walked through her house, everything was the way she had described it all those years ago. I felt as if I'd had the life squeezed out of me."

Behind the glass, Ruth shifted in her chair. That was why

Tracey's study was devoid of technology. She had designed it in her head almost thirty years before.

"All little girls have dreams," Fran Powell continued, "but Tracey was the only person I've ever known who lived hers exactly. She put every ounce of her tremendous focus and energy into making her daydreams come true."

"Except for the baby daughter," Moscone said.

Fran Powell gave a rueful smile. "I looked for that little girl for a long time," she said. "She was completely real to me, because all the other tales Tracey had spun became reality. I'm convinced the daughter would've arrived in time. Tracey and her brothers are only eighteen months apart. Tracey would have spaced her children so that each one could be lavished with the attention she felt her mother had no time to give. In any case, I couldn't ask Tracey what had happened. We weren't as close in the second round of our friendship as we were in the first."

"Because you were sleeping with her husband?" McGrath, still on his feet, spoke from the other side of the room. McGrath boomed on. "That's the third lie," he said.

"Not a lie," she protested.

"Omission, then," Moscone brokered peace.

Fran Powell's choices flickered across her face. Through the glass, Ruth watched closely. Would Fran deny the affair outright? No, she didn't know what they had. Full disclosure, then? Perhaps unnecessary at this time. In the end, she tried a dodge. "What did or did not happen between me and Stephen doesn't have anything to do with any of this."

"You slept with the husband of a murdered woman and you don't think it's relevant?" McGrath was incensed. "Your job is to tell us the truth. We decide what's relevant. We know you're lying about this because you have even bigger things to hide."

Fran turned to Moscone to see if he would help her out. "Your affair began a year ago," Moscone offered, his voice was low and even. "When Susan Gleason put pressure on Stephen to produce a show for her new gallery. It continued until this October, when Hannah Whiteside replaced you."

Fran opened her mouth and then closed it.

"Did you do it to get back at Tracey?" Moscone asked. His voice was conversational, inviting gossip from a friend.

Fran Powell shook her head. "It had nothing to do with Tracey. I didn't seduce Stephen. He seduced me. Not that he had to try hard. Here's a tip—when a woman is married to a stupid, drunken slob, you don't have to try too hard. Tracey wasn't the only one who talked about her dreams. I lived alone with my drunken mother. Before Tracey and I became friends, I think my most vivid daydream was about coming home and finding something hot that smelled good on the supper table. But on those summer days in Tracey's bedroom, I had to come up with something better. Tracey didn't respect anyone who didn't have ambitions. In our stories, Tracey was the successful businesswoman married to the artist. I was the glamorous movie star, known all around the world. Successful in my own right, I was married to the son of a fabulously wealthy, very classy family.

"When I wasn't accepted at any college, I went out to Los Angeles. I figured by the time anybody realized I hadn't gotten a degree, I'd be such a star it wouldn't matter. It didn't work out that way. Four years later, when most of my classmates were graduating from college, I was working as a dancer, in a bar. By the next year, when Tracey finished Princeton, I was finally working in film, but not the kind of movies I wanted anyone at home to see. I hated every minute of it and I hated myself for doing it. That's when I met my husband."

Fran Powell dabbed at her pink nose, threw the used tissue away and took a new one. She took a deep breath. "Sandy was rich. He came to Hollywood to be a big producer. He was handsome then, or at least not so ugly. And he wanted me, desperately, pursued me for months. So I thought, why not? Why not at least let the other part of the daydream be true? The rich husband. So I married him."

Her tears flowed again. Behind the glass, Ruth leaned in, studying the scene. Were the tears real this time, she wondered, or were they for the benefit of the male detectives?

"Sandy came from money, all right, but the money came from a trust left by his grandmother, money he came into when he turned twenty-five; seven million dollars. In the ten years we were together on the coast we burned through every dime of it and then some." Fran Powell managed a sardonic smile. "It's terrible when you marry a man for his money and then find out he hasn't got it anymore. We were in real trouble by the time Xander was born. We couldn't pay our mortgage and the house was worth half what we'd paid for it. I hadn't worked since I met Sandy and he never did package a single deal in Hollywood. He just threw his money into other people's pictures, one disaster after another. His parents have the real money, of course, but they're still alive, so a fat lot of good it does us. They finally stepped in and bailed us out, but there were conditions, terrible conditions. They built us the house on the service road and moved us back East. Sandy went to work in his father's firm where he can't even pretend to be important. I shut myself up in the house and stayed there as much as possible. That's where I was, in my own driveway, when along strolls Tracey Noonan, tanned and fit only weeks after having a baby."

"You hated her," McGrath said from the shadows. "You decided sleeping with her husband would hurt and humiliate her, knock her down a notch or three."

"I hated myself," Fran Powell insisted. "So when Stephen Kendall said he wanted me, he thought about me day and night, that I was his energy and his inspiration, I thought, at last I am useful. I am something."

"Did Tracey know?" McGrath asked.

"We took elaborate precautions."

"How did it end?" Moscone's voice was almost tender.

Fran Powell covered her eyes with her hand. "The way it always does. Hannah Whiteside arrived to take care of Carson in September. By October, she was Stephen's inspiration, and I was back to being just a neighbor." Fran pulled her hand from her eyes and looked back at Moscone. "I will always be proud of the work he created in the one year, seven months and ten days we were together," she said. "No one can take that from me."

"Your affair with Stephen Kendall ended in October," Moscone spoke it as a statement not a question, "and you decided to console yourself with Al Pace."

"Your fourth lie, Mrs. Powell, and the one that will cook you." McGrath ticked them off on his fingers. "You knew Al Pace. We can prove it. You were sleeping with Al Pace. We can prove that, too. You gave Al Pace money. We can prove that. In fact, you gave Al Pace ten thousand dollars to kill your oldest friend, the wife of your former lover, because you were jealous of everything she had. You hated Tracey Kendall." By the time McGrath was finished, he was nose to nose with Fran Powell, his finger jabbing the empty air just inches from her chest.

Ruth's eyes were glued to Fran Powell's face, evaluating her reaction. In the interview room, Moscone quietly Mirandized her. Fran Powell's eyes mirrored her terror at McGrath's accusations. Her mouth hung open. She gulped air twice and then her entire being deflated. Her body slumped on the tabletop and she burst into noisy sobs.

An hour later, McGrath and Moscone were in Ruth's office. Ruth was leaning back in her desk chair, palms pressed to her eyes. McGrath sat slumped in the chair across from her and Moscone had his elbows on the conference table, holding his chin up with his hands. All three were exhausted, McGrath and Moscone because they had painstakingly led Fran Powell through her story again and again, Ruth because she had sat outside, staring at the glass, reading every nuance.

Fran Powell admitted to sleeping with Al Pace. She said Pace had come on to her and that she had once again gone without a struggle. She was deeply wounded by the end of her affair with Stephen Kendall. She knew that Tracey and Pace had some sort of special relationship. She believed they were lovers.

Ruth hadn't been able to follow the twisted logic that made sleeping with the wife's boyfriend revenge against the husband. It wasn't clear Fran herself could reconstruct her thinking now. In any case, she had later discovered Al Pace and Tracey Kendall were more than acquaintances, but less than friends, and certainly not lovers.

Fran and Al's affair continued through October and November. The meetings at the Hightide Motel in Rockport were as frequent as three times a week. It was just after Thanksgiving when Al Pace first asked for money. She gave him two hundred dollars cash. He said he needed it to buy Christmas presents for his boys.

It was remarkable to Ruth that both the sex and the payments had continued. Fran Powell said there had been an air of menace in Al Pace's demands for money, but she had been unclear about whether the threat had been to expose her or to stop seeing her. "If Al Pace were alive today, would we charge him with extortion or prostitution?" Ruth wondered aloud. McGrath shrugged and Moscone shook his head.

Fran Powell had absolutely denied paying ten thousand dollars to Al Pace, five thousand in February and five thousand the day Tracey Kendall died. After the first time, her payments to

Al had been fairly regular, but had run in the hundreds, not the thousands of dollars.

"Look, I swear," Fran Powell had finally said, "I just don't have access to that kind of money. Sandy's father pays him a salary that meets our basic needs, but we have to go and grovel for every little 'extra'—like Xander's nursery school tuition or a working car. I couldn't very well have gone to my dear in-laws and said, 'I need ten thousand dollars to have a friend rubbed out.' "

In the end, they'd believed her. McGrath would spend the rest of the morning with her going through bank accounts, but it would be a formality.

Moscone spoke from his chair. "It seems to me that we have an awful lot of people coming on to Fran. First Stephen, then Al. What's so special about her? I don't get it."

"Stephen Kendall is what he is," Ruth answered. "We already know that. I believe Al Pace targeted Fran Powell specifically. Her house, her car. He must have believed she was rich. His plan was always to take money from her. His bad business judgment was going to result in losing his wife's favorite thing in all the world—her grandmother's house. He was desperate for money."

"The threat of foreclosure turned him into a killer?" Moscone sounded doubtful.

Ruth shrugged. She wasn't ready to answer that question.

CHAPTER TWENTY-ONE

After McGrath and Moscone left, Ruth sat at her desk, turning the investigation over in her mind. She knew they were closer to solving the mystery of Tracey Kendall's death than they'd ever been. She was sure the answer was . . . somewhere, perhaps somewhere close. What had they missed? After a few minutes, she rose and made her way down the long central hallway of the headquarters building to the basement stairs.

Inside the property room, uniformed officers were completing a post-break-in inventory under the watchful eye of Lieutenant Lawry. Ruth craned her neck to see the window where the thief had tried to cut the bars. It was boarded up with plywood and secured with metal rods that ran horizontally across the inside.

Ruth returned to the section of shelving that held Tracey Kendall's things and took down the box. Once again, she walked down to the furthest of the old jail cells, put on a pair of surgical gloves and laid out the contents of the box in the circle of light on the table.

Ruth looked at Tracey Kendall's gym bag, briefcase, and pocketbook. She had pinpointed the detail gnawing at her. Stephen Kendall knew that Ruth knew about Tracey's appointment with Wink Segrue and her subsequent three-day disappearance. Yet, in their last conversation, Kendall had again asked about Tracey's property. The attempted break-in at the property room had occurred that night.

The conclusion was inescapable. Tracey's possessions had not yet told everything they had to tell.

Ruth started with the gym bag. It disturbed her. Tracey Kendall, the woman who had everything, had been so scared she kept old clothes in her car in case she had to run. "Tracey, who were you so afraid of?" Ruth muttered into the bag.

It broke Ruth's heart that Tracey Kendall had been so alone she could tell no one her troubles. But whom would she have told? Brenda, Jane, and Ellie were subordinates. Hannah, Susan, and Fran were Stephen's lovers or ex-lovers. Tracey wouldn't have confided in them. It would make her look weak.

Why, as Tracey drove herself to her perfectly imagined future, hadn't she created a role for a friend, an equal, a confidant? Tracey couldn't admit to vulnerabilities. People who can't ever show the chinks in their armor can't have friends, Ruth reflected. There's no intimacy, no shared trust because there is no need to trust. Alone in the property-room cell, Ruth winced in recognition.

Ruth removed everything from the gym bag, layer by layer. She shook out each piece of clothing, even examined the tags inside looking for extraneous markings. Then she slowly felt her way from one side of the gym bag to the other. She crinkled the sides looking for hidden pockets, false linings. Nothing.

She opened the pocketbook and was struck once again by how impersonal it was. She emptied all the pockets and checked for false linings, papers stuffed up in the fabric, secret compartments. There were none.

She went through the pile of reading material in the briefcase next, looking for something that was more than met the eye, a paper shoved onto the pile that didn't belong there, something underlined or highlighted that had extra significance. If there was anything like that, Ruth lacked the sophistication to understand it.

The computer and the personal organizer remained. She turned to the organizer first. Unzipping it, Ruth felt her excitement rising. This organizer was Tracey Kendall's most personal possession. It might be left by a phone at home or locked in a locker at the gym, but it would never be far from her. This was where anything Tracey Kendall wanted to hide would be hidden. It was also where anything she wanted found would be kept. Ruth turned the pages carefully, mindful that the calendar had already yielded a clue. She went through the calendar section, the To Do lists, and the notes.

Carefully, Ruth began to disassemble the organizer. She removed the business cards, writing instruments, and photograph and felt down to the bottom of each pocket. She opened the rings and slid the calendar, To Do lists, telephone directory, and note pages out. All that remained was a pad of blank paper, held in place by its backing cardboard, which fit in a special slot on the back cover. Ruth slid the note pad out, then slowly put her hand down the opening created by the slot.

Her gloved fingers touched it almost instantly. She grasped gently and pulled. Seconds later, she was blinking at the thing that she'd been looking for—a small square, made out of a piece of white paper, taped shut and squashed flat.

The group that met around Ruth's conference table fifteen minutes later was unnaturally quiet.

Lawry, McGrath, and Moscone were passing around a photocopy of the sheet that had made up the paper square. Ruth gazed out the window. The big clouds had broken up, revealing patches of blue. Upstairs, Detective Miller was working on the original note. After all three men had examined the photocopy, Ruth placed it on the table. It read:

Do you think that you can cast me off? Now when I need

you the most? Nothing's changed and nothing will change. Not if you know what's good for you.

It was unsigned, printed by inkjet printer on plain white paper.

"This note," Ruth said, "was terrifying to Tracey, as well it should have been. It is an overt threat."

"When did it come, do you think?" Lawry asked.

"It's hard to say," Ruth answered, "but I think it may have been the catalyst for Tracey's unexplained disappearance in January. After she returned, she kept the emergency bag of clothes in the car, in case she needed to disappear again. But weeks went by, then months. Tracey probably let her guard down. She didn't know that her killer had already set a plan in motion."

McGrath picked up the note again, squinting at it through his reading glasses. "Not very helpful, is it? Who was she about to cast off? The unfaithful husband? The business partner who had become a dead weight? Or the art dealer who had risked everything to retain the husband as a client?"

There was a soft rap on the open door. "Excuse me, Chief." Officer Cable stood there.

"Yes?"

"Detective Miller's cleaning up upstairs," Cable said, "but he sent me down because there's something he wanted you to know right away."

"Yes, Officer Cable." Ruth thought if Miller wanted her to know something immediately, he'd sent the wrong person.

"Chief, he said there were only two sets of prints on the note you found."

"And they belonged to?" Ruth's patience was worn out.

"One belongs to Tracey Kendall."

"And the other?"

"He matched it to the set on the acetylene torch from the

property-room break-in, just like you said he would."

Ruth turned to face her men. "The torch belongs to Stephen Kendall. I saw it at his studio the day of the funeral."

McGrath stood up. "Let's go."

"Yes," Ruth said, looking directly at them. "It's time to bring him in."

"You coming?" Moscone asked.

"No," Ruth answered. "I have one more thing I need to do."

CHAPTER TWENTY-TWO

Ruth paced back and forth in the Fiske & Holden parking lot, talking to herself. The high clouds were breaking up, yielding larger and larger patches of blue. A stiff breeze moved them steadily across the sky.

Ruth walked out of the parking lot, thinking things through carefully. *Tracey accelerates out of the lot. She's driving confidently. She's come this way thousands of times before.*

Does she brake where the lot meets the road? Ruth looked to her right. *No. The flat at the top of the hill allows her to see both to her right and down the hill to her left. She can tell no one's coming, she hasn't got enough speed to need to brake for control. She rolls out slowly, talking on the cell phone as she leaves the lot.*

Ruth started walking down the hill. When she had careened down the road on her wild ride, not touching the brakes, she still hadn't reached nearly the speeds Tracey had. *Something causes Tracey to accelerate. She steps on the gas hard about fifty feet down the hill. Here or so. Why? Over-confidence? She had a lot of experience with this road. She didn't know she had no brakes. Something more.*

Ruth went back to the parking lot, passed it, and kept walking toward the Deli-Cater. Despite the rain of the last two days, it didn't take long to find the place where the vegetation was broken and bent.

Ruth returned to the lot and got into her car. As she pulled away, she looked into her rearview mirror. Ellie Berger, Brenda

O'Reilly, and Jack Holden were staring at her from Fiske & Holden's windows.

Hannah Whiteside answered the Kendall front door. "Your detectives are down at the studio with Stephen," she said before Ruth had a chance to speak.

"I know. I saw the car down there. I need to speak to Carson."

"Carson? Are you sure? Shouldn't Stephen . . . ?"

"I'd like to talk to Carson alone."

Hannah straightened up, made a decision, and called the boy.

"Thank you," Ruth said and led him into the empty living room. She sat with him on the couch.

"Carson, do you remember you told me your mom was mad at you when she had her accident?"

Carson nodded miserably, staring at his shoes.

"Why did you think she was mad? Did you have a fight?"

Carson shook his head from side to side. A single tear squeezed from his eye and traversed along his cheek.

"Then why, Carson? Why did you think she was mad?"

"She called me a name." His voice was so soft, Ruth wasn't sure she had heard. She took his hand.

"What, honey? What did she call you?"

The little boy shook his head. "It's a bad word."

"Carson, you can tell me. I won't be mad."

Carson leaned in and whispered in her ear. "She called me a bastard." He began to cry.

"Oh, Carson." Ruth had fifteen years training as a parent and twenty years as a policewoman, and it took everything she had not to cry with him. "She wasn't mad at you. When she said that, she wasn't talking to you."

Ruth hugged the boy to her. He was crying hard now, crying out the days since his mother's death, days filled with his father's remoteness, his mother's family's tension, the screaming accusations between his father, Hannah, and Susan Gleason.

"Your mother loved you very much, Carson. I'm sure of it." Ruth felt Carson's face against her breasts, the dampness of her uniform shirt from his tears. As he cried Ruth lifted her head to hug him to her chest. She gazed out the window just in time to see Detective McGrath huffing and puffing as he ran toward the house.

She met him on the porch. "Chief, you gotta come quick," he gasped. "We've got a situation—"

"I left Moscone with him," McGrath explained as they hurried toward the studio. "He went to that hostage negotiation school. Of course, there's no hostages, but we thought—It doesn't matter. Moscone's just marking time. Kendall says he'll only talk to you."

On the studio step, Ruth took a deep breath. "Okay. I'm going in there. You coordinate backup when it arrives." Ruth stepped out of the bright sunlight into the interior of the studio. Off to her right, Moscone called, "Chief's here, Mr. Kendall. It's okay. She'll talk to you now." Moscone slipped up behind Ruth, put his hand on her back, and gently guided her to the center of the floor.

"It's me, Stephen, Chief Murphy." Ruth looked up toward the ceiling. The sun was pouring through the skylight. She shielded her eyes with her hand and looked again.

She was astounded by what she saw. Stephen Kendall must have been working non-stop over the last two days. T. Rex's face, head, neck, and back had their finishing coat of fiberglass. The surface was rent with giant holes, Kendall's trademark decay. The sculpture looked grotesque, like its skin was melting.

Stephen Kendall was standing stock still on the crown of the tyrannosaurus' head. He had a rope taken from the pulley system fashioned into a noose around his neck. The other end was tied to a rafter. From the ground, Ruth could see him trembling.

"Why are you up there?" she called. Her voice echoed in the cavernous space.

"I killed my wife!" Stephen Kendall screamed. "And you found out. I knew you would. You sent those men to arrest me."

"They didn't come to arrest you," Ruth shouted back. "They wanted to ask you some questions."

"That's what the detective said, but I knew what he meant."

Moscone leaned down and whispered in Ruth's ear, "Try not to argue with him." Outside, one of the high clouds moved across the sun. The studio grew dark. Ruth took her hands from her eyes and looked up at Kendall again. His face was contorted from crying.

"I can't talk like this," Ruth whispered back to Moscone. "I'm going up." She motioned to Moscone to steady the scaffolding beside the dinosaur sculpture and started up, placing a foot on the metal piping that formed its framework. "I'm coming to talk to you, Stephen," she called. "Hold on."

She stopped a third of the way up and took off her pumps. They weren't climbing shoes. She tossed them to Moscone one at a time. She didn't want to startle Kendall with the noise of them clattering to the floor. Then she continued climbing. The metal of the scaffold was cold on her feet, but she felt faster, surer in her hose. The ladder ended with a plywood platform at the top of the tower. Ruth gripped the plywood, climbing up until she could lay the top portion of her body across it. The buttons of her uniform dug into her chest. She pushed herself forward. The ridiculous uniform skirt caught the edge of the plywood. Ruth grunted. One last push and she slid across the platform, splinters searing her legs above the knees.

She stood up on the platform. Suddenly, the cloud moved

away and she was blinded by the skylights. She froze, afraid she'd fall off the edge. She blinked, focused, and found herself face-to-face with T. Rex. Up close, his expression was terrifying, his teeth enormous. Ruth pulled her eyes from the sight and stared at the dinosaur's creator above her. Stephen Kendall, bathed in sunlight, looked ravaged, exhausted. Ruth felt her chest tighten with a surge of adrenaline.

"Don't do this," she said quietly.

"It's better," Kendall answered. He sounded sad.

"No, no it isn't. You know it isn't."

He didn't respond. Ruth waited. "Did you write it down anywhere? Tell the whole story? Leave a note?"

Stephen Kendall shook his head. Outside, the noise spiked as patrol cars, an ambulance, and a fire truck arrived. "Keep them out of here!" Stephen yelled. "Anyone comes in here and I'm gone. I mean it."

"Stephen," Ruth kept her voice as low as she could and still be heard, but she could not keep out the emotion. "You cannot do this. Listen to me. This cannot happen."

"Why not?"

Ruth drew a deep breath and came as far forward as she dared. "Because of your son, Stephen. Because of Carson. Just a few years from now, he'll be asking questions. Not the kind he asks now, but detailed questions that will demand answers. And someone, your mother-in-law, one of your brothers-in-law, someone will have to tell him. Your mother died in a car crash. We don't know why. And then your daddy killed himself. We don't know why he did that, either. Carson is a smart boy, Stephen. He'll draw his own conclusions. And he'll be wrong. Don't leave the boy to grow up thinking he's a monster's son."

Stephen Kendall looked down at Ruth and wiped at his eyes. He made a mewling, hiccupping sound, suppressed, but full of fear. Ruth sat down on the scaffold. She hoped Kendall would get the impression she intended to stay. As soon as she sat, he surprised her by dropping to his haunches. The rope around his neck remained slack.

"We found the note, Stephen," she said quietly. "It had your fingerprints on it, just yours and Tracey's. I won't lie to you. It looks terrible."

A sob ripped up from Stephen Kendall's gut so violently Ruth feared for his balance. The noise he made was loud and awful. "I killed her. I killed her. I killed her."

Ruth rolled up to her knees and leaned as far forward as she dared. "Stephen," she called. "It can't be left this way. I know you didn't kill your wife. In fact, I know who did, but you have got to help me prove it. If you die, the truth will never be known. Let me solve this case. Come down. Release Wink Segrue from his privilege." When Kendall didn't respond, she continued. "Don't punish a little boy forever because you can't live with the compromises you and Tracey made. I know you loved your wife. I know you love Carson. I know you've been too sick with guilt to comfort him. But you must. Come down."

Kendall didn't answer. Ruth's heart contracted. The silence expanded. "I'm coming over," she said. He didn't say no. Ruth walked to the edge of the platform and felt the dinosaur's head. It was slippery, but the contours of the face, the jaw, the eye sockets, offered some footholds. She was nearly forty feet above the hard wood floor below. Stephen Kendall remained crouched, rocking slightly. "I'm coming," Ruth said again. She removed her jacket, ripped the feet off her ruined hose and stepped out.

Her foot found Rex's jaw and held. She crept along it as it curved upward toward the back of his head. At the end of his mouth, she reached up and around, trying for purchase on the top of the slick head. The neck sloped downward. If she could lie across it and pull herself up, she could move onto the head. Above her, less than five feet away, she heard Kendall's weight shift. He was on the move.

Ruth tried. Once. Again. Her arms couldn't reach around the head with any kind of grip. She shivered. She was covered in sweat. Out of the corner of her eye, she saw Moscone slowly, silently making his way up the scaffold. And then she heard the slight noise of friction, hemp against wood. Kendall was trying the noose, pulling on it to test its attachment to the rafter. He was getting ready to jump.

"No!" Ruth pushed off from the jaw, twisting herself as she rose. She landed across the back of the monster's head with a thud that nearly knocked the wind out of her. Scrambling to her feet, she saw Kendall running for the end of T. Rex's snout. Ruth leapt forward, arms flailing. "No!"

Kendall turned to face her, the noose still loose around his neck as he headed for the side.

"No! No! No! Think about Carson!" Ruth's scream transformed into a beseeching wail. "Think about your son!"

Kendall's expression changed. Determination turned to fear, panic, regret. He reached out, but it was too late. He started to go over.

Ruth ran to him and grabbed for his shirt. For a split second, she thought her momentum was all wrong, that she had pushed them out over the studio floor where her colleagues would find her, swinging from Stephen Kendall's corpse.

But his descent stopped. At the last moment, he aimed his feet for the beast's mouth and caught. He had saved himself.

Ruth gripped his shirt as tightly as she could and pulled him toward her, easing him back up over the side until they were lying on top of the monster's head. Then she closed him in her arms, cradling him as he wept.

Chapter Twenty-Three

On the ground, Ruth demanded a cell phone. She banged at the buttons, listened briefly, then thrust it at McGrath. "Find him. Track him down," she commanded. "We've got to get out of here."

Outside, the lawn was awash with emergency vehicles and the ubiquitous television satellite trucks, attracted by all the scanner activity. Ruth motioned to Moscone. "Let's go."

On the grass, Ruth waved away the microphone of the first reporter who reached her. "Not now," she yelled. "I need something from you." She pulled the reporter aside, gesturing to Moscone to keep the others away.

"Are you interrupting regular programming?"

"Yeah."

"How have you been playing the story?"

"Murdered woman's spouse threatens suicide."

"Have you broadcast that he's down?"

"Yeah, that he came down with you."

"Give me ten minutes, then you can report he's not a suspect. He's cooperating with us."

The reporter grinned. "Thanks. I owe ya."

Ruth pointed to Bob Baines marching up from the street, flanked by the state trooper who acted as his driver. "Talk to him," Ruth urged in a loud voice. "He knows everything."

The reporters flocked toward the D.A., but he was too smart to be ambushed. As Ruth and Moscone jumped into her car,

Baines and his driver reached their car and followed right behind.

Ruth made it from Derby Hills in eleven minutes with lights and siren blazing. Moscone, riding shotgun, was buckled at her side. Baines's car was right on their tail, driven by the trooper.

As they came to the top of Willow Road, Ruth saw Jack Holden's expensive black coupe as it raced out of the lot, veering left onto the roadway.

"There he is!" Moscone shouted. Ruth accelerated across the flat. Holden's car started down the hill.

The cars began their descent, one after the other. Ruth lifted her foot from the accelerator as the "dangerous curves" sign flew by. Ahead of them, the coupe bounced over a bump, gathering speed.

The scene of Tracey's accident and the railroad bridge beyond flashed into view. Ruth's foot hovered over the brake.

"Not yet!" Moscone's voice was urgent.

Ruth held off. Behind them, she heard the squeal of the state trooper hitting his brakes. Twenty yards in front of her, the black coupe made the turn and headed for the underpass.

"Now!" Moscone screamed.

Ruth pumped the brakes three times. The rocketing car barely seemed to slow. Behind them, she heard Baines's car begin to spin. She prayed they would be out of the way.

Ruth hit the curve and held. Glancing in her rearview, she saw Baines's car come to a stop facing backwards on the grassy verge, just as she had the first time. Just as Tracey Kendall would have—if she'd had brakes. Baines jumped out and lost his stomach contents in the grass.

Moscone twisted in his seat, looking back. "They're okay," he yelled. "Keep going. You can catch him now. Step on it."

A thousand yards beyond the underpass, lights still going,

Ruth drew even with Jack Holden. With one deft turn of the wheel, she forced him from the road. He bumped along the grassy shoulder, slowing as he went, until his back wheels hit the ditch. Stuck, he sprang from his car.

Ruth yanked her vehicle to a stop and jumped out. Her breath came in short gasps.

"Fuck you," Holden screamed, backing toward his car.

"You're a clever killer," Ruth called to him, "and you had a brilliant plan. But you made one stupid mistake, you son-of-a-bitch, that's going to cost you."

Holden looked to the right and left, assessing his chances if he ran. Evidently, he didn't like them.

Ruth shouted after him. "Adam Bender got an e-mail from Tracey Kendall's mailbox on the day of her murder asking him to wait to discuss a trade. But Tracey didn't send the e-mail. The person who sent it knew something was going to happen on the street at lunchtime he didn't want Adam Bender to see."

Holden went pale, then red, but held his tongue.

Ruth walked toward him, until she was about six feet away. "It could have been something as simple as the act of passing Al Pace an envelope containing five thousand dollars cash. But it wasn't. The money must've been put somewhere for Al to retrieve. The person who paid Al Pace to disable Tracey's brakes was already somewhere else." Ruth looked hard at Holden. His face was flushed with barely suppressed rage. "When Tracey pulled out, her killer was sitting in a car just below the rise on the other side of the driveway. He pulled up tight behind her, tailgating. At first, she didn't recognize him. His regular car was still sitting in the Fiske & Holden parking lot. She responded by accelerating, trying to put some distance between them. She was halfway down the hill, already going far too fast, when she tried the brakes. Nothing. The grade continued and she kept going faster. Her killer watched her hit the wall, braking slowly so he wouldn't leave skid marks. Then he continued calmly around the curve, under the railroad bridge and away from the scene. By the time the salesman found Tracey, her killer had parked the second car at the Deli-Cater, walked back to his office, and was calmly eating a sandwich at his desk."

"That is brilliant," Jack Holden jeered. "You'll never be able to prove it."

"Ah," Ruth said. "But here's where a brilliant plan turns to crap. Al Pace had no idea what the killer was going to do. Pace was desperate for money, desperate enough to blackmail, to intimidate, but not to kill. He was horrified when he saw the second car. But to finger the killer was to implicate himself. So he ran."

Ruth's eyes drilled into Holden's. "If Pace hadn't run, we never would've known. We might've questioned him, but he could've claimed he hadn't touched the car that day. We never would have begun a murder investigation."

Ruth took her time, making sure Holden understood her words. She inched forward until she stood less than two yards away. Holden had pressed himself against his car. His face was purple, every muscle in his body tense. He was in a towering rage. "So the killer's mistake," Ruth continued, "was the same as Tracey Kendall's. He picked a weak and ineffective partner, a man not bright enough to hold up his end."

The dam burst. "The dumb bastard," Holden shouted. "I told him over and over to come back and take it like a man."

Ruth yelled back. "I bet you did. I bet you told him when you put the muzzle in his mouth. I bet you said it over and over right up until you pulled the trigger."

"Bitch!" Holden lunged at her, hands going for the throat in a blur of motion. He was inches away when he hit the ground, tackled from the side by Moscone.

Holden's habit of ignoring those of lower rank had finally cost him everything.

CHAPTER TWENTY-FOUR

"When I understood that there had been a follow car, I knew Stephen Kendall couldn't have done it, no matter what he said," Ruth explained. She, McGrath, and Lieutenant Lawry were gathered in her corner office, enjoying a quiet postmortem. "Stephen Kendall was at his studio when his wife died. He couldn't have been in two places."

"How'd you know Holden followed her?"

"Carson told me days ago that when she died, his mommy was mad at him. He believed she was mad, because Tracey screamed, 'Bastard!' through the phone. Of course, she wasn't calling Carson a bastard. She'd just recognized Jack Holden in the car behind her."

"The nanny could have lied when she told us Kendall was in his studio at the time of the accident," McGrath pointed out. "She had a reason to lie for him."

Ruth smiled. "But she didn't. Moscone was pretty definite she was telling the truth. Stephen Kendall's fingerprints were on the note because his wife had showed it to him. He knew she was in business with a man who was increasingly dangerous, who was making overt threats. He begged her to stay at Fiske & Holden until after his show, not to take the financial hit that would come from breaking up the firm. They fought terribly about it. Tracey even took off for a while, but then she returned and went back to work."

"They couldn't have needed the money that badly," Lawry

said. "They were rich."

Ruth shook her head. "Breaking up Fiske & Holden would have frozen almost all their assets for a protracted period. The limited partners could pull out their funds on a change of management. Tracey would have had to wait through a lengthy dispute with Holden and probably expensive litigation to start her new business. Kendall didn't want that, and even more, he didn't want the mess and distraction while he was getting ready for his show. It was pure selfishness."

"Why did she ever agree to it?"

"I don't know. Because she loved him. Or because she was in love with the idea of being married to a famous artist and had been since her childhood." Ruth paused before continuing. "When Tracey was killed, Stephen didn't want anyone to know what he'd done. He was so guilty, so ashamed, he tried to break into headquarters to steal the note back. Finally, the burden was so great, he tried to end his life. He believed he'd killed her."

"It'll be impossible to convict Holden." McGrath was his cranky self, but the awful sports coat was gone and he was wearing a nice gray suit. It was the first time Ruth had seen that suit in quite a while.

"Not in New Hampshire," she answered. "Holden was present at the scene that time, and not nearly as careful. He didn't have months to plan. The New Hampshire M.E. feels certain he can show from the brain splatters Al Pace couldn't have pulled the trigger at that angle with the muzzle in his mouth. And the gun must have come from somewhere. They'll find out how Holden got it. Even Lieutenant Thibodeaux feels good about his evidence, and we know he doesn't like 'complicated.' Don't be so sure we can't get Holden here, either. Stephen Kendall has released Wink Segrue from privilege. Segrue confirms Tracey came to him about splitting up the firm. Holden stood to lose everything."

The television lights were hot and bright. The timing was elegantly orchestrated, live on the six o'clock news. Bob Baines, Sussex County District Attorney, stood behind the podium, jacket off, sleeves rolled up. "We're elated," he said as flashbulbs popped, "to have brought this difficult case to a successful conclusion. It's a tribute to the value of teamwork and co-operation."

It was all Ruth could do to keep from rolling her eyes on camera.

When the press conference broke, District Attorney Baines energetically pumped Ruth's hand. "Bygones be bygones, Chief?"

"Certainly," Ruth answered positively, but stiffly. She had to work with him, but she didn't have to like him.

As Ruth moved away from Baines, Mayor Rosenfeld grabbed her elbow. "You okay?" he asked. "You're bright red."

"Television lights," Ruth mumbled.

"I'm happy things are going well." Rosenfeld inclined his head in Baines's direction and pulled Ruth forward, putting more space between them and the D.A. "It was gracious of you to defer to him during the press conference."

"I'm not a complete idiot."

"Anyway, this should put any lingering fears among the aldermen to rest. Congratulations, Chief."

In the main corridor of the station house, Ruth caught up with Lawry, who looked as fresh and unwrinkled as he had at the start of the day shift. "What are you still doing here?" she asked. "And where's Moscone? He loves this stuff. Press conferences, publicity. You think it's ridiculous, yet you're hanging around."

"I'm filling in on the front desk for our lovely Lieutenant Carse tonight. She had an important date," Lawry winked, "with someone you know."

Ruth was thunderstruck. "You're kidding!"

"Not a bit of it. Moscone's loved her from afar for years, the whole time he was on the night shift, but he didn't think it was 'professional' to ask her out. Brenda O'Reilly convinced Moscone to go for it. He said if not for Brenda, he'd still be pining. Their first date was Saturday night. It must've gone pretty well. I found him at Carse's apartment when you wanted him at the Pace scene in New Hampshire."

Ruth slapped her hand to her forehead. "Have I fallen off the grapevine completely?"

"Well, Chief, they say it's lonely at the top."

Ruth smiled. "So they do, Lieutenant. Anyway, it's been a good day."

"Or mostly a good day."

"Why mostly?"

"There's a complaint on your desk. The department is being sued. By Mr. Chiarousco."

"Mr. Chiarousco?"

"Yeah, the guy who fell in the dog poop."

Ruth raised the remote and turned off the television. She didn't need to see Baines do his act again on the eleven o'clock news. It had been a satisfying evening. She'd received congratulatory calls from all over, including special ones from her sister Helen and Anna Abbott. Mrs. Abbott had reiterated the mayor's sentiments. Ruth's appointment was a lock.

With her sister, Ruth had started off deflecting the praise, but then she found herself thinking of Tracey Kendall scared for her life with not a soul to confide in. Ruth pushed to open up, telling Helen about the conflict with Baines and how scared she had been of losing her job. Helen listened carefully and kept up a running commentary about Baines and Mayor Rosenfeld that made Ruth laugh.

After the television darkened, Ruth thought about what Stephen Kendall had said about the armature, how the sculpture had to be right at its core. Tracey Kendall's life had been outwardly perfect, but broken at its center. Her marriage had been flawed. Her business partnership had been flawed—fatally, as it turned out, and she'd had no one in her life to talk to about either.

Marty came in and sat down. "See," he said, "I told you it would all turn out okay."

"You never did."

"You're right, I didn't. You had me scared there for a while. But everything's all right now, isn't it?"

Ruth moved closer to Marty on the couch, and kissed his familiar cheek. "Yes," she said. "Everything is fine."

ABOUT THE AUTHOR

Barbara Ross is the mother of two children and lives with her husband in Somerville, Massachusetts. Like her character, Chief Ruth Murphy, she knows something about the stresses of being the boss.

Her short stories, *New Derby, New Year's Eve* and *Winter Rental* have appeared in anthologies of New England crime stories published by Level Best Books. *Winter Rental* won an honorable mention for the Al Blanchard Award sponsored by the New England chapters of Mystery Writers of America and Sisters in Crime.